CROOKED TOP MOUNTAIN

AARON BLAYLOCK

CROOKED TOP MOUNTAIN

Aaron Blaylock

An Imprint of Praystez Publishing

ISBN-13: 978-0692961728
ISBN-10: 0692961720

Cover design by Aaron Blaylock
Cover design © 2017 by Praystez Publishing.
Edited and typeset by Lola and Aaron Blaylock
Printed in the United States of America

*This book is dedicated to all those who love the
Superstition Mountains, and to those who've devoted
their days to its exploration and preservation.*

VENI VIDI

"No no no no," he breathlessly muttered. "Not like this, not like this."

The dank hole which he wriggled through closed in around him and pinched his hunched shoulders. He scurried on his belly as quickly as his old bones would allow. His own odor, of sweat and dirt, offended his nostrils. Still, it was a welcome reprieve from the monstrous smell from which he fled. The rock tube he crawled through quaked all around him, a quake that emanated from behind his ribs. His own heartbeat sounded in his ears like a bass drum and his head throbbed from the rhythmic pulsing.

In his right arm he clutched his long sought prize, wrapped in burlap and held close to his chest. At long last, his fortunes had changed and yet in a horrifying instant all his elation was swept away. *That smell*, he thought. *The smell of death*. It was his only warning. If not for that smell he would have been a goner, a footnote in history, just another lost miner claimed by the cruel wilderness.

He reached a squeezing point, where he could no longer hope to proceed without a painful contortion of his body. Hastily, he shoved his burlap covered prize through the hole and followed it quickly with his left arm. He tilted his neck to force his head and shoulder through the opening together. Sounds of clawing and snatching were just below his feet.

Impossible, he thought. Surely his pursuer was too large to have come this way. He prayed it was his mind playing tricks on him but hurried forward nonetheless. In a few tense moments he had freed himself from the accursed rabbit's hole and was able to get to his feet. He stooped down and felt around in the darkness until his fingers brushed against the coarse burlap. With his newly acquired prize once more held to his chest, he felt his way forward in the pitch black tunnel.

In his panicked flight, he had broken the rusty old head lamp and extinguished his only source of light. Initially, he hoped it would prove to his advantage but it seemed as if his adversary could see in the darkness. In the deep black, he was accosted at every turn. It was through sheer luck or providence that he fell back into the crevasse that led to the hole through which he had come. His head throbbed with a dull pain and he could not be sure if the warm moisture on his skin was perspiration or blood. In either case it did not impede his flight for the moment and that was all he concerned himself within. What did slow his escape was that he lacked a bearing. Fortunately, he prepared for such an eventuality. Not fleeing for his life but for navigating through the ancient shaft in the darkness.

With great difficulty, he hobbled forward and bent low to the ground to feel along the cold rock floor. His hip ached and he could feel the metal pins in his surgically repaired joints. Just as doubt began to creep into his mind, he felt his twined salvation and took a firm hold of the rope with his free hand.

"Thank the Good Lord," he whispered to the darkness.

A furious yell echoed throughout the narrow passage. It seemed to come from all sides, and he had no indication of the exact direction it had come from. In the frenzied darkness he could not decide whether he was pursued by a man, a monster or some myth or apparition, so he feared them all equally to be sure. He took a deep breath and clung tightly to the rope and to his prize.

"Ya get me out of this and I swear my sin'n days are over."

Sliding his hand along the rope he made his way forward and moved much faster, despite the darkness. He encountered a small ledge, about head high, just a few hundred feet from the hole. He placed the burlap bag atop the shelf and hoisted himself up and over the ledge with great difficultly. He retrieved the bag and once again clung to the rope as he limped upward to the world above.

Another shout bellowed in the blackness. This time he was certain it was a good distance behind him. Still, he could not tell if it was a shout of anger or pain. In either case, he knew it would not be good for him if the bellower caught up with him. He was fairly certain that, in the melee, he had injured whoever or whatever it was. In his wild flailing during the escape, he struck something which prompted the first of many bone chilling screams. He plodded ahead hurriedly, to put as much distance as possible between himself and the epicenter of the bellowing.

A soft gray dot shone up ahead in the distance. His steps hastened as he began to see a literal light at the end of the tunnel. The shaft began to take shape as he drew closer to the exit. The dot had grown considerably and he could see the dark blue light from the night sky. He dropped the rope and galloped to the opening, as fast as his aging body would allow. As he stepped out into the twilight he peered up into the starry heavens, framed beautifully by the canyon walls that rose up before him.

"Thank you," he prayed as the moonlight bathed his creased and worn skin.

With a glance over his shoulder, back into the dark shaft behind him, he listened for signs of pursuit. He held his breath and remained deadly still while he waited. There was a faint sound of pebbles grinding against the stone floor. Although not yet upon him, there was no mistaking, danger was coming. Beside the entrance, his carry bag and a hostler with his pistol lie right where he left them. How foolish it now seemed for him to have left his sidearm. With no time to lose, he grabbed the hostler and threw it over his shoulder before he leapt from the opening and began to claw his way up the canyon wall.

Suspended in air, a few feet up the wall, was the end of the rope he had used on his descent into the eroded crevasse. He took hold of the thick twined support and tugged hard to test its honor. When he was satisfied he could trust it, he tucked the burlap sack tightly underneath his left arm and began to pull himself up the steep incline. The strain on his aching muscles paled in comparison with the stabbing pain in his old mended joints.

The long ago admonition of his so-called friends returned to his consciousness. Their shared mantra was that he was too old for such an expedition. Although it was premature to celebrate victory, he had already come further than any of them would have believed. At the moment though, he needed to reach the top if he had any chance of rubbing his success in the faces of those still living. Due to its not insignificant weight, it took great effort to maintain his grip and keep his prize tucked safely beneath his arm. *Just a few more feet,* he thought. *You're almost there.*

As he pulled himself over the ledge, the bag slipped from his armpit and he was forced to let go of the rope with one hand to catch it. He desperately clung to the ledge with his arm, elbow and his chin, any part of his body that could grab hold of something. As he flung the sack to the surface, he grabbed hold of the ground with both hands. His boots scraped against the cliff until they found a footing. He forced his body upwards and rolled onto his back atop the ledge. Stabbing pains shot through his hip and down his leg. He lay there for a moment, breathing heavily. All his strength had been sapped from his flight and the arduous climb. The thought of getting up and continuing on seemed well beyond his capacity.

His hopes of resting for a time were dashed at the sound of crumbling rocks and a terrible shout came from the shaft at the bottom of the canyon. The howl echoed off the walls and seemed to reverberate through the ground beneath him. Without looking back, he scooted away from the ledge and rolled up onto his knees next to the rock where he had fastened the rope. He let the hostler fall from his shoulder as he frantically unwounded the rope from the rock. In one motion, he picked up the burlap sack and struggled to his feet as the rope disappeared over the ledge like a suicidal snake.

Unsure of how much that would slow his tenacious pursuer he hobbled further into the wilderness in search of a place to hide. He had no chance of out running the cat to his mouse but hoped he might be able to conceal himself and wait it out. As luck would have it, the moon was full and illuminated the vast desert landscape, from the towering saguaro giants to the dark silhouetted mountain skyline in the distance. Up ahead he locked eyes on a plateau, littered with thorny brush. As fast as his weary and broken-down legs could carry him he rambled for the mesa. There was no time to cover his tracks and no point in wasting energy on stealth. If he did not make the plateau before his attacker reached the top of the canyon he was as good as dead.

The beige face of the desert bunker was too steep for him to climb with any speed, so he made his way to the western end. There was a sloping incline that lay out in front of him like a grand staircase. He ascended the incline with relative ease and reached a patch of thorny bushes near the top. With all his strength exhausted he fell amongst the thorns and brush with a pathetic thud.

It seemed as if he had used up all of the air in the desert, as he gasped for breath. Like tiny daggers, the thorns scratched and tore the flesh on his arms and face. His shaggy beard caught on a branch as he rolled onto his back and clutched the prize he had risked his life for. The heavens above sparkled with more stars than he could count in a lifetime, which would be especially true if that lifetime were to end tonight.

Holding the burlap close to his chest seemed to help calm his racing heart. He wanted to open the sack and get a better look at his prize but did not dare move. Instead, he listened for sounds of danger. All he heard at the moment was the chirping of insects and the breeze that swept through the cacti and brush. Ever so slowly, he lifted his head off the ground and peered over the brush toward the ledge of the crevasse. It was only when he spotted a dark figure claw its way over the top that he remembered his pistol. He dropped his head hard back to earth and clenched his eyes closed tightly while he cursed himself for twice leaving behind his sidearm. *I'm a dead man,* he thought.

With his eyes still shut he listened to the footsteps as they drew ever closer. Although he was too afraid to watch, he played the scene out in his mind of an imposing animal stalking its prey. Louder and louder the sounds grew as his end drew nearer. When he could not stand it any longer, he opened his eyes and slowly and carefully turned his head to peer through the thorny branches, which were all that stood between him and death. Through the brush and dry leaves, he spotted the hairy top of a head. He heard the panting and deep breaths of his pursuer and tried unsuccessfully to suspend his own breathing.

There was no escape now, he knew that, and it was only a matter of time before he was discovered. His flight had proved unprofitable and now came the fight. Surprise was his last card to play and he would only get one shot.

He shifted slightly as the thorns dug into the back of his skull. He hefted his prize gently off his chest to gage the weight. It would make an effective implement for inflicting pain, perhaps even death. How had it come to this? Kill or be killed. In all his wildest dreams and fantasies, he had never considered a reality like this one. He mustered all the strength he had left and took one more look through the brush. The dark hair atop the head of his pursuer was still in plain view and he would not find a more opportune moment.

One final breath and he leapt up and sprang from the summit with the burlap sack held over his head. With a sickening thud, his prize impacted the skull of his foe and both bodies fell to the desert floor in a heap. The moonlight shone down on a pair of unconscious bodies and waited for a victor to arise.

HOMECOMING

The old church building never looked so brilliant and white. Gideon took a moment to gaze on his childhood meetinghouse, as the early morning sunlight bathed the walls in its soft glow. He shifted his weight from side to side and looked around the packed parking lot. The passengers had likely exited their suburbans and minivans more than an hour ago, to file in through the glass chapel doors. Gideon's original intention had been to join with them, but due to his late arrival he just stood quietly and enjoyed the Sunday morning solitude. He remembered a hymn from his primary days *'The chapel doors seem to say to me "Shh" be still*'.

A large ash tree in the center of the grounds caught his attention. Although the top of the tree had surpassed the grand steeple, Gideon remembered a younger ash tree under which he played tag after church. His fondest memory was chasing a specific brown eyed girl around the tree and across the grass. He never could catch her, and in a way, he still pursued her.

Through the glass front doors, he could see a crowd gathering in the foyer outside the chapel. He stopped a good distance from the entrance and considered whether he ought to wade into the fray or wait for the throngs to disperse. Before he could make up his mind the herd parted and for the first time in years he laid eyes on the brown eyed girl. His heart leapt in his chest at the sight of her smile. She was visiting with a portly woman in a floral print dress who stood next to a tall bald man in a blue suit. They all laughed at something the bald man said and Gideon could not help but envy those in the crowded foyer who were treated to her infectious laughter. At that moment, she looked out through the doors and locked eyes with Gideon. He fought a sudden urge to duck out of sight and managed a feeble wave and a smile. She turned her attention briefly back to the couple in the foyer and gave the portly woman a hug before she excused herself and made her way through the throngs of well-wishers toward the front door. Gideon straightened his tie and stretched to his full height as she pushed open the door and stepped into the daylight.

"Gideon!" she shouted with a huge smile.

His heart thumped in his chest as they walked toward one another. Something was different about her. She had the same warm eyes and welcoming smile, the same flowing auburn hair and alabaster skin but there was a change in her walk. She moved with a confidence and grace that surpassed Gideon's memories of her.

"Hey there, beautiful," he tried to match her confident stride. As they drew near he extended his hand just as she threw her arms open. They both fumbled and traded positions with Gideon going in for a hug as she put her hand out to where his had been. Liz laughed and pushed her hair out of her face while Gideon shuffled uncomfortably and placed his hands at his side.

"Get over here," she reached up and pulled Gideon in for a hug. With a great big smile, he stepped closer to her as they embraced.

"Well that was awkward," called a taunting voice from back by the chapel doors. Gideon looked up and Liz turned around to see Todd Colbeck leaning against the opened door. He wore a long sleeved blue shirt and a yellow tie that matched his blond hair.

"Hey Todd," Liz said. "I thought I saw you sneak in the back."

Todd let the door close behind him as he joined the reunion. The three of them grinned at each other as Gideon thought back to the last time they had all been together. It was under fairly similar circumstances that they had said their goodbyes three and a half years ago. Gideon had just spoken in church prior to departing on a mission to Jamaica. He imagined that was probably the last time Todd had been in a church and tried to remember if he was wearing the same blue shirt.

"Nice speech, Lizzie," said Todd as he got a half hug from Liz.

He gave a nod and a wink to Gideon and stepped back to look the pair over. Liz wore a purple cardigan and a beige skirt with a pair of dark brown loafers. Gideon had on a long sleeve white shirt with a purple tie.

"Well aren't you two a pair," Todd remarked. "Did you dress to match or is that a Mormon uniform thing?"

"No," Gideon said looking down at his tie. "Fashionistas just think alike."

Liz laughed and her hair fell across her face as Gideon was anything but fashionable. Growing up, if he wore anything other than a t-shirt and shorts he was either going to church or playing football. She swept her long brown locks back behind her ear and smiled broadly at Gideon. His heart swelled in his chest and he felt as if he stood atop a stool.

"Yeah Todd," said Liz. "Didn't you hear, purple is in."

She radiated a light that was beyond her natural beauty. Gideon attributed it to the devotion and service of her missionary work. It was work to be sure but a work that brought tremendous blessings and happiness. He wished she could have been there when he returned home, to have seen him on his own spiritual high. He wondered how much of that light still remained. His current service, kept secret by design, brought with it blessings and joy of a different kind. While missionaries shared what they had with the world, he now spent much of his time keeping his service unknown to the world.

"Elizabeth," a new voice called from behind them.

Back by the glass church doors stood a tall balding man with leathery skin, on his face shown the wrinkles and wear of a lifetime of laboring in the desert sun. His massive frame nearly filled the doorway. Despite his burly physique there was a gentleness to him that was disarming.

"Hi daddy," Liz answered.

"Hey Brother Hunter," Gideon called.

"Hey Gideon," Liz's dad replied warmly before turning back to Liz. "We're gonna load up and head to the house, darling."

"I'm coming," Liz replied and turned to Todd and Gideon. "Are you guys coming? We're having refreshments at our house."

"Of course," said Todd.

"You had me at refreshments," said Gideon with a wink and a point.

"Great," said Liz. "I'll see you there."

She turned and shuffled off after her father. Gideon watched until she passed through the foyer and disappeared out of sight. He turned to see Todd smirking at him.

"What?" Gideon questioned.

"I knew she'd bring you back."

"Who says I didn't come back to see you?"

"Okay then," said Todd. "Where's my awkward hug?"

"Well all right, but I'll have to tell Bigga you love man," Gideon leapt at Todd with open arms and wrapped him in a big bear hug.

"Get off me you sicko," Todd struggled to free himself from his friend.

Gideon released him and slapped him on the back. They both looked toward the parking lot as a black Yukon rolled into view. Brother Hunter filled the driver's seat and Liz waved at them from the backseat. The suburban turned out onto Crismon Road and pulled away from the peaceful grounds of the old church. A few cars followed suit while the majority of the vehicles remained with their passengers, staying for the entire three-hour block of meetings.

"How did you get here?" asked Todd.

"Taxi," replied Gideon. "Just came from the airport."

"Well then it looks like I'm driving," said Todd. "Come on, I'm this way."

Todd led the way around the back of the church to a blue pickup truck that was very familiar to Gideon. Todd pulled open the door and reached across to unlock the passenger's side door. Gideon climbed in and looked around the cab. The armrest was more faded and worn than he remembered, but outside of a few paper cups and empty burger wrappers everything was just as he left it.

"The old girl's looking pretty good," Gideon remarked.

"Are you talking about your truck or Liz," Todd quipped.

"Ha ha," Gideon rolled his eyes.

Todd turned the key and the Nissan sputtered as the engine roared to life. They backed out of the spot and drove round to the front of the building where the large ash tree loomed to bid farewell to the patrons of the church. The blue pickup turned out of the parking lot and headed south in a familiar route. Gideon had taken this road home every Sunday as long as he could remember. A right turn and they drove past the Circle K where Gideon worked the nightshift, in what seemed like another life. As they turned onto Liz's street a wave of excitement washed over him. He moved to the edge of his seat and smiled broadly.

"Easy there, fella," Todd teased.

Gideon masked his expression with a furrow of the brow and a frown. He pretended to find something of interest out his window but the houses on the street were exactly the way he remembered them except for a fresh coat of paint here or there. It was both gratifying and a little sad that the old neighborhood remained the same.

"I thought you said you let your hair grow out," Todd said, giving him a sideways look as they pulled to a stop in front of the Hunter home.

"I did," Gideon replied. "I just got it cut."

"For Liz?" asked Todd.

"No, for your mom," Gideon retorted.

"Not cool, man," Todd turned off the truck and pulled open the door. "Besides, you know my momma likes long hair."

"Just give me a break with the Liz stuff," Gideon pleaded.

Todd smiled and gave him a nod and a wink. They both exited the truck and walked around to the front of the pickup. The front yard of the Hunter home was always immaculate, a natural consequence of the head of the household owning his own landscaping business. The lawn looked as if a barber had painstakingly cut the grass with a pair of scissors. The towering bushes that flanked the front window were trimmed the shape of giant Christmas lights. A red brick walkway led to the front door and was lined with yellow flowers. There was a handwritten sign taped to the front door that said 'Come on in'.

Gideon turned the doorknob and pushed open the ornate wooden door. The low rumble of conversation from the living room met them just inside. Familiar and unfamiliar faces passed in and out of sight beyond the archway that led into the dining room. Adults transported dishes full of finger foods, snacks and pitchers of lemonade while small children weaved in between them laughing and giggling, unaware of the hustling and bustling cares of the parental figures preparing for guests. A brunette woman in a red apron narrowly avoided one of the children who darted out from underneath the table and held her dish high above her head as she regained her balance. She looked into the entryway with a bright smile.

"Gideon!" she exclaimed.

When she smiled, she looked very much like her daughter. Lorna Hunter had fair skin and light brown eyes and although the lines and wrinkles on her face alluded to her age, you would not know it by her outgoing and vibrant persona. She had always been kind to Gideon and he secretly believed that she was rooting for him to win the heart of her daughter, despite having no evidence to back it up.

"Hey Sister Hunter," Gideon replied with a sheepish wave.

"Get over here," she placed the dish on the table and wiped her hands on her apron. Gideon walked toward her, and she wrapped him in a warm hug. "You're back! It's so good to see you."

"How 'bout me, Mrs. H?" Todd said from behind Gideon.

"Come here, Todd," said Sister Hunter. She drew him in for a hug and Todd grinned and winked at Gideon. Todd had long professed a crush on Liz's mom and although Gideon tried to tell himself it was simply a tactic to annoy him, he feared that his crush was all too real. She released Todd and stood back with her hands on her hips. "So good to see you boys."

"Good to see you too, Sister Hunter," said Gideon.

"Come on in," she beckoned, as she turned and headed back into the dining room. "Liz is around here somewhere."

They followed her into the organized chaos of a family gathering. Aunts and grandmas were busy putting the finishing touches on the bountiful spread on the long oak table. In the adjoining living room, Liz's grandpa had already fallen asleep in an overstuffed lounge chair in the corner. Her uncles were gathered together in an informal circle speculating about the outcome of the Cardinals game later that evening. There was a hoard of unsupervised children chasing a blond-headed boy, who held tightly to a coveted toy fire truck and screamed. Gideon spotted Liz sitting with her father on the couch beneath a large rectangular window at the back of the house. The morning light that poured through the window bathed Liz in its glow, but Gideon imagined it was her glow that added to its glory.

"Egg salad sandwich?" Sister Hunter offered.

"Sure thing, Mrs. H." Todd swooped in and took the tiny plate from her hand, knowing Gideon's aversion to egg salad. "Thank you."

Gideon nodded in gratitude to Todd. Despite a constant barrage of joking, teasing and tormenting, Gideon knew that he could always count on Todd to have his back.

"Make yourself at home," Sister Hunter invited as she picked up another plate and turned her attention to a conversation between her mother and mother-in-law on the opposite side of the table.

Not wanting to seem too eager, Gideon gravitated toward the men at the center of the room and casually listened to their amateur sports talk analysis. With an ear toward the guy talk his eyes watched and waited for an opening to speak with Liz. She beamed as she recounted a story or experience to her father. He wanted to join in but thought it best not to intrude on father daughter time. After all, her family had not seen her for eighteen months and was sure to have missed her. Todd busied himself loading up a small plate full of sandwiches, crackers and yogurt dipped pretzels, while Gideon tried not to appear so obvious in his intentions. One of Liz's aunts walked up to her and offered her a clear plastic cup full of lemonade which prompted her father to glance back toward the kitchen table. He then excused himself and made his way toward the refreshments. Gideon wasted no time and stepped around the group of sports enthusiasts to talk with Liz.

"Hey," he said as Liz took a drink of lemonade.

"Hey!" she placed her cup on the floor and stood up to greet him. "So glad you came."

They stood and smiled at each other until the momentary pleasantness began to lean into an awkward silence.

"Please, sit down," she said, taking her seat on the end of the couch.

Gideon looked over his shoulder to see her father happily talking with Todd as they both grazed their way through the offerings on the table. He took a seat next to Liz and put his arm on the back of the couch.

"So, what have I missed?" Liz smiled with big bright eyes. "Tell me everything."

He withdrew his arm from the back of the couch as a nervous reflex. Gideon understood the question but recoiled slightly because he knew he could not tell her everything. He wrapped his arm around a throw pillow and tried to look casual.

"What do you want to know?" Gideon asked with a nervous grin.

"Well, I get a postcard from you, from Jamaica of all places, and then boom, six months of nothing," she punched him playfully in the shoulder. "What's up with that?"

"Yeah," he replied sheepishly. "Sorry about that. I got caught up in some stuff."

"My mom tells me you are some kind of an estate manager?" Liz questioned.

"Something like that. I have some property I look after and some other varied responsibilities. It keeps me busy and out of trouble," he said, anxious to change the conversation. "I'm more interested in what you've been up to. How was Holland?"

A vague response and a subject change was almost a conditioned response now. His life had become veiled by a secret that made it nearly impossible to talk about himself, or what he did from day to day. In this case, however, he also genuinely cared about Liz and wanted to hear about her mission experiences.

"It was amazing!" she exclaimed. "Such a beautiful country and the people, oh my gosh, I just love them. It was hard to leave, but I'm glad to be home."

Gideon knew exactly how she felt. When he returned home from his mission he was happy to see his friends and family, but it almost hurt how much he missed Jamaica and his life as a missionary. As he sat next to Liz on the couch, he had those similar feelings when he thought about returning to Jamaica. However, his desire to get back to his life on the island waned as he looked into her eyes.

"I know what you mean," he said. "What will you miss most?"

"The work," she answered without hesitation. "I already miss serving all day every day. It's unbelievable how much joy you find in helping and serving others."

"Yeah," he nodded along as she spoke. "Totally."

"So how long are you back for?" she asked.

"Just a week," he replied with a slight grimace.

"That's all?" she said. "What brings you back?"

Before he could answer Todd plopped down on the couch between them. A piece of cheese and a couple of crackers fell from his plate into Gideon's lap.

"What are we talking about?" Todd asked, oblivious to his intrusion.

"Just talking about being home," Gideon said as he brushed at the cracker crumbs that assaulted his black dress pants.

"Isn't this awesome," Todd said. "All together again, like old times."

"You certainly haven't changed," said Liz.

"Why would I?" asked Todd. "You can't improve perfection."

Gideon shook his head as they all chuckled.

"So what kind of trouble do you get up to with Gideon off enjoying the island life?" Liz asked.

"I'm taking classes at MCC and on the weekend I work with my pops back in the Superstitions," Todd said.

"What work do you do out there?" asked Liz.

"They're looking for Glenn's Apache wind cave," Gideon answered.

Liz looked down at the floor as the smile fell from her face. The jubilant conversation quickly changed to a melancholy silence at the mention of Glenn's name. Gideon had only just realized that the quartet of their childhood was incomplete without him and he was ashamed that it had taken him this long to notice his absence.

"Actually," Todd finally spoke up and broke the silence. "We think Glenn was onto something bigger."

"What do you mean?" asked Gideon.

"Well, at first we were looking for the legendary Apache wind cave because that's what we thought Glenn was after," Todd began. "But then Mrs. Bicklesby let us look through his things and we found that he'd be researching something else, something he didn't want anybody to know about."

"What?" Gideon and Liz asked in unison.

"The Lost Dutchman," Todd popped a finger sandwich in his mouth and chewed proudly.

The legend of The Lost Dutchman's mine had colored the history of the Superstition Mountains for over a century. It was said to be the biggest cache of gold in the western United States. Supposedly, Jacob Waltz, a German miner known as the Dutchman, whispered the location of his mine on his deathbed. Since then men and women have worn out their lives in search of the mythical gold. Locals sell copies of maps to tourists and cartoon caricatures of an old bearded miner can be found throughout local restaurants, shops and even in schools. Despite the commercialization of The Lost Dutchman, Gideon always chose to hope that the gold was out there somewhere to be found.

"You're kidding," said Gideon. "You think Glenn was looking for the Dutchman's gold?"

"I don't think he was looking for it," Todd said. "I think he found it."

"Based on what?" demanded Gideon.

"The last time I spoke with him he was going on about how he'd found the key," Todd replied. "He said he knew where it was. When I asked him what he was talking about he said that he wished he could tell me."

"So?" asked Gideon.

"So!" exclaimed Todd. "He was ranting about how he'd found the key and then he disappeared in the Superstitions the next day."

"Mines don't have keys, genius," rebutted Gideon.

"But maps do, codes do," argued Todd. "Then I found this."

Todd reached into his back pocket and pulled out a tattered envelope with a red, white, and blue striped border. It was addressed in Glenn's handwriting to Elder Gideon Goodwin 22 Charlemonte Drive, Kingston 8 Jamaica.

"Where did you get that?" Gideon demanded.

"It was in the box of mission stuff you left in your closet," Todd said as he opened the letter.

"Those are my private things," said Gideon.

"I know, but I think he wanted you to come looking for him," said Todd as he gestured to the letter.

"That's crazy," Gideon argued.

"Gideon," Liz interjected. "I don't think that it is."

Todd and Gideon both turned their attention fully toward their hostess with eager anticipation for what she had to add on the topic.

"Glenn called me," she continued. "It was the middle of the night, the night before he went missing. He sounded hurried, almost frantic; one of the things he said was to tell Hansel to follow the breadcrumbs. He said that he would know where to start. I told his mother and the police, but he was acting so erratic and so little of what he said made sense. We all just thought he had lost his mind. But now that we're sitting here together I feel so stupid for not connecting it earlier."

"Exactly," said Todd.

"What are you talking about?" asked Gideon.

"Hansel!" they both shouted and gestured at Gideon.

All at once a flood of memories came back to his mind. In the third-grade production of Hansel and Gretel, Gideon had played the title role. Glenn was one of the stage hands and Todd and Liz were narrators. In the German fable, Hansel and Gretel left a trail of breadcrumbs to follow. Gideon sat dumbfounded. The helplessness he had felt when Glenn had gone missing returned. He had been thousands of miles away and with the delay of the mail system it was all over before he even found out about it. There was nothing he could have done to help, and he always felt guilty about it. Now with this revelation that Glenn may have expected him to come after him he could hardly stand it. Todd unfolded the letter and handed it to Gideon pointing at the last line.

"The path to me starts at the AC," Gideon read aloud.

"That's what we can't figure out," said Todd. "We checked the air conditioning unit on top of our house and even checked the A/C at the Bicklesby's and your folk's old house. We couldn't find any clues. Joe's got a theory that he meant the American Civil War 'cause near the end of the war some soldiers cut a path from Fort McDowell to Picket Post Mountain and it cuts right through the Superstitions. That's where we're making camp for now."

"The path to me starts at the AC," Liz excitedly. "Ammo-can!"

"What?" asked Todd, matching her excitement.

"Gideon," she continued. "Your ammo-can. Remember? When you left you hid a present for me to find and clues to follow. Glenn helped me find it. The present was in an ammo-can!"

"Well, where was it?" Todd exploded with anticipation.

Liz and Gideon both stood up and turned toward the window. Todd nearly dumped his plate on the ground as he spun around and peered through the lace curtains. Beyond the window, beautifully framed, was the face of the Superstition Mountains jutting up out of the valley floor like a stone cathedral. Todd slowly came to his feet and the three of them stared at the magnificent mountain wall as if they were seeing it for the first time.

"Are you guys up for a little hike?" Todd asked.

"Tomorrow?" asked Liz.

"First thing," Gideon nodded.

JEDDEDIAH STANDAGE

Tiny pebbles and dirt burrowed into the open wound on his forehead. He lifted his head off the ground and stared blankly at the brush and cacti in the distance. All at once he became aware of a sharp stabbing pain in his side, which only intensified as he attempted to roll away from it.

"Ah!" he cried out.

The pain dropped him mid-roll, and he laid out flat on his back. He peered up into the starry night sky and felt his left side in search of the source of his discomfort. It did not take long to discover that his ribs were the culprit. Unable to draw in a deep breath, he wheezed and struggled to fill his lungs. A soft breeze swept through the brush and carried with it the unsettling sounds of breaths that were not his own.

He scrambled to his feet as the nightmare of his pursuer returned to his mind. Like a fleeing crab he scurried away from the dormant figure lying near his feet. Each movement brought a jolt to his ribcage and stung as if he was set upon by a giant unseen bee. When he had retreated to a more comfortable distance he surveyed the wreckage of his desperate act. Next to his fallen victim lay his burlap wrapped prize, which he guessed was the most likely cause of his broken ribs. Besides cracking a rib or two, it had done its work on his assailant as he was clearly unconscious amongst the dirt and brush. The hulking figure's torso rose and fell with each laborious breath, leaving no doubt that life still clung to it.

"Pistol," he whispered to himself as he stared at the slumbering giant.

He rose and twisted around as fast as his old bones would allow him. A few hundred feet ahead, near the ledge of the canyon, his sidearm lay beside a rock that jutted up into the night. With all the haste he could command, he hobbled toward his pistol. The shuffle of his feet and the pain in his ribs told him he was moving, but he did not feel like he drew any closer to his destination. Unable to take in a proper breath, he quickly tired and stopped to rest for a moment. He could have sworn he heard the sound of falling rocks echo down the canyon. *Are there more of them?* He thought.

With renewed determination, he lumbered forward. When he reached the large rock, he fell to his knees and pulled the pistol from its holster. After a moment to catch his breath, he laid flat on his stomach and scooted to the edge of the canyon wall. Excruciating pain shot through his torso with every pull toward the side. He peered over the side and scanned from one end to the other as far as he could see in both directions. Everything was still and quiet, he could not see or hear any movement, but before the calm could settle into his heart he remembered that his prize lay back by the plateau beside his relentless pursuer.

He struggled to his feet and spun around in the direction he had come from. With pistol in hand he walked with purpose back toward the beige rock face of the mesa. He watched for a silhouette to rise from the ground and listened for a sign of his monstrous pursuer's awakening. All he heard were his own labored breaths and the sound of his boots tromping through the dirt and gravelly stones beneath his feet. When he reached the high point of the desert incline and cleared a row of prickly bushes he could see the scene was just as he left it minutes earlier. His prize lay undisturbed by the slumbering body that was felled by it. He flew to the burlap sack as if a rope had drawn him there. At last he stooped down and retrieved the sack. Reunited with his prize he turned his attention to the next most distressing subject on his mind. He tucked the burlap sack underneath his arm and checked the rounds in his revolver. *Him or me*, he thought.

"It has to be done," he whispered.

With rough and callused fingers, he stroked at the long gray whiskers on his face. He reached up to wipe the perspiration from his forehead and winced as he brushed past the open wound on his right eye. He pulled the sack from under his arm and moved around near the head of his unconscious foe. The long scraggily hair atop his assailant's head cascaded out in every direction and gave him the looks of a great fallen palm tree. He raised his right arm and leveled the pistol at the center of its head. His usually steady hand trembled slightly, whether from exhaustion or nerves he could not be sure. This pistol had taken life before but this was very different. He had never shot at anything bigger than a coyote. He was certain he could justify himself to the authorities. After all, he had been attacked. It was a clear case of self defense. Justifying himself to his maker was another matter. He pulled back the hammer and took a step closer, no reason to leave anything to chance. With the barrel of the gun just inches away from its scalp he stared blankly down the sights.

Suddenly the sound of rocks and breaking branches brought his focus off his cold-blooded intentions. A new figure appeared just beyond the butte and was stumbling towards him. He raised his pistol and fired. The shot echoed off the nearby canyon walls and reverberated down the mountains in the distance. The newcomer dropped at once and immediately began to writhe and squirm on the ground.

"What have I done?" he said as he leapt over one victim to head toward another.

In seconds, he was standing over the twisting and turning young man, whom he had just shot. The young man wore a white canvas hat with a long brim and a sunshield that fell over his shoulders. His round face was contorted and he was moaning through grit teeth.

"You shot me," cried the young man.

Unsure how to respond he instead looked the young man over thoroughly. He wore a backpack and a five-gallon canteen over his shoulder. The young man pressed his hands on a fresh hole in his blue jeans where the bullet ripped through.

"What're ya do'n out here, boy?" he demanded.

"I heard a scream come from up the canyon," the young man replied.

Even in the mute moonlight he could see the blood spreading out from the wound and soaking the young man's blue jeans. He squatted down next to him and placed his pistol and the burlap sack gently in the dirt. His second victim of the night recoiled as he reached out to touch his leg.

"Relax boy, I'm try'n to help," he contended.

"Who are you?" asked the young man with a quiver in his voice.

"My name is Jeddediah," he replied. "Jeddediah Standage. Now hold still and lemme have a look at it."

The young man took his hand from the wound and lay back with his face still clinched and contorted. Jeddediah scooted closer to the boy and tried unsuccessfully to get a better look at the consequences of his trigger finger. The young man removed his hat to reveal a bulb of straight hair that fell in a perfect line all the way around his head.

"Am I dying?" asked the young man as he tilted his head forward to look down at his leg.

"You're not dy'n," Jeddediah assured him. "Do you have a light?"

"Back at camp," the young man grimaced.

"You came out here without a light?" Jeddediah questioned his young victim.

"It's a full moon," replied the young man. "Where's your light?"

Jeddediah ignored the unwelcomed and impertinent retort. He scratched the top of his head in the hopes of it unearthing a plan. When no such inspiration came, he stood up and glanced back over his shoulder where his pursuer still lay motionless, undisturbed by all the commotion. As he drew in a breath his cracked ribs bit at his side. The young man cried out again and slid his wounded leg across the grainy desert floor. Jeddediah looked down at fruit of his shooting and pulled at the long whiskers on his face.

"Do ya have a first aid kit in there?" Jeddediah gestured to the young man's backpack.

"It's back at camp," the young man answered with a distressed shake of the head.

A small fit of frustration reminded Jeddediah again of his own ailment as the stabbing pain tore into his side. He knew that unless the bleeding could be stopped, he would be responsible for the young man's death and would not be able to claim self defense before God or man.

"Where's your camp at?" he questioned.

"Back there, just west of the canyon," the young man answered and pointed over the butte behind him.

"Can ya walk?" he asked.

"Dunno," replied the young man. With great effort, he leaned forward. Jeddediah reached down and took him by the hand. The young man braced himself with his good leg and attempted to stand. When he tried to draw his wounded leg in, he winced and fell back to the ground.

"Hold on," ordered Jeddediah.

He quickly scooped up his burlap sack and walked over near the beige colored rock ledge. After a brief survey, he found a suitable spot behind a young Palo Verde tree. He bent over and dug a hasty hole with his bare hands. Carefully, he removed his prize from the burlap sack and buried it in between the Palo Verde and the rock ledge. He returned to the young man with only the burlap sack. With the knife from his boot he cut the sack at the seams and spread it out lengthwise. The young man looked on as Jeddediah lifted the wounded leg and laid the burlap underneath it.

"This is gonna hurt," he warned the young man before he pulled the ends of the burlap together and cinched it down tight above the gunshot. The young man cried out as he finished tying his best square knot. "Let's get you on your feet."

Jeddediah reached down once again and helped the young man up, with stabbing pains tormenting his every movement. As the young man retracted his lame appendage, Jeddediah moved closer and slid his shoulder under his arm for support. Jeddediah's old frame quaked beneath the weight. He worried he barely had the strength to keep himself upright but knew he owed it to his victim to give it all he had.

"Gonna get ya to that kit," Jeddediah groaned.

They had only shuffled forward a few feet when he remembered his sidearm. He led the wounded young man backwards and squat down to retrieve his pistol from the ground. As a new ache surged through his ribs he peeked behind him to ensure the body was still where he left it. With one hand supporting the young man and the other holding tight to his pistol, the involuntary duo hobbled into the desert night.

Their labored breaths joined in concert to produce a rhythmic melody that accompanied the pounding footsteps of the two-man band. Although his body headed north, his mind was buried back between the rock ledge and the Palo Verde tree. After all the searching and toil to obtain his prize it pained him to leave it behind, a pain as real and poignant as his cracked ribs. They stayed west of the canyon for thirty harried minutes. Each of them remained silent as they saved all of their energy for the journey. Among the uneven rock covered hills and brush he spotted an unnaturally symmetrical dome in the distance. They altered their course at once and headed straight for the two-man tent.

The young man collapsed as they entered his camp. Seeing no equipment outside of the tent, Jeddediah pulled on the zipper and threw the flap open. Shaded from their only source of light he could not make out any of the shadowed contents of the tent. One by one, he began to pull things out under the moonlight and discard what was of no use at the moment.

"Hey!" protested the young man, who had risen to a seated position to watch the bearded gunman rifled through his things.

"Where's the first aid kit?" Jeddediah questioned as he found the young man's flashlight and switched it on. He shined it over on the young man. His freckled face was pale and drenched with sweat and his eyelids began to droop. "Stay with me, boy, where's the kit?"

"Big pack, top pocket," the young man responded.

Quickly, Jeddediah shined the light into the tent. The last thing remaining was a large blue backpack. He ducked under the domed threshold and scooted inside. In a flash, he tore open the zipper on the top pocket and pulled out a plastic case with a red cross on it. He snapped open the lid and pulled out bandages, pads and antiseptic wipes. When he failed to find a needle, he discarded the kit and rummaged through the blue backpack. Just as he began to lose hope he discovered a long knife with a metal handle and a compass on the end. The compass twisted off to reveal a tiny stash of emergency survival essentials. There was a plastic bag with matches, a hook and some fishing line. Jeddediah grinned as he looked down at the miracle he sought.

"Thank you, Lord," he prayed.

When he emerged from the tent, he found the young man lying face down in the dirt. He hobbled over to him and turned him over onto his back.

"Hey," he shook the young man hard by the shoulders. "Stay with me, boy."

The young man's eyes opened slightly and fell closed again.

"Talk to me, boy," Jeddediah pleaded. He drug the young man over to a sleeping pad he had pulled from the tent. Shooting pain grabbed him by the side. "What's your name?"

Jeddediah laid his upper torso on the pad with his legs still resting in the dirt. He fumbled with the bandages, wipes and fishing line he had scavenged from the young man's things.

"Hey, hey!" he shouted at the young man as he pulled a small metal flask from his boot. "Boy, stay awake. Tell me your name."

"Glenn," the young man replied behind flickering eyelids. "Glenn Bicklesby."

With that, the young man closed his eyes as his body fell limp and lifeless on the cold hard desert floor.

FLATIRON

The muted morning daylight was only just perceptible as the trio started up Siphon Draw Trail No. 53. The terrain sloped steadily up toward the base of the mountain as the trail cut southeast across its imposing face. Gideon wore a borrowed hoodie from Liz's father that was two sizes too big, but provided respite from the cold winter air. Steam clouds puffed from their mouths with each breath as they chugged up the hill. They walked side by side when the trail allowed it, but as they rose higher the trail narrowed and Gideon was forced to quicken his pace to stay in his preferential lead position.

"Why didn't you put this thing at the bottom of the mountain?" Todd asked as they reached the lower edge of the cliff face.

"Where's the fun in that?" asked Gideon through labored breaths. Secretly though he regretted his decision to hide the cache in such a hard to reach location. He and Glenn had conceived the idea of hiding the ammo-can near the peak of the mountain. The very top of the Superstitions was called Flatiron, named because it resembled an upside-down iron. It was meant to be part of an elaborate treasure hunt for Liz after he left on his mission. Gideon never imagined that Glenn would use it to reach out to him from beyond the grave.

A wide crevasse cut between two monumental cliffs and the trail disappeared over the rocky uneven surface. As they paused for a drink break, Gideon noticed that while he and Todd were huffing and puffing Liz remained composed. Her breathing pattern was only slightly more elevated than normal. She wore a maroon Arizona State University windbreaker with a matching baseball cap. Her hair was pulled back in a ponytail that pushed the bill of the hat downward slightly. Gideon watched as she took a drink from her water bottle and saw Todd grinning at him over her shoulder. He quickly shifted his attention out toward the sprawling valley to the west. Homes and buildings filled a landscape that, until a few years ago, had been mostly cactus and brush. He had grown up among the cacti and partially mourned the progress that crowded out the desert with so much civilization.

"Mind if I lead the way up the draw?" Liz asked with an enthusiastic smile.

"Of course not," Gideon lied. He did mind, not only because of his innate desire to be first but because he had hoped to impress her with his hiking acumen. That hope quickly disappeared as he struggled while she was entirely unfazed by the ascent to this point. "Lead on my lady."

Gideon stepped to the side with a grand sweeping gesture, and Liz led the way into Siphon Draw. The trail vanished into the polished rock of the draw as the crevasse opened into a huge natural amphitheater. The rock was cut and smoothed out by the water runoff that funneled down from the peaks above during the torrential seasonal rains. Although the surface appeared quite slippery, their shoes gripped the rock particularly well. With Liz leading the way they climbed the steep draw at a remarkable pace. The distance from the top of the rock chute to the bottom was only a couple hundred yards, but due to the rapid elevation change in such a short distance, they took another break atop a rocky crow's nest when a fresh trail once more led the way upward.

This time all three of them drew heavy breaths, and Gideon could see patches of sweat forming on the brim of Liz's hat. His heart pounded and his lungs burned but he felt somewhat better knowing that his friends were toiling on their journey as well. Todd moved around by Gideon and leaned back against the ledge to rest. They peered up to their destination at the top of the mountain. Somehow it seemed further away than it had prior to the start of their climb.

"Seriously, G," Todd panted. "What were you thinking?"

"I don't know," Gideon replied. "It seemed like a good idea at the time."

"I thought it was perfect," Liz chimed in. "A little hidden treasure in the mountains just for me. It was so sweet."

"What did you leave in there anyway?" Todd asked.

Gideon paused for a moment to appear as if he needed to think about it. He remembered perfectly well what he left for Liz in the ammo-can but did not want to give away how much thought he had actually given to his love ploy.

"There was a letter," Liz answered in the gap Gideon left. "And your football jersey with a peppermint from the restaurant we ate at before the homecoming dance. You remember?"

"Yeah," Gideon answered with a big smile.

"You wrote that you "mint" for me to hold on to your jersey until your homecoming," she smiled back at Gideon.

"That's so lame," Todd exploded with laughter.

Gideon grimaced and threw a half empty water bottle at his friend. Todd blocked it with his arm, and it fell into his lap while he continued his laughing fit.

"It wasn't lame," Liz argued. "It was sweet. Gideon has always known how to make a girl feel special."

She winked at Gideon, and his heart swelled in his chest. Gideon gave a slight bow and a broad smile. They gazed at each other for a moment before Todd tossed the water bottle back at Gideon.

"Okay then," Todd said. "How about you two sweethearts hike up to the top and bring back the can, while I sit here and think about how I can make you feel special when you get back."

"I thought you were all about staying in shape," Gideon said. "Think of this as your workout."

"Uh, when I go jogging there's zero chance of me sliding off a cliff to my death," Todd replied and gestured to the steep drop offs on either side of him. The descent back down the draw was a perilous one that Gideon did not look forward to on their return journey, but the path forward was fraught with peril as well. The trail cut along the edge of a deep bowl, filled with cactus and brush. On the other side of the bowl the real climb would begin. Jagged cliffs rose up to the north and south of the crevasse with only one way forward up a rocky incline to the top. Although the climb was not without its dangers, Flatiron was popular among hikers and the path was well traveled, so Gideon was not overly concerned with the prospect of injury or death.

"You are being overly dramatic," Gideon said.

"Are you telling me nobody has ever died up here?" challenged Todd.

"Are you saying no one has ever died while jogging?" Gideon retorted.

"Touché," Todd relented.

"If you boys are done we should get going," Liz said. "The sun is about to peek over the ridge."

They turned and looked up at the iron shaped summit above. Tiny pins of white light burst from the ledge and cut through a soft blue sky. There was not a cloud to be seen, which made the canyon feel deeper as they peered up into the heavens.

"All right then, once more into the breach dear friends," Gideon recited in his best Shakespearean accent.

"You're such a nerd," Todd said as he collected his day pack and shook his head.

Besides one minor slip from Todd along the narrow trail, their journey around the bowl was uneventful. As they started their climb, it occurred to Gideon that they had not seen another soul since they left the ranger station at the entrance to The Lost Dutchman State Park. He attributed their solitude to the earliness of the hour and the cold winter temperatures that had most likely put off hikers until later in the day. He was glad they had the mountain to themselves and hoped to make the most of his time with Liz. Although he held a burning curiosity for what they might find in the ammo-can, he was unsure they would find anything more than an echo from the last few days of their friend's life. What was certain was that their little expedition meant several hours shared with Liz.

"You know, I still need to return that jersey," Liz said, looking back over her should. "I left before you got back. It's hanging safely in the back of my closet."

"No worries," Gideon replied. "I know where you live."

She smiled and turned back to the climb ahead of her before Gideon could return an adoring smile. They climbed over small boulders and ducked under overhanging branches as they sought out the path of least resistance. When Gideon stopped to survey the way ahead, he noticed a shadow move across the sunlit horizon of the peak above them. He spun around and looked up in an attempt to see who or what it was, but whatever it was had disappeared.

"What's wrong?" Todd asked

"Nothing," Gideon said. "I thought I saw something move up there."

"Probably just a curious critter," Todd said. "It's probably wondering what we are doing up here so early when everybody else in the valley is still asleep."

"Yeah, probably," Gideon answered dreamily, as his thoughts had already left their conversation, and his imagination drifted to the top of the peak to who or what his shadowy apparition might be. He was uncertain whether the shadow had been man or beast, but had the distinct impression they were being watched.

They climbed within a hundred yards of the top when Liz stopped for another drink break. Gideon was grateful as he too was in need of water and a break, but his pride would not allow him to ask for a halt. Todd rested against a large boulder to the south, and Gideon gulped down the remains of his primary water bottle. Then he looked in his pack to check his backup water and provisions. He brought an apple and two granola bars along with his old boy scout pocket knife and a first aid kit, which he had had since he was twelve. Liz finished her drink and returned her bottle to her daypack.

"It sure is beautiful up here," she remarked.

"Yeah," Gideon agreed. "Do you know what the original inhabitants of the area called this mountain?"

"Oh, here we go," Todd teased. "Mr. History."

"They called it Kakatak Tamai," Gideon continued ignoring Todd. "It means Crooked Top Mountain."

Liz gave a feeble patronizing nod and continued the arduous climb. Todd grinned and shook his head as he passed Gideon and left him to his disappointment.

"Caca talk," Todd chuckled underneath his breath.

Jagged towers rose up from the top of the cliffs above them like pipes from a giant stone organ. The newly risen sun shone brightly on the beige rock towers and Gideon was reminded of the story of Crooked Top Mountain. He shook off his initial failure and sought once more to impress his friends.

"There's an ancient Pima legend that says the Earth Maker once called to all his people from the four winds to live in peace," Gideon began. "He sent a prophet, Suhu, to them. When they rejected the prophet and few would heed the call, he gathered the good people to the top of Kakatak Tamai and flooded the earth. Only those who followed the prophet to the top of Crooked Top Mountain were spared."

"Really?" Liz asked. "Just like Noah?"

"Yeah," Gideon replied, grateful he had at last piqued her interest. "It is said that the Earth Maker turned all the wicked to stone and that's where many of these rock formations came from."

"Do you think there's a connection to the story in the bible?" asked Todd.

"Dunno," replied Gideon. "But it's one heck of a coincidence if there's not."

Gideon wished he had more to share but had exhausted his limited knowledge of the Native American lore associated with their current position. He stared back up at the cliffs above and noticed a light grey spot between two of the rock formations. As he peered up at this anomaly, it moved. He blinked quickly and shook his head to clear his vision. A figure wearing what looked like a grey cloak came into focus. Gideon opened his mouth to call attention to this strange sight. But before he could speak, the cloaked figure began to run along the cliff that skirted the top of crevasse they were climbing. With each step, baseball sized rocks slipped free and began to cascade down the wall to their left.

"Look out!" Gideon shouted. "Rocks!"

Todd and Liz frantically looked above them to both sides. They spotted the falling rocks and quickly ducked and covered their heads. Gideon rushed to Liz and sprawled out over top of her. He braced against the wall, like a human boulder ramp. In bunches, the rocks bounced off the edge and rained down on them like a hail storm. Gideon was struck in the back several times, across his back and shoulders. Todd was hit on his arm and ankle by the same rock. In once tumultuous moment it was over and the quiet of the morning returned.

"Are you okay?" Gideon asked Liz.

"I'm fine," she said while looking up at the cliffs above with trepidation.

"I'm fine too," Todd said. "Don't worry about me when you're handing out human shields."

"I'm sorry, man," Gideon said. "I didn't have time to think. I just reacted."

"It's nice to know where I rank," Todd said as he examined the gash on his ankle.

"You know you're my boy," Gideon responded. "I just…"

"Save it," Todd interrupted. "You made the right call, hero. I'd have done the same thing if you hadn't scared the crap out of me with all your screaming."

"That was crazy," said Liz. "I've never seen a rock slide come out of nowhere. We're lucky you saw it."

"Somebody's up there," Gideon said.

"What?" asked Todd

"There is some guy up there in a cloak with a hood over his head," explained Gideon. "He ran along the ledge and caused the rock slide."

"A cloak and a hood?" Todd questioned. "Is he from Middle Earth?"

"I know it sounds crazy, but I'm telling you I saw it," replied Gideon. "Some dude in a cloak was watching us and he took off when I spotted him."

"It could be a woman," Liz added. "Under the cloak and hood, it could be a woman. Don't just assume it's a man."

"Right," Todd said. "So, Legolas or Galadriel is up there waiting for us. What's the plan?"

Gideon stepped back out into the middle of the crevasse and surveyed the cliffs above them. He could see no signs of the cloaked figure and wondered where he or she had disappeared to. With no way to know the intentions of a lone person out in the wilderness or the mental state of someone who chose to dress themselves in such a way, Gideon was left to imagine what they might be in for should they reach the top. There was no evidence that he or she had any interest in them at all, but Gideon was nearly certain that whoever was behind the cloak had been watching them.

"The plan hasn't changed," Gideon declared. "Find the ammo-can and see what Glenn left for us."

"We're not concerned with a person who dresses up like Moon Knight and trumps around the mountains hucking rocks down on people?" Todd asked.

"I'm with Todd, Gideon," Liz agreed. "People just don't hang out on cliffs with a cloak on. This person could be seriously disturbed."

Gideon placed his hands on his hips and pursed his lips. He considered for a moment the wisdom of their caution and the possible danger that lie ahead. When coupled his friend's apprehension, the fact that he only agreed to the hike as a chance to catch up with them, left little reason to continue. Still there was something about a hasty fearful retreat that did not sit well with Gideon. He had never been one to withdrawal, a trait that had served him well and also gotten him into a considerable amount of trouble.

"We're so close," Gideon pleaded. "It would be a shame to turn back now. We'll keep a sharp eye out for anything suspicious. Let's just have a look in the ammo-can and see what there is to see. Then we won't have to wonder. Besides, if crazy cloak guy…or girl wants to roll more rocks down on us he…or she will have an easier time if we are going down than if we are up top."

He watched and waited for them to come around. Gideon was confident that Todd would go with him no matter what, but he was less sure what Liz would decide. She looked over at him, and he gave her a playful raise of his eyebrows and flashed a cheesy grin.

"All right," she laughed. "But if we spot your cloaked cuckoo..."

"Don't worry," Gideon interrupted. "I'll look after you."

"No," said Liz. "I was going to say just get behind me, it's been a few years but I've still got a couple of gifts, courtesy of Sensei Zabka."

Daryl Hunter had made sure that all his daughters were enrolled in classes at the Zabka Dojo before they were enrolled in kindergarten because, in his words, "Boys are the worst." Gideon had mistakenly boasted to Liz that, despite the years she had dedicated to the skill, he was still the safe bet in a fight due to his size and strength advantage. He had hardly finished speaking when she spun him around and tossed him over her hip into the nearest trash can. Todd got months of entertainment retelling that story to anyone who would listen.

"Very well," Gideon conceded with his hands raised in surrender. "If we are accosted by a hooded lunatic with a cloak he...or she is all yours."

They all smiled and with that continued on their journey to the top of Flatiron. The rocks ahead were organized into a series of crude steps that weaved around several car sized boulders. At last they reached a ten-foot wall that blocked their way. It was the last hurdle before they would reach the top. Gideon was the first to shimmy up the hand and foot holds to their right. When he was safely atop the wall, he reached back down and extended a hand toward Liz. She took hold of his hand and pushed off the last foothold as he pulled her up. Todd followed her lead. In no time, the three of them stood side by side atop the wall with a beautiful view of the Flatiron peak and the sprawling valley beyond. This vista alone was worth the journey for most hikers who came up this way, but Gideon, Todd and Liz had another less scenic objective.

"Lead the way," Gideon said to Liz, after a cursory check for their hooded adversary.

"Me?" she replied. "I don't remember where it is."

"You don't?" Gideon responded with disappointment. "Oh, well then I guess I'll lead the way."

"I'm sorry," Liz said. "Glenn actually led me to it. He tried to give hints and told me when I was getting warmer, but eventually he just showed me where it was."

Glenn and Gideon had hidden the ammo-can together, and Glenn had come up with a series of clues that would lead Liz to the cache. When Gideon questioned whether or not she would be able to solve the puzzle and reach her destination, Glenn assured him that she would find it. Gideon smiled as he imagined Glenn impatiently prodding her along as she failed to decipher his all too cryptic prompts.

"It's this way," Gideon pointed. "East of the three sisters, beneath the jewel of the king's crown."

"Ha," Todd laughed. "That totally sounds like Glenn. That kid was something else."

"What does that even mean," asked Liz. "I couldn't figure it out."

"It's the rock formations," Gideon replied and pointed over to three identical rock spires. "Over there are the three sisters and there is the king's crown."

He turned to the east and pointed to a stone fortress that rose up from the mountain's summit which most certainly resembled a crown. The sun beams poured through the jagged points of the crown and added to its natural majesty. They left the primitive trail and made their way toward the regal rock formation. In the shadow of the statuesque pinnacle of the crown was a diamond shaped stone that was several shades darker than the rest of the beige colored spires.

"There," Gideon pointed up at the dark stone. "The jewel of the crown."

They altered their course and headed straight for the jewel. There was a forty-five-degree slope all around the base of the crown about eight feet high. The trio ascended the slope until they reached the bottom of the rocky circle. Gideon stooped down near the ground and peeked under a diagonal overhang directly beneath Glenn's jewel stone. He smiled broadly and his heart rate accelerated as he saw the ammo-can resting undisturbed in the secreted nook of the crown. With a moment's pause to give thanks that their faith had not been in vain, he reached into the nook and pulled out the dark green ammo-can. He turned his back to the crown and sat on the sloping base as he placed the can between his legs with a faded No. 053 stamp facing out toward Todd and Liz. They crouched down in unison next to Gideon, all eyes on the battered old military container. Gideon looked up at his friends and smiled as they reveled in the moment of anticipation. He popped the metal latches off the sides and lifted the lid. His heart sank as they looked inside at the bottom of an empty can.

"Are you kidding me?" Todd exclaimed. "What the crap?"

"It can't be," Gideon muttered as he stared at the can with disappointment and disbelief. Although he refused to let his hopes rise too high, he had allowed himself to believe they might find some message from their departed friend. More than he cared to admit, he had indulged the fantasy that they might find a clue that would lead them to Glenn. The empty ammo-can in his lap was a painful manifestation that his friend was gone.

"But the path, the bread crumbs..." Liz spoke to a disheartened choir.

"Maybe somebody found the can and emptied it," Todd speculated.

"Or maybe there was never anything to find," Gideon said as he kicked the can with contempt. "Maybe he never made it back here or maybe…maybe he was crazy."

"Gideon!" Liz rebuked.

The ammo-can skidded to a halt several feet from them. Todd threw his hands on his head and paced back and forth near the base of the crown. Gideon hung his head, ashamed of his outburst. Quietly and gracefully, Liz stooped down and picked up the can. She gently brushed the dirt from the side and looked over at Gideon.

"I'm sorry," he said with his head still hung low. "I let myself believe that Glenn had left something for us. That maybe he…"

His voice trailed off as his glanced up at Liz. She nodded back at him, and in her eyes, he could see that she knew exactly how he was feeling. Gideon opened his mouth to speak but could not find the comforting words they all needed. After a moment of silence, Liz stood up and carried the can back to the diagonal overhang. She paused and stood over Gideon looking at the can.

"I'll feel better knowing this is out here somewhere," Liz said.

She bent down and Gideon reached over and fastened the lid back on the can. He knelt next to Liz and together they started to return it to its hiding place. Before they slid the can into its spot, Gideon noticed something he had not seen before.

"Hold up," he said and pulled the can back. Partly buried in the dirt floor of the tiny nook were three black arrowheads. Gideon reached down and picked up the one nearest him. It was made from an Apache Tear, a polished transparent stone that was abundant in the area. Glenn, Gideon, and Todd used to collect them where they were children. He turned it over in his hand and studied it.

"What did you find?" asked Todd.

"It's an arrowhead," answered Gideon. "An Apache Tear."

"I knew it!" exclaimed Todd. "I knew he left a clue!"

"What clue?" asked Gideon. "We don't even know if this is from Glenn."

"Apache Tear," Todd repeated. "Apache wind cave. It's got to be Glenn."

"I thought he was looking for the Dutchman?" Gideon questioned.

"That's not his style," argued Todd. "You know he likes to be all cryptic. Besides it was under his can, so it's got to be him."

"Gideon let me see that," Liz said.

She took the arrowhead from his hand and returned it to its original position with the other two. They lined up in a straight row, each of them pointing in the same direction. Todd joined Liz and Gideon as they squeezed together to peer down into the nook. Slowly they turned around in unison to face the direction the arrowheads pointed. They looked directly to the west toward the triple peaked stone formation.

"The three sisters," Gideon whispered, almost to himself.

Without another sound, the three of them walked toward the stone monument. Gideon tried to walk in a direct line; however, the bushes and cacti in his path caused some slight diversions. Before they reached the rock formation, Todd pointed to a marking near the bottom of the nearest boulder.

"Look," he enthusiastically called. "Look!"

Gideon saw three faded etchings back to back to back, three arrows drawn with some kind of white chalk-like implement.

"It's hieroglyphs," Todd proclaimed. "It's Glenn!"

They galloped the last ten yards to the rock formation. Gideon fought the impulse to rebut Todd's ascertain and allowed himself to join in his excitement. The three white markings pointed northeast to another cluster of boulders that lay atop a mound of earth. He quickly pressed his head against the rock to verify the direction the arrows indicated.

"There," he pointed to the boulders. "That way."

Each of them scrambled forward as if they were in a race to reach the rocks to the northeast. They had to beat a path through and around the brushes and rocks that blocked their way. All doubt had left Gideon's mind. His renewed hope lifted him and carried him forward as if he had wings. Liz was the first to reach the boulders, followed closely by Todd with Gideon right on his heels. There was a moment of disappointment when a scan of the shoulder-high rock in front of them did not reveal anything of interest.

"Spread out and look for a clue," Gideon said.

Liz moved to her left and Todd to his right, each of them inspecting the boulders as they went. Gideon chose to follow Liz around the west side of the cluster of boulders. They had no sooner moved into the shadow of the rock pile when Todd shouted. "It's here! I found it!"

Choose the right, Gideon thought. *Always choose the right.* He and Liz hurriedly continued around the boulders back to Todd. Gideon stumbled and fell directly onto a sharp rock. He suppressed an outburst from the pain and a curse word. Liz stopped to help him up and he quickly came to his feet.

"You okay?" she asked.

He nodded although the pain was still intense. Liz turned and headed toward the sound of Todd's beckoning call. Gideon hobbled around behind her with a slight limp, the greater blow being dealt to his pride. They came around the corner to find Todd triumphantly pointing to three white arrows etched on the side of the eastern facing boulder. Once again, the arrows all pointed in the same direction, due south. Gideon spun around to discover that they pointed back toward the king's crown. The looks on his friend's faces told him they were just as perplexed by the arrow's indication as he was. They marched back toward the crown at a slower but deliberate pace. Todd and Liz began to drift back toward the west end of the crown where they had started.

"Wait," Gideon called out.

They stopped and looked back at him. Gideon turned back to the boulder cluster and then to the crown. He closed one eye and held his arms out to his sides. With a swivel of his head he shuffled his feet backwards, when he was satisfied he was lined up properly, he lowered his right arm and kept his left arm pointing toward the crown.

"They aren't pointing to the jewel," he said. "They're pointing to the back."

Liz and Todd joined him and judged the lay of the land. They exchanged nods of agreement and made their way together to the east end of the crown. Gideon was uncertain where these arrows would lead them, but he trusted that if they were left by Glenn, the route would be precise and well thought out. Glenn had a history of laying out elaborate courses and trials when they were younger and took great pleasure in the details of his plans. As they approached the crown Gideon saw no arrows. He looked back at the boulders and was certain this was where the arrows had directed them. Todd put his hands on his hips, and Liz took her water bottle from her back pack.

"What now?" asked Todd. "Should we back track and make sure this is where they were pointing?

"Maybe," Gideon replied.

"Wait," said Liz. "Look."

She pointed at the ground by the base of the crown. Tucked back in the dirt behind a large bush was an oval stone with three white arrows etched on the top. This time the arrows were not in a line but they all pointed back towards each other to the center of the stone. They surrounded the stone and peered down at the arrows.

"What does it mean?" Liz asked.

"It means we're here," replied Todd. He bent down and slid his fingers underneath the stone. "Grab hold."

Liz and Gideon readily complied and bent down on opposite sides of the oval stone. When they all had a hand hold they lifted together and tossed the stone to the side of the large bush. Underneath the stone was another, dark green, military grade, ammo-can buried in the ground. Like small children opening presents on Christmas morning, they tore at the rocks and dirt on all sides attempting to unearth the can. As soon as they uncovered the handles, Gideon pulled the can from the ground and popped open the lid.

Inside the can was a plaster statuette of an angel. Gideon gently lifted the angel out and handed it to Liz. Beneath the angel was an old Topps football card of Dallas Cowboys quarterback Roger Staubach. Todd reached across Gideon and grabbed the card.

"I know this," Todd said. "The NFL player's party. Remember? Our senior year. We met Roger Staubach when the Super Bowl came to town. Glenn didn't even know who he was, but they talked for like ten minutes while they waited in line for the bathroom."

"Yeah, I gave him this card when he didn't believe us that he had met a Hall of Famer," added Gideon.

Liz reached into the can and retrieved the last item from the bottom. It was a tattered and worn piece of paper. She unfolded the brittle document to reveal a handwritten message.

"To get to me you must find the key," she read aloud.

"See, I told you!" shouted Todd. "The key!"

"Calm down," said Gideon. "That doesn't help us. What key? Where? How do we find it?"

"The bread crumbs, the clues," said Todd. "Follow the clues."

"We have an angel and a football card," said Gideon. "Does that mean anything to you?"

Todd furrowed his brow and looked down at the card in his hand. "Well the card could be to let us know that it's him," he reasoned.

"Okay," Gideon with a gesture of his hands for him to continue.

"And the angel…" Todd's words trailed off as he stared intently at the statue in Liz's hand. "The angel has got to be the key."

"Or a clue to the key," said Liz.

"Right," Todd agreed.

"So, what does it mean then?" asked Gideon.

"I don't know Mr. Smart Guy," said Todd. "What have you got?"

"Dunno," he answered. "But nothing is jumping out at me."

"Maybe there's a clue inside the statue," suggested Todd. "We should smash it open."

Todd took the angel from Liz and raised it over his head.

"Todd wait," shouted Gideon. He reached up to catch his arm but Todd had already flung the statue into the oval stone beside them. It shattered into several pieces that shot in all directions. Todd bent over and picked up a piece to examine it. He shot a sheepish look at Gideon when he discovered the statue was one solid piece of plaster.

"Nice, Todd, real nice," chided Gideon as he collected the pieces of statue that spread out in the dirt.

"What now?" Liz asked after several silent moments.

"We should go see Joe," Todd suggested. "He's great at figuring out stuff like this."

"And where exactly is Joe?" Gideon asked.

"Can't tell," Todd replied. "Top secret. I'll have to show you. We'll need to pick up some supplies though, it's a half days ride at least."

"I wish I could go with you," said Liz.

"You have to," Todd said.

"Excuse me?" she said.

"Three arrows," he replied. "Glenn left three arrows. You, me, and Gideon. He wanted all of us to come."

"Todd," Gideon began his rebuttal before he quickly withdrew his protest. Glenn had always concerned himself with the meaning of things. If it did not have meaning it was of little interest to him. Glenn did not do things without reason, especially when it came to his puzzles. The three arrows likely meant something and it was possible that they represented the trio of Glenn's closest friends.

"Well I don't think daddy would be too happy with me sleeping out in the wilderness alone with a bunch of men," said Liz.

"You need a chaperone?" asked Todd.

"A companion," Liz answered.

"What about Becky?' Gideon asked.

"She's up at BYU," replied Liz.

"Sarah?"

"Married, up in Idaho I think."

"Lydia?"

"She hates camping," said Liz. "And she doesn't really like you much either."

Gideon smiled as he recalled all of the pranks he had played on Liz and her friends growing up. Lydia had unintentionally been on the receiving end of more than her fair share. Like most things, Liz had a good-natured response to Gideon's immature attempts to entertain himself.

"No worries," Todd said with a huge smile. "I've got the perfect companion for you."

The continued back and forth between Liz and Todd, over his mystery suggestion, fell from Gideon's ears as his attention had been caught by the sight of a grey cloak disappearing around the corner of the three sister's monument behind Liz. He watched and waited to see if the cloaked figure would emerge on the other side. When no one presented themselves, his thoughts drifted back to the crumbled remains of the angel statue in his hand and where they might lead them.

SCENE OF THE CRIME

Dawn had at last broken, after what seemed like an eternal night. A glorious desert sunrise cast long shadows in his path. Jeddediah had patched up his victim the best he could. In some ways, he was grateful the young man had passed out as it allowed him to work without disruption. In his day, he had treated scrapes and minor abrasions along with several sprained ankles but never a gunshot wound. Considering the crude tools he had at his disposal, he was quite proud of the work he had done. Although he was careful not to let himself revel in his accomplishment, being that it was by his hand that the young man came to be in this state in the first place. However, circumstances being what they were, he could not have hoped for a better outcome. He had removed the slug, stopped the bleeding, and, at least for the moment, the young man was alive and breathing.

With no path to follow he weaved through the barrel cacti and brush that dotted the landscape. In reality, he did not need a path as this particular piece of remote wilderness had become like home to him in the past few years. There were precious few trails that cut through these parts, and they did Jeddediah no good any way. What he sought no trail would lead to. For the most part, he used landmarks to guide his way. He knew that the canyon was behind him to the east and set his course directly between the distant Weaver's Needle to the north and the highest mountain peak on his left. When he reached an expected wash, he looked back to the campsite before he descended. Although he worried the young man might awake while he was away it was a chance he was willing to take. His singular and burning desire was to reclaim his buried prize.

As he hobbled down into the tiny wash his legs reminded him of the weary night he had just endured and all his troubles came back to him. With one deep breath his ribs pulled at his side and brought on a wave of stabbing pains. He considered returning to the young man's campsite and resting a while, but the thought of his prize drew him onward. The sandy floor of the wash only added to his struggles and he wondered if there were some conspiring forces at work to keep him from reaching his objective.

"Dangnabbit," he cursed as he stubbed his toe on an unseen rock at the far end of the wash.

He climbed out of the wash and continued forward with a throbbing toe, sore legs, tired eyes and a cracked rib or two. The unmerciful desert sun had already begun her work, and sweat gathered around the brim of his hat. With a look to his left and right he pulled at his beard and took his bearings. A slight course correction was required and he was on his way again. When he spotted a plateau directly west of his position all pain and discomfort left his troubled mind and he hastened his steps as his secreted prize lay just ahead. He rounded the bend and his heart ached at the sight of the large Palo Verde tree lying on its side next to the plateau.

"No," he muttered. "Can't be."

The distance between himself and the fallen Palo Verde passed like a dream. He stood next to the trunk and looked down in horror at the broken roots jutting up out of the ground. Refusing to believe what his eyes were telling him, he dropped to his knees and began to claw at the dirt between the plateau and uprooted Palo Verde. He scooped up handfuls of disturbed soil and discarded them immediately until his fingers scraped across the harder desert core. When his vain hopes had been extinguished, he pounded his fists into the dirt and the intense pain in his side only added to his fury.

"No!" he shouted at the earth.

His long coveted prize was gone and there was no use denying it. Jeddediah looked over the fallen tree trunk to the spot where he left his monstrous pursuer and saw only dirt and brush. He arose, hurdled the tree trunk, and staggered over to where he had stood in the wee morning hours. It was at that moment he realized, once again, he had forgotten his pistol, this time back at the young man's campsite. With a furious kick at the impression the massive body left in the dirt, he nearly lost his balance and fell over. Only then did he notice the large foot prints that covered the area. They led in several different directions, but all seemed to originate from the spot where the body had fallen. He followed the patterns as they drew near the Palo Verde tree. A careful survey of the tree and its surroundings revealed just one set of footprints left the area, heading away to the east. He had no doubt where they led but followed them nonetheless, right to the edge of the canyon. From the spot where they disappeared over the ledge, he could see the entrance to the shaft from which he had emerged in a frantic retreat, hours earlier. His arms and legs began to shake as he peered down at the dark hole on the opposite canyon wall. The thought of venturing back into the tunnel was terrifying. He collapsed to the ground and lie motionless. The labors of a long night and morning having finally caught up with him. His side ached and he focused on the throbbing sensation while he stared at the tiny scattered pebbles among the dirt.

A black ant moved deliberately across his field of vision. The ant dragged what appeared to be a beige seed behind it. Jeddediah peered through his one open eye and followed the insect's progress. He felt a kinship with this ant and was certain its days were full of labor and toil just like him. Still he was certain this ant could not possibly be suffering a day like he was. Just then a smaller ant came dashing past the old ant. The smaller ant carried a seed just as big as the first ant, if not bigger, and yet the younger insect moved at twice the pace. Pebbles fell from Jeddediah's cheek as he peeled his face from the dirt and raised his head off the ground. He stared at the young ant as it darted over the ledge. All at once he sat up and looked down the canyon to the north.

A new seed of hope blossomed in his mind and gave him strength and energy that had abandoned him just a moment ago. He left his woes at the edge of the canyon and pursued his hope as swiftly as his old bones would allow. All the long shadows pointed to his left as he weaved between the bush and cacti in a beeline to his intended destination. Despite his quickened pace the return trip felt interminably long. When he reached the expected ridge and lay eyes on the red dome tent his stomach leapt up into this throat.

Casually kicking at a piece of debris with his foot was a slender dark-haired man with a wide-brimmed hat, khaki dress shirt and matching khaki pants. Unable to find his voice Jeddediah scrambled over the ridge toward the campsite. The man in the khaki shirt surveyed the chaotic campsite and turned to inspect the tent. Jeddediah was still half a football field away when he saw the unwelcomed guest reach out toward the tent.

"Hey!" Jeddediah shouted, at last finding his voice. "Get away from there!"

The khaki clad man spun around toward Jeddediah and adjusted the brim of his hat. Jeddediah stopped his hurried descent into the campground and tried to calm his breathing. He walked casually as the man in khaki placed his hands on his hips and waited.

"What do you think you're doing here?" demanded Jeddediah.

"Jeddediah, you scared the dickens out of me," the man said.

"You got no right to be here, Stanky," barked Jeddediah.

"It's Starkey," replied the man as he removed his hat and wiped at his brow. "And we've been over this. I'm a ranger and I have every right to be here."

"W-well," Jeddediah stammered. "These are my personal belongings and you don't have the right to go poking through them."

"This?" Starkey questioned as he tugged on the tent's rain fly. "This really isn't your style, is it?"

Jeddediah cast a worried look at the tent and hoped the interior remained still and silent.

"What's it to ya?" he said with disdain and slapped the ranger's hand away from the rain fly.

"Nothing," replied Starkey. "Just, what happened to your reclusive hermit shacks?"

"You know darn well what happened to 'em!" Jeddediah shouted. "You had 'em torn down for spite."

The slender ranger hung his head with an exasperated sigh and removed his wide brimmed hat. He gazed for a moment at the distant mountain peaks before he turned his attention back to his accuser. Resolve filled his face, casting off the inquisitive expression he had worn a second earlier. Jeddediah drew in a deep breath ready for a fight.

"It wasn't out of spite," Starkey replied. "It's the law. Section 2 of the Wilderness Protection act of 1964 says..."

"Ah pig spit," interrupted Jeddediah. "I weren't hurting nobody an' ya know..."

"Section 2," Starkey continued louder. "States that no structure or manmade road way or residence is to be erected in a protected wilderness area."

"I only used materials I found out here," Jeddediah argued with arms opened wide. "I was as outta the way as ya could git an'..."

"You carried lumber in on your donkey," Starkey cut in. "And that's not the point. It's my job…"

"First off, she's a mule. And it's your job to harass and hassle law abiding citizens trying to enjoy God's splendor," Jeddediah rebutted.

"Enjoy God's splendor?" Starkey questioned. "Article I Section II of the wilderness protection act specifically prohibits mining activities including…"

"I've read the blasted law!" Jeddediah shouted, waving his arms at the ranger. "An' there's provisions made for prospect'n an' survey'n. It ain't against the law to look."

The ranger shook his head and sighed deeply again. "You really think you're going to find anything? People have looked for that mine for a hundred years. It's not out here, probably never was."

"Fools have searched for the mine," said Jeddediah. "Wasted their lives look'n for what can't be found, I ain't no fool."

"If you're not looking for the mine, then what are you doing out here?" asked Starkey.

"Did the quest for Erebor end with them saunter'n into the Lonely Mountain?" he asked. "Did it matter one lick the fellowship knew where the entrance was to the mines of Moriah?"

Starkey furrowed his brow and tilted his head sideways as he tipped his hat back. Out of the corner of his eye, Jeddediah spotted his pistol atop a flat rock where he left it. It took considerable concentration not to cast a worried glance in that direction. He needed to keep the ranger's attention on him. To his right lay the pistol and to his left lay a young man who had fallen victim to the pistol. Each posed their own unique brand of trouble if discovered by the khaki clad busy body under the wide-brimmed hat.

"What are you talking about?" asked Starkey.

"Ah hells bells, would ya just git already?" Jeddediah yelled. "Ain't noth'n here for you to…"

The tent behind Starkey shook slightly as the patient inside moved. Jeddediah froze and his eyes widened. His mouth fell open but he was unable to draw in a breath. If the young man were discovered it would surely lead to questions and those questions would certainly lead to jail. The slender ranger studied Jeddediah closely for a moment. With eyes still locked on the old miner his shoulders shifted slowly back toward the tent. Panic swept through Jeddediah's body and one frenzied thought sprang to the front of his mind.

"That's it!" he shouted and tossed his floppy hat to the ground.

The startled ranger jerked back around to face Jeddediah and he crouched down in a defensive posture. Jeddediah pulled at the buttons on the front of his shirt and one by one undid them from the top down to the bottom. When his buttons were undone he pulled off his flannel shirt and cast it aside.

"What are you doing?" Starkey asked with a slight quiver in his voice.

"You can stay if ya like, but this here is my camp an' I can do as I please," Jeddediah said as he loosened the latch on his pants and let them drop to his knees.

"Stop that," protested Starkey as he slowly backed away.

Jeddediah lifted his good leg and tugged at his boot. He winced from the pain in his side but continued to undress.

"What is the matter with you?" Starkey asked as he took several steps away from the nearly naked old man.

The tent shook again as the young man shifted inside. The movement caught both of their attention, and Starkey paused in his retreat and looked over at the tent. Jeddediah acted quickly and kicked his boot off at the ranger. It stuck him in his bony shoulder and sent him careening backwards. By the time he recovered from the boot blast, Jeddediah had removed his other boot and shook free from his pants.

"You're crazy," cried Starkey.

"You bet I am," Jeddediah replied. "Now git!"

Starkey stumbled as he turned around and scurried up the small hill to the north. He stopped at the top and turned back toward the campsite.

"Go on, git!" shouted Jeddediah as he waved his arms wildly. All that covered his wrinkly body was his grey beard and a pair of dingy red boxer shorts. Without another word, the frightened park ranger disappeared over the ridge and a victorious calm settled over the camp site.

Jeddediah chuckled to himself as he sauntered over triumphantly to his pants that were dangling from a prickly bush. As he hiked up his britches and fastened them to his waist, the tent rustled gently again. He glanced back over toward the ridge to ensure that their nosey ranger had not returned. When he was certain the coast was clear he reached under the rain fly. The metal couplers made the customary zipping sound as he drew down the handle and pulled open the front flap of the tent. Inside, the round faced young man, with hair that matched the bright red tent, scrunched up his face as he sat up slightly and rested back on his elbows.

"Is he gone?" Glenn asked.

"Yep," Jeddediah replied as he examined his bandaged leg. There was a small circle of blood on his upper thigh where the bullet had entered the young man's body, which he figured was reasonable considering the size of the wound.

"Why aren't you wearing a shirt?" questioned Glenn.

"Never mind that," Jeddediah barked. "How's the leg?"

Glenn lifted it gingerly off the sleeping pad and set it back down. He sat upright and rubbed at the bandages.

"All right, considering it stopped a bullet," replied Glenn.

"Yeah, about that..."

"Don't worry about it," Glenn said with a wave of his hand. "It was my fault as much as yours. It was dark, I should have announced myself. Besides, now I can say I've been shot. So that's cool."

Jeddediah cocked his head sideways and studied the young man. He could not imagine a scenario where he would be okay with getting shot and was puzzled by the guileless expression on his victim's face. Unable to come to any certain conclusion about the young man's sanity, he turned around and hunted for his shirt. One of his boots had landed atop his old flannel shirt. He scooped up the shirt, knocking over the boot, and dusted it off. With his eye trained on the pistol atop the flat rock, he slipped his arms through the sleeves and began to button from the bottom.

"My mom said she'd never seen anybody button up a shirt from the bottom except me," Glenn said, still lying on his back inside the tent.

Jeddediah ignored him and continued to button up his shirt, still looking down at his pistol.

"So, did you find it?" asked Glenn.

"Find what?" Jeddediah replied.

"Did you find what you're looking for?" asked Glenn

"What do ya know about what I'm looking for?" Jeddediah questioned.

"Just what I heard you tell the ranger," replied Glenn.

"And what do ya think ya heard?" Jeddediah asked, as he turned his full attention on the red-headed young man.

"I heard you're a fan of Tolkien," Glenn began. "And I heard you're looking for a key."

Glenn's eyebrows bounced up and down like ginger caterpillars on a trampoline as he shot him a playful grin. Jeddediah brushed at the whiskers on his face and could not suppress a grin of his own.

"Well I'll be," he whispered.

OUTLIER

Gideon leaned against the brittle wooden fence post and watched a trio of horses quietly gazing on a pile of hay. His admiration for the majestic creatures was interrupted when the dark brown steed on his left lifted her tail and dropped three large turds in the dirt. He covered a childish smile with his hand even though there was no one else around. The sound of approaching footsteps on the loose gravel drew his attention away from the horses. Liz walked up beside him and gently brushed his arm with her shoulder as she too leaned against the old fence post.

"Hey," Gideon greeted her.

"Hey yourself," she said with a smile and a wink.

They both turned from the corral to face the rundown ranch house with their elbows draped back over the fencing. A charcoal gray dog lay on the front porch, fast asleep. Todd's pickup truck was parked around the side by a sun-beaten barn, which appeared to be held together with nothing more than rusty old nails and faith. The house, barn and the corral were all tacked together with the same cracked and twisted wood that Gideon imagined must have been warped by at least half a century in the harsh desert heat. This morning, however, heat was not an issue as they were in the middle of the fleeting Arizona winter cold. Gideon peered through the doorway of the old ranch house at Todd who was talking with someone he could not yet see.

"You ready for this?" asked Liz.

"I guess we'll see," replied Gideon. "You?"

"I think so," she answered.

"Well you sure look ready," said Gideon.

She wore brown leather boots that came to a point at the toes, a pair of blue jeans with a matching jean jacket and a beige cowboy hat. Gideon looked her up and down with a respectful tip of his Diamondbacks baseball cap. She laughed and gave him a half-hearted shove.

"Are you checking me out Gideon Goodwin?" she asked.

"Did you just have that get-up in your closet?" he asked.

"My uncle has some horses up in Alpine," she replied. "I go up there most summers to help out."

Gideon cocked his head to the side and raised one eyebrow. She placed her hands on her hips and returned his quizzical stare. He reached up and flicked her pristine cowboy hat with a smirk.

"Fine!" she exclaimed. "I bought it for a Brooks and Dunn concert. Are you happy?"

He turned a satisfied smile back toward the ranch house as Todd emerged with a rugged looking cowboy. They walked toward Gideon and Liz almost in slow motion. Todd was a couple inches shorter than the man to his left but the 5-gallon Stetson atop the man's head made the difference appear much greater. The cowboy wore a pair of leather riding caps over his blue jeans and walked slightly bowlegged as dramatic clouds of dust kicked up and blew in the breeze behind him.

"Oh my," Liz remarked in a whisper.

Gideon scowled at the ground as the square jawed cowboy drew nearer. He looked down at his black Reeboks and lamented his less manly attired. At first he had counted it a great blessing when he found his old black hoodie from high school in the back of Todd's closet. Now he wished it was a rugged jean jacket or even a leather jacket. If he could have magically transformed his favorite baseball cap into a Stetson or even a fedora he would have; anything to compete with the picture of manhood that stood before him. What added to his distress was that, with his thick wool shirt and boots, the cowboy and Liz looked like a perfect match for a western themed prom, while Gideon and Todd were literally wearing the same clothes they wore in high school.

"Gideon, Liz," Todd said. "This is Cal."

"Of course it is," Gideon muttered.

Even his name was as if he had escaped from the pages of a Zane Grey novel. Liz reached out immediately to shake his hand while Gideon forced his hands into the front pocket of his hoodie. He took little comfort in the fact that his olive complexion was just a dark and sun-kissed as the cowboy, only not as hardened and rough looking.

"Howdy ma'am," Cal greeted her. He flashed a smile with his perfectly straight teeth. Liz blushed and Gideon cursed the cowboy's cleft chin and dimpled cheeks that were, of course, covered with a blanket of man stubble.

"Cal is going to take us out to camp to make sure we get there all right," said Todd.

"Do we really need that?" asked Gideon. "Don't *you* know where Joe is?"

"I know where he is, but it's in the middle of a hundred and sixty acres of wilderness," replied Todd with a 'what's the matter with you' expression. "There's a lot of ground to cover between here and there and Cal knows the Superstitions as well as anybody. Besides that, he's going to help carry supplies that we need."

"Gideon, this is wild country," Liz added. "It will be good to have someone along who knows the lay of the land."

"No worries ma'am," Cal said to Liz. "I'll take good care of ya."

The rugged cowboy winked at Liz with his sky blue eyes, and Gideon felt the blood vessels in his neck expand until they nearly choked him. He grabbed Todd by the arm and pulled him to the side with their backs to the cowboy.

"What is your deal?" Todd asked as he wrestled his arm free.

"Can we trust this guy?" Gideon questioned. "How much does he know?"

"He knows you're look'n for the Dutchman," Cal said in a louder than normal voice. "And he ain't deaf."

Gideon glared over his shoulder as Cal tipped his cap toward him with a mischievous grin.

"Relax, G," Todd said. "Cal's been doing this for years."

"Just let me saddle the horses, and we'll be on our way," Cal said as he gracefully swung his leg up and over the fence and sauntered to a group of saddles laid over the railing.

Liz leaned over the fence post and watched Cal approach the horse nearest him, with a blanket he had retrieved from a pile near the saddles. Gideon leapt into action and hopped the fence into the corral. He grabbed a blanket and draped it over the dark brown horse in front of him. Cal smiled at Gideon as he rolled up the sleeves of his shirt and grabbed hold of one of the saddles. Gideon followed suit and pushed the sleeves of his hoodie up to his elbows and picked up the next saddle in line. He flung it on the back of the horse just moments after Cal and began to work frantically to try and beat the cowboy. To his disappointment he cinched down the last strap only to turn around and find Cal leaned against his horse watching Gideon with a satisfied expression of victory on his face.

"That's pretty good, kid," he said.

Gideon gritted his teeth at both the condescending tone and the fact that Cal called him 'kid' though it was clear he could not have been more than five or six years older than him.

"Horsemanship merit badge, '94," Gideon replied in an attempt to shake off his emasculation.

Cal laughed and picked up the last blanket from the ground. Gideon looked over his shoulder back toward his friends. Liz wore a puzzled expression that took Gideon aback.

"What's that on your arm?" she asked.

Gideon held up his right arm, knowing full well what she referred to. He displayed the tattoo of the backward facing bird in the middle of his forearm. When he looked back at Liz she wore a disapproving grimace.

"It's Sankofa," he answered. "It means learn from the past."

"What about learn from the prophet?" Liz asked as both hands returned to her hips.

Gideon sighed and forced himself to meet her judgmental eyes. He was well aware of the counsel they received from the prophet regarding tattoos and body piercing. In this case, however, he had justified his choice as a prerequisite to taking up the mantle he had been given and to fully joining with the secret he hoped to protect. Under the weight of her stare those justifications melted away to reveal the shed of shame they had been insulating.

"Ya know," Cal's deep voice rose over Gideon's shoulder and broke the silence. "I treat my body like a temple. No mark'ns or pierc'ns for me. I'm just the way God made me."

"That's great, Cal," Gideon responded as he attempted to unclench his jaw. "Thanks for sharing."

Cal tipped his hat to Gideon and received the gratitude with all the sincerity that the giver lacked. Only then did Gideon realize that Cal had saddled the last horse while his back was turned.

"Should we load up the horses?" Todd asked.

"Yep," Cal replied. "Once we get 'em loaded, we can head out."

"Wait," Liz said to Todd. "Where's this mystery companion you've got for me?"

Todd checked his watch and turned around to look up the lone dirt road that led to the ranch. In the distance, a yellow car moved deliberately toward the rod-iron gate with the letters RB welded onto the top. A cloud of dust trailed behind the car like smoke from a rocket.

"Here she is now," Todd said. "Right on time."

The yellow taxi rolled to a stop around the front of the old ranch house. Todd walked over to the car and pulled open the back driver's side door. Out stepped a sleek muscular woman with dark brown skin and black hair. She greeted Todd with a one armed hug as she shouldered her backpack with the other. Todd paid the driver and they walked side by side toward the corral as the taxi backed down the driveway.

"Wha pun, Tara," Gideon greeted the new arrival. "Wha ya say?"

"Boy, mi nearly died from boredom on dat drive up 'ere," she replied.

"Yeah, there's really nothing between here and Tucson," said Gideon.

"Noth'n but cactus an' dirt," she agreed.

"Liz, this is Tara," Todd made introductions. "Tara, this is Liz."

"Pleased to meet you," Tara said as she slowed down her speech and enunciated.

"The pleasure is mine," said Liz.

"Tara is a friend of ours from Jamaica," Gideon explained.

"I figured," said Liz. "You didn't come all the way from Jamaica for this, did you?"

"No, mi live with mi son down a Tucson," Tara answered.

"How's Corey doing?" Gideon asked.

"'im real good," she said. "'im love school an' dem tek good care of 'im."

"Her son is deaf," Todd said to Liz while he signed with his hands. "Gideon got him into a really good school for deaf children."

Tara smiled at Gideon until it looked as if her dimpled cheeks might pop. Gideon nodded and smiled back as the two regarded each other. Cal stepped in between them on his way to grab some rope looped around a distance fence post. Gideon glowered at him as Tara followed the cowboy with her dark brown eyes.

"You sure he'll be okay without you?" Todd asked.

"Yeah man," replied Tara. "We live on campus an' 'im 'ave plenty of friends an' teacher fi look after 'im."

"It was really nice of you to come all this way for our little expedition," Liz said.

"No problem," said Tara. "Mi know what it is fi go out into di wilderness with these fool fool boys. Yu were right fi wan' company."

Gideon and Todd laughed as memories of their adventure in the cockpits came flooding back. It had been a little more than five months since they traveled through the Jamaican backcountry on a quest that had altered the course of all their lives. At the time Gideon had given little thought to the consequences of their choice to go searching for answers. Even if he had could not have imagined the consequences would follow. He felt a similar feeling at the outset of this journey. He had no idea what they might find or if their time in the wilderness would prove fruitful. This time, however, he was acutely aware of the unknown dangers they might face and the potential that they might indeed discover something extraordinary. The thought caused a knot to form in the pit of his stomach, as he had no desire to ever place his friends in harm's way again, especially not Liz.

"Well I'm glad you're here," Liz said. "You can tell me what Gideon was like as a missionary."

Tara scrunched up her round nose and shrugged her shoulders with a look toward Gideon.

"I met Tara after the mission," Gideon explained.

"Oh," Liz replied. She looked down at the ground and folded her arms across her chest.

"Ya'll ready," Cal asked as he joined the group.

"Tara, this is Cal," Todd introduced them.

"Howdy ma'am," Cal said. He tipped his hat to her and Gideon was certain her dark cheeks redden as she giggled like a school girl. Gideon rolled his eyes and sighed. Cal swung himself back over the fence into the corral and the group followed after him, climbing one by one over the creaky old wooden barrier.

"This here is Moses," Cal said with a pat on the romp of the tan horse with a blondish white mane. "He's gonna lead us into the wilderness to the promised land. I'll be rid'n him."

Cal walked in between the brown horse and gray spotted horse. He took hold of their respective reigns and led them in front of the group.

"This here is Pepper," he said with a nod toward the gray spotted horse. "And this is Hercules. Pepper can be a handful so she needs an experienced rider with a gentle touch."

Without a word Liz stepped forward and took the bridle from Cal's hand. She grabbed the horn, put her foot in the stirrup and gracefully swung her leg over the black leather saddle. Pepper took several jittery steps backward. Liz calmly leaned forward and patted her while she whispered soothingly. In moments Pepper stood calm and still with Liz sitting triumphantly atop her.

"Nothing like a woman with a soft touch," Cal remarked.

Gideon's ears reddened and he felt as if his blood was boiling. He did not like the way Cal looked at Liz and liked even less the way she looked at him. Before he had the chance to say or do something regrettable a new realization dawned on him and he looked around the corral for confirmation.

"There are only three horses," Gideon stated.

"Two of us will have to double up," Cal said.

"I'm with da cowboy," Tara said as she raised her hand and shuffled quickly over to stand next to Cal.

"Hercules can handle you two just fine," Cal said.

Todd jogged forward and mounted the tall brawny horse. Gideon watched Cal help Tara up onto Moses dark brown saddle and then climbed on behind her. Liz had done a lap around the interior of the corral and came to a stop next to Cal and Tara. Hercules walked slowly over to Gideon with Todd on his back.

"You want front or back?" Todd asked.

Gideon shook his head and put his foot in the stirrup that Todd had vacated for him. He swung up onto Hercules and settled in behind Todd, atop a rolled up blanket. Without another word, Cal led the group out of the corral northward, into the heart of the wilderness. Todd gave Hercules a nudge with his heels and the hulking horse lumbered up next to Liz, who looked completely at ease atop of Pepper. Cal whistled back toward the ranch house.

"Come on, Dog," he commanded.

The charcoal cattle dog leapt from the porch and trotted joyfully to join the group.

"What's your dog's name?" asked Liz.

"Dog," Cal replied

"His dog's name is Dog," Todd whispered to Gideon. "This guy is the man."

"Seriously, how do we know we can trust him?" asked Gideon.

"Would you relax," Todd said. "Cal knows the Superstitions like Tara knows the cockpits. He'll get us where we're going."

Gideon did not reply but it was not Cal's sense of direction that bothered him. He was uneasy about having an outsider join their journey, albeit temporarily. And although he could not put a finger on it, something about the cowboy made him uneasy.

"Keep an eye out for rattlers," Cal called back over his shoulder.

"It's winter," Gideon responded. "Snakes are all sleeping."

Cal eased back on the reigns and sidled up next to the other two horses. He glared over at Gideon and sat up tall in the saddle, with his arms still around Tara.

"There are always outliers," Cal warned. "Creatures who don't conform to the rules of God or man. It's them that are the most dangerous of all."

A cold chill shot up Gideon's spine. He wished he could attribute it to the winter weather but reluctantly attributed it to Cal's solemn warning. With a nudge and a click from the cowboy's tongue, Moses trotted up ahead of them in the lead position. Liz and Gideon exchanged wide-eyed looks before she too prodded her horse forward and followed behind Cal and Tara. No sooner had they fallen into formation than the trail narrowed and the incline steepened. They ascended a ridge that dropped back off the other side into a wash. From the top of the ridge Gideon looked to the west and could just make out Flatiron peak in the distance. He thought of Glenn's clues and how much he would have loved playing cowboy. Cal and Tara were already at the bottom of the wash, and Liz was halfway down, before Hercules began the descent. Gravity forced Gideon into Todd's back as they were tossed from side to side with each loping step. When they reached the bottom, Gideon adjusted himself back onto the blanket behind the saddle and wished he had a horse of his own. They headed straight down the sandy wash for nearly a mile before Cal abruptly turned left, and Moses climbed to the ridge on the opposite side from where they had entered.

"So, you're not from around here?" Gideon heard Cal ask Tara as they made their way down a well-worn horse trail. While he heard her answer audibly Gideon did not pay particular attention to their conversation as he was certain it would only lead to aggravation. Instead he focused on the peaks that they were approaching to the west. He wondered where exactly they were headed and looked forward to seeing Joe again. Saguaro cactus dotted the face of the mountain and looked like a band of warriors assembled for battle.

"You know," Gideon said aloud. "This area used to be inhabited by Apache."

Liz glanced over her shoulder and Todd simply shook his head and prodded Hercules onward. When no objections were offered Gideon decided to continue.

"They were fierce warriors and drove out or killed anybody who traveled through these parts," he went on. "The other tribes feared this area and the Apache thunder god. It's part of the legend of this place. Some say..."

A shadow moved between two of the cacti near the top of the peak. Gideon shook his head and squint his eyes. His mouth fell open as a hooded figure with a grey cloak came into focus. He did not want to believe what he saw, but the figure moved again across the peak's face and there was no denying their cloaked watchman was following them again.

"Some say, what?" asked Todd.

Before he could answer, Pepper reared up just in front of them and threw Liz to the ground. On sheer instinct Gideon dismounted and ran to her side. He reached her just as she began to sit up. She stopped abruptly and Gideon froze as well at the dreaded sound of a rapid rattling just ahead of them. Pepper bounded away as Hercules lumbered backward and Todd tried to steady him.

"Woah," Todd called.

Gideon and Liz stared at the coiled-up snake just off the beaten path. Its black and gold body pulsed and rippled with each ominous rattle. Gideon slowly slid his body between Liz and the snake as she clutched his arm. They were close enough to see the tongue protruding from its diamond shaped head. A shot rang out and the snake's head exploded into a plume of dust that leapt up from the desert floor. The blonde-haired horse came bounding down the trail and Cal dismounted right in front of them with his pistol still drawn. Tara took hold of the reigns and drew Moses to a halt. Dog trotted up next to Cal, as the gun toting cowboy kicked at the remains of the snake's still coiled body with his boot and holstered his sidearm. Gideon came to his feet and turned to help Liz up. Dog growled and pawed at the dead snake. They joined Cal next to the corpse of the venomous serpent.

"Outlier," Cal said. He spit on the rattlesnake and turned to Gideon. "Well he's sleeping now."

With the immediate danger departed Gideon waited for his elevated heart rate to return to normal. Although he was grateful for their rescue from harm, he struggled with his feelings of resentment for their rescuer. Tara and Todd had climbed down from their mounts and walked the horses over to what was beginning to look like a memorial for the rattlesnake. For several moments, no one spoke. Gideon thought of what a snake bite would have meant for him or their journey and shuttered to think what he would have done if it had been Liz. He turned to the cowboy and swallowed hard.

"Thank you," he said with an outstretched hand.

Cal reached out and grasped Gideon by the hand. His grip was just as firm and manly as Gideon would have expected. He would have tried to give him an extra squeeze if not for the fact that his callused hands already felt like granite.

"Yes, thank you," Liz added. "That was amazing."

"Weren't noth'n ma'am," Cal replied. "Besides, I couldn't bear to see a beautiful thing like yourself marked up by a pair of fangs."

Liz blushed and Gideon's newfound gratitude quickly retreated from the onslaught of jealously. Cal did not wait for further adulation. He hopped up on Moses and turned the horse back the way they had come.

"Dog, go get her," he said. "We're gonna run down Pepper. Be back in a jiff. Gitup!"

Moses galloped away after Dog at the sound of Cal's commanding voice. The quartet watched him ride away toward a tiny gray spec up the trail.

"Do you think I should go help him?" asked Todd.

"I don't think he needs any help," replied Liz.

"No man, 'im a bad man," added Tara. "Dat boy is...hot like da sun."

"Yeah," Liz agreed as the two ladies gawked toward the clouds of dust left by Moses' hoofs.

Gideon turned back toward the peaks, unwilling to participate in the Cal appreciation party. All at once the gray hooded figure returned to his thoughts. He scanned the mountainside but saw nothing more than cactus and rocks. His mind whirled as he tried to discern the motives of their mysterious stalker. He began to worry that rebellious rattlesnakes would not be the only menace they might face out there in the wilderness.

CORONADO'S CHILDREN

"How much further?" asked Glenn.

The redheaded young man limped along in a pair of gray sweatpants. He wore a faded blue t-shirt with a black and yellow Batman symbol on the front and a white canvas cap with a long flap in the back that covered his neck.

"We'd already be there if you'd pick up the pace," replied Jeddediah.

"Oh I'm sorry!" Glenn exclaimed. "Some old coot shot me in the leg."

Jeddediah brushed him off with a dismissive wave. He wished he could offer a better response but he had indeed shot the poor young man earlier that morning. Despite that tiny face, he considered them even since he had patched him up afterwards, although he knew very few people would take up his side. They stopped to rest from the unrelenting sun in the shadow of the cliff face to their west. Jeddediah scanned the way ahead and pointed toward a mountain top shaped like a medieval castle.

"We're headed to the other side of that mountain there," he explained. "Are you good to go on?"

Glenn nodded and pushed off from the rock he had been resting on. He picked up his backpack and slung it over his shoulder. Jeddediah took up the remaining bag as a painful jolt stung his side and led the way toward the castle-like rock. He began to worry that Glenn's wounded leg would prove to be a fatal flaw in his scheming. Even in his old age and with his cracked and weary bones Jeddediah made better time on their march than the hobbled young man. Time to recover was required but just how much time was unclear. That particular unknown caused Jeddediah a good deal of internal torment and anxiety. To make matters worse, he had held his obsession in his hands and then all too quickly it had been taken away. His hopes now, ironically, rested with the young man whose rescue had necessitated the separation from his prize and ultimately led to its loss. They dropped down into a ravine and lost sight of their mountain destination.

"How long have you lived out here?" Glenn asked.

"Technically speaking I live in Superior," said Jeddediah. "But I made the Superstitions my home over ten years ago."

"Are you from Arizona then?" asked Glenn.

"Yep," Jeddediah replied.

"Me too," Glenn said between labored breaths. "Born and raised. I grew up in AJ."

Jeddediah looked back at the red haired young man with an acknowledging nod. He had been alone in the desert for so long that he was unaccustomed to all the chatter. The solitude of the Superstitions was the thing he loved best about it. On any given day, especially in the heat of the summer, he took comfort in the assurance that he was the only human being for miles. It was as if he was the king of the desert and the rock, cactus, reptiles, and birds were his subjects. This newcomer posed a threat to his kingdom and his peace, but he knew that for now he could prove to be a useful ally. The heavy bag in his hand scraped along a rock protruding out of the ground. He adjusted his grip and strained to lift it higher with another stabbing pain from his ribs.

"Whatcha got in this bag anyway?" Jeddediah demanded.

"Food," Glenn answered. "Mostly Dinty Moore."

"Dinty Moore?"

"Yeah, you know, beef stew," Glenn replied.

Jeddediah dropped the bag on the ground and opened it up.

"Are you tell'n me you've got me haul'n around cans of stew?" he exclaimed.

"My mom packed them," Glenn explained. "She wants to make sure I eat good when I'm out here."

Jeddediah shook his head and gave the cans a kick. With his hands on his hips he gave the bag a good long look before he hefted it off the ground. They turned left and ascended a jagged rock formation out of the ravine. From the top, the castle rock formation once again came into view only much closer. To the west, the desert sprawled out toward far off mountain tops. Behind them to the south the up and down terrain was rocky and mostly bare, with tiny blue gray peaks miles away on the horizon.

"And what is it again that you're do'n out here?" asked Jeddediah.

"Same as you I guess," said Glenn. "Looking for something extraordinary."

The old miner faced north and gestured with open arms from right to left.

"Wouldn't ya say this is extra ordinary?" he asked.

"It sure is," Glenn agreed.

They both stopped and took in their majestic surrounding. Each peak and valley was unique, as if hundreds of artists had worked in concert to compile their talents into a single masterpiece. Jeddediah considered how few people on earth had beheld this awe inspiring view and counted himself one of the luckiest men in the world. Still those who dared to tread into this wilderness left an indelible mark on its history and any pilgrim who chose to follow after them could feel that these mountains guarded great secrets.

"But I didn't come out here for the view," Glenn added, breaking their silent worship. "I'm looking for what lies in the shadows, for things not easily seen."

"You're look'n for treasure," Jeddediah clarified.

"Not necessarily," said Glenn. "There's something out here though, I can feel it. Whether it's a treasure or a secret lost to time, I intend to find it."

He could not keep the smile off his face as he studied his sincere, young friend. Despite nearly half a century that separated them, Jeddediah felt a kinship with this young man that he had not found in all his long years.

"It's not much further now," he assured Glenn.

They took a longer but flatter route, swinging wide around the base of the castle rock mountain. Jeddediah checked all sides to ensure they were not being watched or followed. Then he took a straight course directly toward the smallest stone tower of the mighty rock formation. The sun shone down from the west, directly behind him so his shadow reached the mountain long before he did. He followed his shadow through a breach in the rock. Glenn followed behind and Jeddediah looked back to see him wince in pain as he lifted his leg over a rock at the narrow opening. Beyond the breach the gap widened significantly and joined with a small valley in the shape of a crescent. It was filled with cottonwood trees and hackberry bushes. There were dozens of knee high green bushes which grew along a small track of smooth rocks and cut through the valley. Beside the row of brushes was an ancient broken down wagon with a dingy white mule tied to it and beyond that a one room wooden shack.

"Here we are," Jeddediah announced. "Find a place to rest and I'll fill the canteens."

"Wow," Glenn remarked. "How long did it take you to build that thing way out here?"

"I didn't build it," he replied. "I found it."

"You found it?" asked Glenn. "Who built it then?"

"Look, one question will only lead to another," Jeddediah snapped. "You get off your feet and I'll get some water. Then I'll tell you what I know."

Glenn limped over to a pair of round rocks beneath one of the cottonwood trees and wedged his bottom in between the rock and the tree with his wounded leg propped up against the farthest rock. Jeddediah made his way over to a round wooden barrel. He lifted the dusty old lid from the top and submerged the canteen into the murky water in the lower portion of the barrel. Another stinging pain shot through his ribcage as he swapped one canteen for the next. After he replaced the dusty lid he returned to Glenn and handed him one of the canteens before taking a seat beside him in the dirt.

"It ain't clean or cold but it's wet," the old miner said. "Drink."

Glenn took a hasty gulp of water and wiped his chin with the back of his hand.

"So, who built the shack? Is that your wagon? How did you find this place?" Glenn opened his mouth and released a flood of questions.

"Easy," Jeddediah said while raising his hands to calm his excited friend. "One thing at a time. I found this place on a tip from an old friend."

The dilapidated old shack looked as if it were about to collapse to the ground. Large gaps shone between the warped rotting wood. The roof provided only slightly better coverage from the sun than the cottonwood trees above it, but when the seasonal rain came it was impossible to ignore the holes and cracks over head. Still, Jeddediah had an affinity for this old place that had nothing to do with comfort or function. He counted it a great blessing that this place had not been discovered by the Park Services and destroyed.

"The wagon has been here as long as the shack," Jeddediah continued. "The man who built it was called Walt."

"Waltz?" Glenn asked excitedly.

"No!" Jeddediah exclaimed. "It's not the Dutchman. His name was Walt-t-t."

Glenn's freckled cheeks fell as he leaned back against the cottonwood tree. Jeddediah drew in a healthy breath and continued.

"They said Walt was a Dutch Hunter looking for the lost mine," he said. "He built this here shack in the early 30's."

The mule took a break from grazing on a patch of grass and whinnied loudly to no one in particular. Jeddediah turned around to ensure all was well with his four-legged companion.

"And the mule?" asked Glenn.

"Well, she's considerably younger than that," replied Jeddediah.

"No," said Glenn. "What's her name?"

"Bernice," Jeddediah said. "She's a good ole girl, but like most females it's best not to cross her or you'll have to deal with an uncooperative nag until she's satisfied with your suffering."

Jeddediah shouted the last several words over his shoulder at the old mule. She simply returned to her grazing, unconcerned with the ranting old miner or his new guest.

"But you are looking for the Lost Dutchman though?" asked Glenn.

"No," Jeddediah replied incredulously.

"Then why are you holed up in an old Dutch Hunter's camp?" asked Glenn.

"Cause that doggone ranger drove me out of every other camp I had," said Jeddediah. "Besides, this place ain't too far from where I want to be."

"And where's that?" asked Glenn.

"Not sure you're ready for that just yet," Jeddediah replied after a long pause. "You know about the Dutchman, what else do you know?"

"What do you mean?"

"The mountains, the superstitions," Jeddediah clarified. "Didya just wander into the wilderness without know'n what you were gett'n into? What do you know, boy?"

"First of all, I'm nineteen," Glenn said. "I'm not a boy. And I know plenty."

Jeddediah eyed the young man skeptically for a moment. The shadow from the western ridge had reached the base of the cottonwood tree by which they sat. Its shade would offer a welcome respite from the desert heat and also meant that night would soon follow. He stretched his back and tiny tinges of pain fired through his old bones like fire crackers. He waited for the young man to collect his thoughts and hoped his answer would not disappoint. If he truly was a kindred spirit then he would know much more than legends of lost gold spouted to every tourist that came to the east valley. Glenn took another drink from his canteen and set it to the side as he sat up and adjusted his wounded leg.

"I know that this area is marked by the names of those who lived and died out here," Glenn began. "Reavis Ranch is named after Elisha Reavis. He was the hermit of the Superstitions and grew fruit and stuff back in the hills. I've hiked down to the apple orchards he planted. I know that Weaver's Needle is named after an explorer, and I've hiked to that too. I know Jacob Waltz was German, not Dutch, and that he told tales of a mine full of gold to anyone who would listen and left cryptic clues about its location. Supposedly, he gave directions to Julia Thomas on his deathbed. I know that people have been chasing after the Dutchman for over a hundred years and I know that he wasn't even the first to find gold in these mountains. The Peralta's beat Jacob Waltz by thirty some odd years and took lots of gold back to Mexico, and I've hiked Peralta trail too."

Glenn leaned back against the cottonwood with a satisfied grin on his face. Jeddediah pulled at the whiskers on his face and considered the young man. He had recited little more than one could learn from a trip to the Lost Dutchman museum but that was more than most. If this young man was to be his partner, he would need some schooling but Jeddediah was hesitant to give him his education all at once.

"So you've hiked the Superstitions," Jeddediah replied. "Is that it?"

Glenn grimaced and said, "What exactly do you want me to say?"

"Noth'n," he replied. "You mentioned the Peralta's. What about before them?"

"Well, I know they were ambushed and killed by Apaches," said Glenn. "So I guess the Apaches were before them."

The red haired young man looked as if he were melting into the tree beneath the withering gaze of the old miner.

"The Hohokam?" Glenn guessed.

"You went a might too far," Jeddediah said. "The first who came to this country in search of gold were the Spanish. Most famously was Coronado, in search of the fabled city of gold."

Glenn leaned forward again and his eyes widened. Jeddediah was pleased at the level of interest that he showed and also that this information seemed to be a revelation to his young apprentice.

"But Coronado brought more gold with him, thanks his suit of armor, than he ever found," Jeddediah continued. "When Coronado gave up and headed back to Mexico City, he left three priests behind. Several years later a party was sent to find them, but they was already dead. What they did find were deposits of rich minerals which they marked for them what'd come after 'em, only the age of the conquistadors was over and those that followed them were missionaries."

He paused to gauge the investment of his would-be accomplice. When he stopped talking Glenn leaned closer and appeared eager to learn more. Satisfied that he had sufficiently captivated the young man, Jeddediah continued.

"Father Francisco Kino, The Great Black Robe, founded a mission down in Tucson and built the oldest church in Arizona in 1700," he said.

"San Xavier del Bac," Glenn interrupted. "We went there on a field trip."

Jeddediah nodded and forgave the minor disruption to his story. "From San Xavier, Father Kino traveled all over the southwest and was the first to map the area. For fifty years after his death, the Black Robes amassed great wealth all throughout the region which they kept from the Spanish crown. When King Charles III heard of their deception, he called them back to Spain. Before they left, the Black Robes hid their wealth in these mountains for the day when they returned. Only they never did."

"How do you know all this?" a wide-eyed Glenn asked.

"I ain't ready to share that just yet," replied Jeddediah. "You wouldn't be the first skeptic."

"No," said Glenn. "I believe you. So, you're looking for the key to find the priest's gold?"

"I found the key," Jeddediah proclaimed with his head held high. Then the events of the day played through his mind. "But then I lost it."

"You lost it?" asked Glenn. "How?"

"I had to save your life, that's how," he said with an accusing wag of his finger.

"Well, you did shoot me," replied Glenn.

Jeddediah picked mindlessly at a patch of grass next to him unable to formulate a valid defense.

"Is that what you buried by the tree?" asked Glenn.

He nodded and rolled the uprooted blades of grass in his fingers.

"And you can't return and get it?" asked Glenn.

"I tried," Jeddediah said. "It's gone."

"What do you mean it's gone?"

"Gone!" Jeddediah exclaimed. "Reclaimed. Taken back into the darkness."

"Taken back?"

"Something's guard'n it," Jeddediah's voice trembled.

"Something?"

"Something," Jeddediah spat. "I don't know if it's a man, a monster or an unholy demon. Whatever it is, it took the key and returned to the underworld."

"Then you know where it is," Glenn asserted.

"Yeah, I know where it is."

The young man smiled brightly and sat up straight and tall. He rubbed at his bandaged leg for a moment. Then he rolled over unto one knee and braced himself again the tree. With a good deal of effort, he slowly came to his feet. Jeddediah mirrored his ascension and stood next to Glenn with a quizzical look.

"Why are you smil'n?" Jeddediah asked.

"Are you kidding me?" Glenn exclaimed. "This is the most amazing day of my life! I got shot and lived. Now I've been enlisted by an old man on a quest for a secret key to an old Spanish treasure guarded by a monster deep in these legendary mountains! So epic!"

"Are ya crazy, boy?" asked Jeddediah. "This ain't no game. I barely escaped with my life."

"But ya did," Glenn grinned. "And now there are two of us."

Jeddediah looked over in disbelief at the enthusiastic redhead. In his wildest dreams, he had hoped to be able to con or cajole this young man into helping him face the demon in the darkness. Not only had he come to it on his own but he welcomed the prospect, and not in spite of the difficulty and danger but because of it. Jeddediah could not help but take this new alliance as divine providence.

"He'll know we're com'n," Jeddediah warned.

"Then we'd better get working on a plan," Glenn said. He hobbled over to the old mule and began to gently brush her mane. Jeddediah shook his head and looked up into the afternoon sky. Out of the corner of his eye he caught the movement of an unnatural shadow. He spun back toward the west ridge and was blinded by the horizon that was bathed by the slowly setting sun. As quickly as his old bones would allow he crouched down into the shade of the cottonwood and peered earnestly back at the top of the ridge. There was no doubt in his mind he had seen something up there move. Whether by man or beast, they were being watched.

MONSTER

Gideon examined the crude lean-to propped up against a waist-high boulder. He squatted down and looked underneath blue tarp to find a navy blue sleeping bag and a ragged pillow with several tiny feathers protruding out of the seams. There was no doubt in his mind that a strong breeze would completely blow this structure apart and he could not imagine that Joe would have constructed such a flimsy shelter.

"Are you sure this is his camp?" asked Gideon.

"This is it," replied Todd.

There was a stone ring surrounding a pit of ashes and Todd stood over it next to Cal, Liz, and Tara. Cal bent down and placed his hand over the dormant embers in the fire pit. He stood up back up and brushed his hands on his blue jeans.

"This was lit this morn'n," Cal proclaimed.

Along with the rest of the party, Gideon scanned their distant surroundings. The camp was in the middle of an expansive incline that rose up to the eastern horizon. Out to the west were a multitude of hills and valleys that stretched to the high mountain peaks of Crooked Top Mountain. Gideon wondered why Joe would have chosen to make camp in such an exposed area. There was no cover of any kind from trees or hills or cliffs. The tallest object in throwing distance was the boulder that held up the lean-to. With the cooler winter temperatures it was a livable arrangement, but in the summertime choosing such a spot would be suicide.

"Where do you think he went?" Liz asked.

"Knowing him, they're following a clue or a hunch or something," said Todd.

"They?" asked Gideon. "Who they?"

"I didn't tell you about Juan Carlos?" replied Todd.

"Uh, no," said Gideon. "Who's Juan Carlos?"

"He's been helping us out," Todd answered. "He wants to learn the trade. He's kind of like Joe's intern. He's a good kid."

Gideon drew closer to Todd and turned with his back to the rest of the group.

"How many people are we going to bring into this club?" he whispered.

"What is your deal?" Todd questioned loudly. "And why are you whispering?"

"I don't know this Juan Carlos," Gideon said. "What if he's crazy?"

"Of course he's crazy," replied Todd. "He's living out in the Superstitions with Joe. Sane people wouldn't choose that. And we're chasing clues our dead friend left in an ammo-can at the top of a mountain, who are we to judge?"

Liz covered her mouth but not in time to keep Gideon from seeing her smirk. She turned away while Tara simply smiled broadly at Gideon. He felt the blood rush to his cheeks and looked back at Todd with his mouth slightly open. There was a time when he had been open and trusting but with the events of the past year his circle of trust had closed significantly. The thought of allowing complete strangers in caused him a good amount of grief.

Cal began to remove the saddle bags and bedding from Pepper and Hercules. Tara and Liz rushed over to assist him. Neither provided much assistance, however, as they stood on either side of him and took turns taking supplies from his hands and placing it on the ground at their feet. Dog pranced around between them and sniffed at each parcel laid before him. Gideon and Todd went to work unpacking the bags and sorting their provisions. Every few minutes Gideon would cast a look around in search of some sign of Joe. When Gideon removed the bottom saddle bag from Hercules the weight pulled it from his grasp, and it landed on the ground with a thud.

"Be careful," Todd said as he stooped down over the saddle bag.

"What the heck is in that thing?" Gideon asked. Todd opened one of the pouches and tipped it to Gideon so he could see the contents.

"I've got two police grade mag lights, two electric lanterns, a deer spotter that's as bright as the sun and a couple of emergency flashlights," Todd patted the other pouch. "And this bad boy is full of spare batteries."

"It's not going to be exactly like last time," Gideon said with a shake of his head.

"Be prepared," Todd said. "I thought a good old boy scout would appreciate that."

"Be prepared," Gideon repeated with a smile. "Well done."

Tara helped Liz clear a pile of ashes from the fire pit and began to build a twig teepee at the center while Cal, Todd and Gideon finished organizing the gear. When the horses were relieved of their burden Cal tipped his hat to the girls and mounted Moses with the grace and ease of a gymnast springing onto a pommel horse.

"Are you leaving?" asked Liz.

"No ma'am," Cal said. "It'll be dark soon. Not safe to travel. Gonna go fetch some water before sunset."

"I'll go with you," Gideon volunteered. He walked up to Pepper and put his foot in the stirrup. Pepper jittered and shuffled away from him. Gideon hung unto the horn and hopped along after the horse until he could free his left leg from the stirrup. Quickly, he abandoned his designs to ride the gray spotted nag, as the last of his pride evaporated in the dust. Without looking up he walked straight to Hercules and pulled himself into the saddle.

"All set?" Cal asked with great amusement.

Gideon acknowledged him with a tip of the ball cap. Liz walked up next to the tall brown horse and brushed her hands gently across his neck. She looked up at Gideon and smiled.

"Be careful, okay?" she said.

His heart leapt up into his chest. With a wink and a tip of his cap he tapped his heels into the haunches of his steed and encouraged Hercules forward to join old Moses. On the short trip over to Cal he contemplated developing a new salute to separate himself from the hat tipping cowboy. Todd reached up and handed him several mostly empty canteens.

"Be careful, okay?" he mocked in a tone that mimicked Liz.

Gideon swung his leg out in a half-hearted attempt to kick Todd. His friend slowly moved out of the way to easily avoid Gideon's pretended attack. With a pair of clicks from his mouth Cal prodded Moses into a trot and Gideon hurriedly compelled Hercules to follow his lead. They headed due west into the setting sun and Gideon tried to imagine their departure from the camp's point of view and hoped they looked half as majestic as the picture in his head.

"There's a spring just over that ridge," Cal said as they rode side by side with their horses at a brisk trot.

"Does it run year round?" asked Gideon.

"No," replied Cal. "It dries up in the summer, 'long with pretty much everything else in these parts."

As they rode over a rocky ridge, a thin thread of brown looking water came into view. Cal dismounted his horse and Gideon followed suit. They left the horses near the top of the ridge and shuffled down the slope to the water. Cal moved right to a patch of large round rocks, where the water appeared clearer, and began to fill his canteen. Gideon squatted down next to him and waited to use the cowboy's prime filling spot.

"Ever run across anything out here more dangerous than rattlesnakes?" asked Gideon.

Cal twisted the lid back on his canteen and sat back away from the spring to allow Gideon room to fill his empty vessels. Gideon moved closer to the spring and dipped an open canteen into the cold water. He watched as Cal stared off into the distance.

"Yep," the cowboy finally answered, without further explanation.

A cold chill shot up Gideon's spine. The glassy-eyed look and haunting tone of the cowboy's voice carried a gravity that startled him. He wanted to know more but knew better than to ask. Silently, he finished filling the first canteen and submerged the second among the round rocks beneath the gently flowing stream. One by one Gideon filled the canteens and capped them, all the while looking for something they could talk about. If he could only connect with the rugged cowboy, even on a superficial level, he felt his hard feelings might subside.

"So, do you lead a lot of groups out here?" asked Gideon.

"Used to," he replied. "Before that boy disappeared last year."

A wave of chills pulsed through his entire body. The blood rushed from his head and Gideon felt dizzy. 'That boy'. The words struck him like a dagger to the heart. He was certain Cal had meant no offense but to hear Glenn's disappearance referenced in such an impersonal way was difficult to take. Glenn had gone missing the summer before last, the summer before Gideon returned home. The loss was so personal to him, his friends, and his family that he had not considered the broader ramifications felt by those who did not even know him.

"You 'bout through?" Cal asked, snapping Gideon from his brief stupor.

Water flowed overtop of the last canteen as it had filled with water and sank. Gideon pulled it out and replaced the lid. He stood up and brushed at a spot of mud on his knee. Cal sauntered back up to the horses on the ridge above them. Gideon collected the canteens and followed the deep impression left by the cowboy's boots. They mounted the horses and swung around to head back to camp. The long shadows from the rocks and bushes all seemed to point the way back to his friends.

To the north, Gideon saw two people walking in front of a horse, headed toward the camp. There was no doubt the burly bearded man in the lead was Joe. He was followed closely by a leaner shorter man with dark black hair who held the reigns of a black horse. Gideon prodded Hercules into a gallop so they might reach the camp together. He could see Todd, Tara and Liz all looking in Joe's direction awaiting his arrival. Gideon eased Hercules to a stop next to the waist-high boulder with the lean-to and climbed out of the saddle to join the group. Joe raised his arm high above his head with a friendly wave and a big smile.

"Hello there," he called when he was within shouting distance.

"Hurry up old man," Todd called back. "I brought you some dinner."

Todd walked out ahead of the group to welcome them. He and Joe embraced and Joe patted him on the back as he moved to greet the rest of the party. Joe was just as Gideon remembered him. He wore a blue and black flannel shirt with the top buttons undone. His floppy wide brim hat sat atop his bushy unkempt hair which converged into his thick black beard. The wrinkles on his sunbaked face were just as pronounced as the last time he saw him. Joe's childlike eyes just beamed on the newcomers.

"Hey Joe," waved Liz.

"Hey there darl'n," Joe replied and threw a pit stained arm around her. "I see the company you keep hasn't improved one bit."

"Nope," said Liz. "Still running with those friends on low places."

"Good for you," Joe responded as he noticed Tara standing back behind Liz. "And who is this?"

"Dad, this is Tara," Todd answered. "I told you about Tara."

"But you didn't tell me she was such a stunner," Joe said.

"Pleased to meet you," Tara said. The dimples in her cheeks appeared between her toothy grin. Joe reached out, took her by the wrist and gently kissed the back of her hand. She giggled but Gideon could not tell if it was due to the kiss or if his bristly whiskers tickled her.

"Easy there, you creepy old man," Todd said as he stepped in and removed his father's hand from the blushing Jamaican.

"Hey there partner," Joe said as he punched Gideon in the shoulder. "Sure glad you came."

"Your son can be very persuasive," said Gideon.

"I'm sure my son's power of persuasion isn't the only reason you're out here," Joe said with a wink.

Gideon looked over at Liz as the last light of day bathed her in orange light. She turned her head sideways with a pleasant look back at him, only then did he realize he was staring. He quickly looked away and noticed Cal over by the black horse examining its hind leg.

"What's wrong with Bean," Cal asked.

"He threw a shoe this morning," Joe replied. "We just walked with him the rest of the day."

"A'right," Cal said with a scowl. "You keep Moses and I'll take Bean back with me tomorrow."

"Thanks Cal, I appreciate it," said Joe. "Now, what's that I heard about dinner?"

Night had come on gradually once the sun set. The sky went through a kaleidoscope of colors from yellow and orange, to red and purple, to blue and grey before finally settling into black. The group all lay around the fire as the flames danced above the wood and ash. Joe leaned back against a rock with his hands over his head looking up at the sky. Gideon, Todd, Tara and Liz sat on top of their bedding while Juan Carlos was already fast asleep beneath his rickety lean-to. Cal was somewhere beyond the light of the fire, tending to the horses. Softly, Todd began humming a tune Gideon recognized from one of their favorite films growing up and Gideon joined in.

"Dopa deeda dopa deeda dopa deeda dope," Gideon sang as Todd and Joe joined in perfect melodic harmony. "Bluuuuuue shadows, on the trail. Little cowboy close your eyyyyyes and dream. All of the doggies are in the corral. All of the work is done. So close your eyyyyes and dream little cowboy. Dream of, some one, whooooooo. Badeeda dopa deeda dopa deeda dope."

The trio laughed as the song finished and Gideon was quite pleased with their impromptu performance. When he was met with curious stares from Tara and Liz, he sat up and shot them a quizzical look.

"*Three Amigos,*" he stated matter-of-factly. "Steve Martin, Martin Short, Chevy Chase? It's a classic."

"If you say so," Liz said with a wink toward Tara. The usually stoic Jamaican smiled back and Gideon was happy she and Liz were getting on so well. Liz rooted around in her pack while Tara and Todd began a quiet conversation on the other side of the fire. Gideon looked over at Joe who scooted into a laying position on his back and place his hands behind his head.

"Hey Joe," Gideon whispered.

"Yeah," Joe replied as he took his eyes off the starry sky.

"What do you make of these?" Gideon reached into his pack and pulled out the broken pieces of the angel statue and the old football card. Joe sat up, took the items from Gideon and held them up in the light of the fire.

"What is this?" Joe asked as he bounced the pieces of the angel statue in his thick callused hands. Gideon looked over at Todd who had suddenly turned his attention to the dirt in front of him.

"It used to be an angel before somebody broke it," Gideon said. "Glenn left them for us in a cache at the top of Flatiron."

"Huh, an angel and a card?" Joe thought out loud. "Does Roger Staubach mean anything to you guys?"

"Glenn met him once at a party," Gideon explained.

"No kidding?" said Joe. "I sure loved watching him play. You know I saw him throw a..."

"Joe, focus," Todd interrupted.

"Right," Joe said. He scrunched up his forehead and looked thoughtfully at the clues in his hand. "Do you all have any guesses? You knew Glenn better than I did."

"We're stumped," Gideon replied. "We were hoping you could figure out what he was trying to tell us. Knowing Glenn, he was targeting Columbo or Sherlock Holmes more than he was targeting us."

Several minutes passed in silence. Cal returned from checking on his four-legged friends and sprawled out on an old horse blanket. Dog trotted in behind him and lay down next to the fire. Cal tipped his hat over his face and lay back on his arms like they were a pillow. Gideon shook his head and wondered if he were even trying to look cool or if that was simply his natural inclination. In the distance, a howl rose up from the desert floor and was quickly joined by a concert of echoing howls. Tara sat up straight and looked out into the dark night. Dog's ears shot up and he let out a faint whimper. Cal reached out blindly and pet the top of his friend's furry head as the chorus swelled and the sound surrounded them.

"A wha dat?" asked Tara with an uncharacteristic concern in her voice.

"Coyotes," replied Todd.

"Dem sound like da dead a go come for wi," she said.

Gideon placed his hand over his mouth to cover his smile. He did not want to make fun of her reaction. Even though he was born and raised in the desert, he still remembered the first time he heard a pack of coyotes in the dead of night. He was twelve years old when he went on his first overnight campout with his Boy Scout troop. He managed to convince Todd and Glenn to accompany him and they made camp at the base of Crooked Top Mountain, the westernmost face of the Superstitions. Just after they had turned in for the night the howling began. Gideon remembered being frozen with fear as he was certain the howling was meant for them and grew ever closer. Todd and Glenn had quickly shuffled the sleeping bags to the center of the tent, away from the paper-thin walls, and Gideon soon found himself squeezed on both sides like a hot dog in a bun. Although his childhood fears were far less pronounced on this night, he could appreciate Tara's reaction to their haunting calls.

"They're just desert dogs, Tara," Gideon assured her.

"They won't come near the fire," Cal spoke up from beneath his hat.

Without hesitation, Tara tossed a few more pieces of wood into the fire pit. Liz got up and walked over to Tara. She dusted off her bottom and sat down on the blanket next to her. With a tap on her knee, Liz leaned toward her and whispered something in her ear that Gideon could not hear over the crackle of the flames. Whatever it was made the worried look on Tara soften.

"T'anks," Tara said.

That moment affirmed everything that Gideon loved and admired about Liz. She was always the first to comfort those in need and had a natural talent to know just what to say. Gideon felt drawn to her and wanted to move around the fire to sit near her. He searched his thoughts for a believable excuse for such a maneuver. Unfortunately, the only thing that came to mind was pretending also to be afraid of the coyotes, which seemed to cut firmly against how he wished her to see him.

"You know what this reminds me of?" Todd asked.

"What?" Gideon replied.

"Remember Camp Geronimo?"

"Oh yeah."

"Remember the campfire outside that old house where they told us about the Mogollon Monster?"

"Yeah," Gideon laughed.

"Man, Glenn was so scared I thought he was going to wet himself."

"He wasn't the only one."

"What's the Mogollon Monster?" Liz asked.

Gideon grinned and looked over at Joe who simply shook his head. Todd joined Gideon in his unspoken plea to insight Joe into one of his classic tales. Joe frowned and bit on his lower lip. The two of them leaned in Joe's direction with Cheshire cat smiles. Todd raised his eyebrows at his father.

"Fine," Joe exclaimed. He stood up and shook his arms out to the side like a sprinter trying to get loose before a big race. Todd and Gideon sat up straight with their legs crossed like kindergarteners at story time.

"Nobody really knows where the Mogollon Monster came from or how long he's roamed the earth," Joe began. "Legend says that he was once a great hunter from a tribe that settled up on the rim. He had won the heart of the most beautiful girl in the village, but when the chief desired her for his son he expelled the great hunter from the tribe. The hunter fled with his love and the chief sent seven of his best warriors to kill him and bring back the girl. The great hunter defeated the warriors but in the battle his love was killed."

"Wha cha," Tara said, completely enthralled by Joe's movements and the inflexion in his voice.

"The greater hunter sought vengeance and struck a bargain with the god of the underworld," Joe continued. "He asked for the strength of a bear, the speed of a deer and the eyes of a hawk, that he might destroy his enemies and replace the wicked chief at the head of the village. The god of the underworld granted his request but for his own amusement cursed the great hunter. His body became deformed as he grew to twice the height of a bear, his teeth turned to fangs and his eyes turned blood red. Long hair covered his body and claws grew in place of hands. This monster returned to the village and laid waste to all he saw. There was no end to his rage. When he realized that he now ruled a desolate village, and that revenge would not restore that which he lost, he disappeared into the mountains."

"Rotted," said Tara.

"Don't worry," said Liz. "It's just a story told to frightened campers."

"Well it worked," Tara said.

"Any way, the Mogollon Rim is like fifty miles from here," Liz assured her. "We're in no danger.

"Don't be so sure," Gideon spoke hushed tones. "For hundreds of years there have been reports of the Mogollon Monster all over Arizona, from east to west, so there's no telling where he might turn up."

"RAW!" Todd screamed as he spun around toward the girls. They jumped backwards and squealed as they embraced each other.

"Todd!" shouted Liz. "You jerk!"

Todd and Gideon high fived each other and shared a laugh at the expense of their friends.

"Easy," Todd said. "We're just having some fun."

"It's just a joke," Gideon added. "There's nothing to be scared of."

"And how would you know that?" Cal asked from the far side of the fire. He had abruptly tipped up his hat and stared over at Gideon. "You don't have the first clue what's out here."

Gideon stared back at Cal, unwilling to break from his dead eyed gaze. The rest of the group fell silent and, after what seemed like an eternity, Cal let his hat drop back over his eyes as he lay back onto his blanket. Gideon looked around the fire at the fallen expressions on his friend's faces. He searched for words to rebut the cowboy's accusation but found none. The truth was none of them knew what might be out in this mysterious region. What made matters worse was the insinuation from Cal that he did. Gideon wished he could chalk it up to the bluster of testosterone and male bravado, but something in his gut told him Cal spoke the truth.

"Roger's Canyon," Joe said breaking the silence as he pulled a piece of paper from his pack.

"What?" Gideon and Todd said in unison.

"Roger's Canyon," Joe repeated. "The football card. Roger Staubach. I'll bet he's pointing us to Roger's Canyon."

Joe unfolded the paper on the ground near the fire. The group gathered around him and Todd produced a flashlight and shined it down on a ragged map. Joe hastily moved his finger over the lines on the map from left to right. He stopped suddenly on the far-right side.

"Here," he declared. "Roger's canyon. It runs north too."

"No way!" exclaimed Todd.

"What does that mean?" asked Liz.

"The Dutchman," Joe explained. "One of the clues he left said his mine is in a north trending canyon."

They all stared down at the map. Gideon's heart rose in his throat. Had Glenn left them a clue that led to the Lost Dutchman mine? He failed to push aside a lingering thought that he had not allow himself to consider. Was it possible that Glenn might still be alive and waiting for them? It was a dream and he knew it, but for a moment he indulged the fantasy. He imagined Glenn's smiling face waiting to greet them at the entrance to the legendary mine. Joe ran his finger up the map along the line that marked Roger's Canyon when it stopped again at the words 'Angel Basin'.

"The angel statue," Liz gasped.

"Ho-ly crap," Todd said.

Gideon's natural impulse was to tell everyone to calm down and think things through but he found himself completely swept up in these revelations. Two clues and two points that intersected on the map, it fit too nicely to be ignored. What's more it gave them a destination and dramatically narrowed the area they would need to search. Gideon racked his brain for something they might be missing but his excitement would not allow him to settle on a single thought. The image of Glenn's smiling face drowned out any skepticism.

"How far away is that from here?" asked Gideon.

"On horseback?" said Joe. "Half a day, maybe."

"Well all right," Gideon grinned. "We ride at first light."

"To Roger's Canyon and Angel Basin," Todd proclaimed triumphantly. "Glenn, you clever son of a gun."

Gideon glanced back over his shoulder across the fire. He could not be sure, in the shadow of the flames, but it appeared as if Cal peeked out from beneath his hat. The good vibrations faded in an instant, replaced by a gnawing mistrust of the stranger in their midst. It was a feeling that Gideon could not define but felt to his core. There was something amiss with the cowboy and he, for one, would be glad when they were rid of him. The distant coyote concert began again and drew Gideon's attention out into the black night. *We're coming, Glenn*, he thought.

OUT HERE

They stood at the edge of the canyon and peered down to the bottom. The hot gust of wind that rushed up to meet them felt as if someone had opened the door to a giant oven. Sweat drizzled from the top of Jeddediah's wide brim hat down into his beard and pooled near the collar of his tattered shirt. Glenn wiped the sweat from his forehead and readjusted his gleaming white canvas cap, with the cloth cover over his freckled neck. He wore his red backpack, which Jeddediah had insisted he empty of all none essential items. It now held nothing more than a first aid kit, a canteen full of water, a flash light and several granola bars. Jeddediah removed a coil of rope from his shoulder and set it on the ground. He carried nothing else with him, except a canteen and his pistol. Behind them, Bernice rested quietly in a shred of shade from a nearby bush.

"So, the key is down there?" Glenn asked as he pointed to the dark hole in the side of the canyon wall.

"Yep," Jeddediah replied. "I believe so."

"And you went in there at night," Glenn asked. "Alone?"

"Yep," Jeddediah replied with his eyes fixed on the opening.

"That's so legit," Glenn said as he patted the old timer on the back. "You're the man."

The pride from Glenn's adulation was blunted by the gnawing feeling that his young companion again showed a lack of appreciation for the danger they were facing. Jeddediah knelt down on the ground and began to draw in the dirt with his finger. Glenn bent down and eyed the lines cut by the old miner's finger.

"This here is the canyon," Jeddediah said as he made the first marking with his callused thumb. "And this is the shaft."

He drew a second line perpendicular to the first that led out away from them. At the end of the shaft he marked an X on the ground and made another X back by the canyon line.

"I found the key here," he said. "The shaft is straight and drops down off a shelf and goes into a rabbit hole. There's a room on the other side of the rabbit hole where you can stand up again. That's where that unholy beast waylaid me."

"What's this one here," Glenn asked and pointed to the second X by the canyon line.

"That's us," he replied.

"And the plan?" asked Glenn.

"Haven't got one," Jeddediah said. "I've told ya all I know. That's what we're up against."

Glenn removed his floppy cap and scratched at his red head. He looked over the ledge down toward the opening and back to the drawing in front of them. Jeddediah felt a sharp pain shoot through his hip and sat down on the ground, only to receive another jolt from his ribs. He rubbed at the spot where the metal plate on his hip had been installed and tried to ignore the dull throbs that echoed throughout his body. His greatest desire was to reclaim his prize. That was rivaled only by his fear of returning into the darkness to face its formidable guardian. Glenn replaced his cap and adjusted the cloth neck cover while he continued to look back and forth between the shaft entrance and the drawing. Jeddediah had at first hoped to use his youth and vitality to retrieve the key but now found himself hanging his hopes on the young man's intellect and cunning as well.

"Is there another way in?" Glenn asked.

"I think I saw a couple of offshoots in the room on the other side of the rabbit hole," Jeddediah said with a shake of his head. "There must be but there ain't no way of telling where they come from."

Glenn sat down on the ground near the ledge and sighed. Jeddediah's hopes for a stroke of genius quickly vanished and they sat across from each other in their shared disappointment. The sun beat down on their backs and added to their misery. Bernice brayed and Jeddediah waved off her complaint with a swipe of his arm.

"Old nag," he muttered.

"Jed?" Glenn asked.

"Yeah," Jeddediah replied and suppressed the urge to correct the unwelcome abbreviation of his name.

"How did you find this place?" he asked. "How do you know about the priests and the key?"

Jeddediah drew in a deep breath and exhaled softly through his nose. He puckered his lips and scratched at the whiskers on his chin. Glenn tilted his head to the side and met his eyes with childlike curiosity. For all his years in the Superstitions the old miner had worked alone. Even prior to his solitude in the wilderness, trusting had never come easy to him. There was something about this young man that disarmed him. It was an uneasy feeling that fought against his natural inclinations. Still, if they were going to partner on this perilous venture, he knew he would have to place his trust in him.

"A few years back I run across this old codger named Cletus," Jeddediah began. "He wandered into my camp one morning, and we shared a fire and a cup of coffee. He struck me like a man who'd been out in the desert sun too long, if ya know what I mean. I was prospect'n and hadn't found much outside of a bit of placer in a dried up old spring. Cletus claimed there weren't no Lost Dutchman mine and never was. He said ole Waltz had found a stash of gold and made up the mine to throw people off. At first I thought it was complete hogwash. I'd spent years study'n and search'n for the mine and wasn't gonna let some wild eyed loon tell me what was what. I told him he was an old fool and didn't know what he was talk'n about."

Glenn shifted his weight from side and side and brushed a black bug off his sweaty arm. The bright smile on his face showed that he was thoroughly enjoying the tale and gave Jeddediah a sense of affirmation he had not felt in some time.

"Well Cletus didn't much care for my estimation of himself or his story," Jeddediah continued. "He pulled out this old journal and waved it at me. Said it belonged to Cristabol Francisco Velasquez, a Jesuit priest. He opened to a page with a hand drawn cross at the top, only the middle of the cross had four interlocking circles and the bottom had a notched paddle sticking out to the side."

Jeddediah drew a likeness of the image in the dirt with his finger.

"Like a skeleton key?" Glenn interjected.

"Yep," Jeddediah nodded. "It was written in Spanish, but he claimed the symbol marked the hid'n place where the Black Robes took their gold. I still didn't believe it and he challenged me to go down to San Xavier del Bac and see for myself. Said I'd find the same symbol etched into an old marker in the graveyard behind the church."

"So, did you go?" asked Glenn.

"Not directly," Jeddediah replied. "I still thought it was all baloney."

"Why would he share that with you?" asked Glenn.

"I asked him that very thing," Jeddediah said. "He told me there was somebody after him. Somebody who knew he was on to someth'n. Said if anything happened to him he wanted someone to know why."

"Did he say who was after him?"

"Nah," he replied as he swatted at a fly buzzing around his beard. "I told him he was welcome to stay with me if he weren't safe. He thanked me and told me there was no need 'cause there weren't no place in these mountains that would keep him safe. Said he was holed up at Walt Pinkman's old haunt between Roger's Canyon and Angel Basin."

"Walt," Glenn said. "That's how you found out about that old shack."

Jeddediah nodded. "A couple of months later, when Ranger Rick tore down my last cabin, I went look'n for old Cletus to see if he'd received the same treatment. It took several days of pok'n 'round the area but I finally found Walt's place. The entrance is only visible in the setting sun if ya don't know where it is you'd walk right by it. I must've passed it a dozen times before I saw it. It was sheer luck that I stumbled on it."

His voice trailed off and he found himself staring down at his liver spotted hands. An image of Cletus rolled through his mind, a wrinkled and ragged man with a gray beard and wild gray eyes set between his rotting teeth and a tattered old sun hat. Jeddediah realized the years had piled up on him faster than he cared to admit and wondered if this young man looked on him the way he had old Cletus.

"I thought he was paranoid," Jeddediah spoke to his hands. "I found him inside, ly'n in the middle of the floor stiff as a board. He was clutch'n that old Spanish journal. His eyes were wide open and wore a look of horror on his pale face"

"He died?" Glenn confirmed.

Jeddediah gave a solemn nod as he looked up into his young friend's worried face. "He wrote four words on the west wall, 'Found the key'. Scratched them in with his own blood-stained finger nails."

"You said there were four words?" questioned Glenn.

"That's right."

"Found the key is three words," Glenn said. "What was the fourth?"

"Monster," Jeddediah answered with a lump in his throat.

They both paused and looked over the ledge back down toward the dark opening. Bernice brayed again and disturbed their moment of silence. With great effort Jeddediah got to his feet. His joints cracked and popped as he straightened himself up and hobbled over to the mule. He brushed the side of her neck and fed her a handful of pellets from his pocket. Glenn stood up and placed his hands on his hips while he continued to study the canyon. When Jeddediah finished calming his pack mule, he shuffled over to stand next to Glenn.

"I buried him up on top of Angel Basin," Jeddediah added.

"You didn't report his death?"

"Nah. That ain't how things are done out here."

"Out here?" exclaimed Glenn. "This isn't the wild west, Jed! There are laws."

"He told me he didn't have no kin," Jeddediah explained. "Besides he'd have wanted to be buried in these mountains, and your laws don't allow for that either."

"You didn't bury him to honor his wishes," Glenn accused. "You buried him so you could use his hideout and keep the journal."

"How dare you!" Jeddediah shouted. "You don't know spit about nothing. We look out for one another out here. Out here we're all we got. Ain't nobody look'n out for us 'ccept us. And for your information I returned the journal to the priest down in San Xavier."

In a huff, Jeddediah turned and stormed off away from the ledge. He grabbed the rope around Bernice's neck and continued his departure. Bernice did not budge and when he ran out of slack the rope pulled him back toward the obstinate mule. With a curse and a tug on the rope Jeddediah dragged his unwilling companion forward. Glenn hobbled up next to him and tried to catch his eye. Jeddediah kept his head down and trudged on, scowling at the ground.

"Jed, I'm sorry," Glenn said as he limped along beside him. "I was wrong."

"This was a mistake," Jeddediah said coming to an abrupt stop. "This ain't gonna work. You git your stuff and be on your way. I ain't got time for some dirty ingrate."

"Dirty ingrate?" said Glenn. "You shot me."

"You shot me," Jeddediah repeated with a mocking high pitched whine. "How long are ya gonna cry 'bout that?"

"It happened yesterday," Glenn replied. "Look, I'm really sorry. I shouldn't have questioned your intentions."

"No ya shouldn't have," Jeddediah said. "And another thing, quit calling me Jed. My momma named me Jeddediah and you ain't got the right to go chang'n it."

"All right," Glenn said with his arms raised above his head in surrender. "I'm sorry."

Jeddediah wiped the sweat from his brow and looked down at his feet. His whole frame shook uncontrollably and he felt a swelling of pressure behind his ears. Bernice nudged her head into his back, and he pushed her away with his forearm. He could not bring himself to look up and was torn between wanting Glenn to leave and praying that he stayed. Glenn's feet shuffled nervously side to side across Jeddediah's field of view. He sighed deeply and kicked haplessly at a rock. Several minutes passed in silence and Bernice drifted over to a little patch of shade from the limb of a lime-green Palo Verde.

"I think I have an idea how we can get that key," Glenn finally said as he leaned down into Jeddediah's line of sight. "But it will take the both of us. What do ya say?"

He averted his eyes away from the grinning redhead and looked out toward the distant mountain peaks. Those mountains had once held such promise and intrigue, but at this moment they seemed to be taunting him. He wanted to be done with them. He wished to be free of his obsession with the gold they hid from him, but he feared he never would be. If he were to ever find rest it would be after he had discovered all her secrets and whether he liked it or not he was going to need help. He forced himself to turned and face his young accomplice.

"A'right, let's hear it," Jeddediah said and wagged his finger at him. "But it better be good."

Glenn walked over to join Bernice in the shade and Jeddediah followed with his hands on his hips. He tapped his foot on the ground while he watched Glenn take his canteen from his backpack and unscrew the lid. Glenn tilted back the canteen and slowly sipped down some water. Just when Jeddediah thought his insides would burst from impatience, Glenn lowered the canteen and wiped his mouth.

"Did you ever play mouse trap?" he asked.

"Boy, if you're talk'n 'bout games..." Jeddediah threatened.

"Never mind," he replied. "We can rig up a trap above the entrance to the cave. Then we just lure it out and drop the trap."

"No good," the old miner shook his head. "You and me ain't gonna build a trap that'll hold that thing. Besides, even if we did we'd be blocking our only way in or out."

"Ever see Return of the Jedi?" Glenn asked hopefully.

Jeddediah cocked his head sideways and scowled at the young man.

"It's a movie," Glenn said. "You've never seen it? Jabba the Hutt, Admiral Ackbar, Lando?"

"Boy, if you don't quit talk'n nonsense," Jeddediah barked.

"All right," Glenn said. "We could make a net out of rope, that way when the trap sprung it would lift him up and out of the way."

"Again, ain't no net is gonna hold that thing."

"What about the tiger trap like in Swiss Family Robinson?"

"You got a plan you didn't see in a movie?" Jeddediah shook his head.

"I don't hear you coming up with any big ideas," Glenn said and folded his arms across his chest. All at once, Bernice lifted her tail and nearly struck him in the eye. Glenn flailed his arms up in the air and stepped back away from the mule. He blinked rapidly and rubbed at his eye.

"Ah!" Glenn complained. "I think a hair got in my eye."

"That's it!" Jeddediah exclaimed. "Bernice, you clever old girl."

"What?" Glenn asked while he continued to rub his eye socket. "Are we gonna poke it in the eye?"

"No," Jeddediah replied. "We're gonna rig up a pendulum. We'll tie up a boulder to the end of a rope and BAM!"

He shouted and smashed one hand into the other with a loud clap. Jeddediah vigorously scratched Bernice along her bushy mane. Glenn wiped at the sweat on his freckled cheeks and looked out into the desert. All at once a smile broke across his sun burnt face.

"Like the Ewoks at the battle of Endor," he grinned.

Jeddediah simply shook his head and grabbed Bernice's rope. He led her back the way they had come with Glenn limping along behind them. The heavens above were a brilliant blue without a cloud in the sky. Although the temperature had reached its peak for the day, he could not help but feel a burden lift from his sweat dredged shoulders. They had a plan and he believed it would work.

"So Jed…" Glenn began.

The old miner stopped him cold with a look of contempt that was so sharp it could have cut glass.

"...dediah," Glenn quickly corrected. "How will we decide who's gonna be the bait?"

"Easy," he said. "That'll be you."

"Shouldn't we flip for it, or draw straws?" Glenn suggested. "How 'bout scissor, rock, paper?"

"No need," he replied. "My plan. My call. Besides, would you really ask a frail old man to put himself in harm's way?"

A sense of relief rested on his old heart when Glenn did not offer any further objection. They had a plan, one that would not require him to face his nightmarish foe alone in the darkness. When he calculated the odds of finding such a willing and enthusiastic partner way out here he had to believe that luck was finally on his side. A smile crept across his face and he gave Bernice's rope a gentle tug toward the canyon, toward his destiny.

SHOCK AND OH

Descending into Roger's Canyon was like descending into another world. Above them was a desert full of cactus and shrubs but the canyon was lush with Juniper trees and green grass. A creek cut down the middle and they followed a trail that looped around and crossed the water back and forth as they weaved their way down the deep crevasse.

"This is beautiful," Gideon called from the back of Hercules, where he straddled a blanket behind Todd.

Tara turned around and nodded from the back of Pepper, where she rode side saddle. Liz held the reigns and guided Pepper back into the shallow creek bed. Joe rode Moses and carried Juan Carlos with him. Gideon had hardly heard a word out of Joe's young helper all morning. From what he could tell Juan Carlos was an eager worker. He had helped Todd cook breakfast and then hurried over to help Cal prepare the horses. Though Gideon had not tried to engage him in conversation he began to wonder, as their caravan pulled through the canyon, if the cause for Juan Carlos's silence was that he did not speak English. He, himself, spoke no more than conversational Spanish which he picked up from a year of Spanish I in high school. If Juan Carlos did not speak English they had little chance of getting to know one another, unless Gideon needed directions to a bathroom.

"Hey Joe," Gideon called. "How much further?"

"About twenty minutes," Joe hollered back.

"You said that twenty minutes ago," said Todd.

"What's the matter, you need a potty break?" Joe taunted.

"I could use a batty break," Gideon replied.

Tara laughed and the rest of the party exchanged puzzled looks. Batty was patios, a Jamaican dialect, for butt. As he and Tara were the only two in the group who spoke patios they enjoyed their little inside joke at the expense of their perplexed friends. Joe raised an eyebrow at Gideon and shook his head.

"The old Salado ruins are just ahead," Joe said. "He can stop and rest there. They are really old so if batty is poop you'll have to find another place to break your batty."

Gideon and Tara roared with laughter to the chagrin of their friends. They rode through a narrow pass where they were forced to ride single file due to the dense vegetation that pressed in on the tiny creek. The horse hooves splashed water and displaced the smaller round river rocks. Beyond the narrow pass, the canyon widened again and on the right side two large caves came into view. Joe steered Moses toward the caves. Pepper and Hercules seemed to naturally follow without much prodding. Moses came to a stop near a long patch of wild grass and began grazing. Juan Carlos hopped off the back of the horse and stretched his arms wide over his head. Liz parked Pepper next to Moses. She and Tara gracefully dismounted and joined Juan Carlos in the grass. Joe swung a stiff leg over the saddle and let out an old man groan as he hung from the stirrup.

"What's wrong Grandpa?" Todd teased. "Getting old?"

"I'm gett'n old all right, but you gotta find a girl who can stand all your fuss'n and primp'n before you can call me Grandpa," Joe shot back with a wink and a smile.

Gideon hopped off the back of the horse and turned to face the massive holes in the canyon wall. From where they stood, he could see the manmade stone walls, housed inside. He took a few steps toward the ruins and tried to squeeze his legs closer together. After a few strides, he abandoned his attempts to walk normally and embraced the bowlegged cowboy walk he had earned on his long morning ride. Gideon was relieved to find he was not alone, as the entire group sauntered up the small incline like John Wayne.

"This is so cool," Todd said. "How old do you think these are?"

"The Salado Indians built these over 600 years ago," Gideon replied. "The mountains provided shelter and protection from rival tribes. They lived here for generations and grew maize. The exact reason they moved on is not known but it is suspected it was due to lack of water."

"Here we go, Mr. History," Todd threw up his hands. "How do you know all that?"

"There's a plaque, genius," Gideon said and pointed to a small wooden plaque posted just inside the cave.

"Oh, right," said Todd. "Well, I know that the Salado and Pima Indians came after the Hohokam disappeared and "Hohokam" is actually a Pima word meaning those who have gone. And I didn't need a plaque to tell me that."

"I was on the same field trip, smart guy," Gideon replied. "Fifth grade, the Southwest Museum."

"Boys, boys," said Liz. "You're both smart and pretty. Okay?"

She smiled at Gideon and he winked back at her. He did not mind in the least being put in his place by Liz. Todd simply scoffed and continued to explore the ruins in the cave.

"A pickney dem lived 'ere?" Tara asked as she bent over and peered inside the miniature doorway that led into the first room.

"Well yes, children lived here but adults did too," Gideon answered.

"Dem likkle 'ee?" she asked.

The top of the doorway was still supported by the original wood beams that were remarkably preserved by the cave. Flat rocks were fitted together to form the walls as mud, grass and reeds sealed it all together like a crude mortar. Most of the hewn wood logs that once formed the roofs had disintegrated over time and they could look over the wall, right down into the tiny room.

"They were short but not that short," Joe interjected. "They most likely built their pueblos this way for protection or because of the difficulty of construction. They would just crawl inside to sleep or escape harsh desert climate."

Gideon turned back and looked out of the cave to check on the horses. Just beyond the patch of grass, that the horses grazed on, stood a figure in a gray cloak with a hood pulled over his head. As a reflex Gideon leapt forward and ran out of the cave toward the unwelcomed voyeur.

"Hey!" he shouted at the hooded figure.

Pepper reared up on her hind legs and bumped into Hercules. The shuffling of the horses blocked the person in the gray cloak from view as Gideon continued to run towards him. The rest of the group hurried from the cave and surrounded the horses. Liz caught hold of Pepper's reigns and attempted to sooth her. Juan Carlos and Todd managed to corral Moses without too much resistance, while Tara and Joe stroked and patted Hercules until he resumed grazing.

"What the heck, G?" Todd questioned.

"I saw him again," said Gideon. "Right there."

"Who him?" asked Joe.

"The guy with the hood," he replied.

"Or girl," Liz added.

"Fine, the person," Gideon replied with extra emphasis on person, "with the hood."

"Where?" asked Todd.

"Right over there," Gideon pointed to a group of trees on the southwest side of the canyon. A quick scan of the area revealed nothing but leaves from the juniper branches.

"Come on Gideon, you think he…"

"Or she," Liz interjected.

"...or she," Todd continued. "Followed us out here from Flatiron?"

"I'm telling you I saw him, her," Gideon corrected. "It, whoever, I saw the same gray cloak and hood standing right over there."

He walked out past the horses toward the juniper trees. Todd followed after him and stood quietly by his side while Gideon searched desperately for some sign of their cloaked stalker or for a potential escape route. To his disappointment, there was nothing but a wall of boulders beyond the trees, far too high for any man to scale without being seen. After a futile effort to explain the disappearance, of what he knew he saw, Gideon hung his head with his hands on his hips.

"Dude, it's all right," Todd said putting a hand on his back. "I believe you."

"You do?" asked Gideon.

"Sure," said Todd. "Why would you make that up? He couldn't have gotten far."

"Or she," Gideon added with a grin.

"Right," Todd said as they both glanced back over their shoulders at Liz. She was still soothing Pepper with long soft strokes along her spotted neck. The concern for the hooded figure became more poignant as he thought of his friends and the potential danger whoever it was might be to them. Quickly, Gideon walked over to where he had last seen the cloak. He stooped down to the ground and brushed at several crushed leaves. There were multiple depressions in the cold earth.

"Here," Gideon said with excitement as he pointed at the footprints. They ran straight into the creek bed and disappeared in the shallow water. He followed them and stood on the water's edge. There were no other discernible signs of the flight of the cloak.

"There's a trail just the other side of the creek that leads up top," Joe called from back by the horses. "Two of us could scoot up there and see what we see."

"Perfect," Gideon said as he hustled back to the group. "I'm with you."

"Actually, the climb is pretty rough," Joe said. "Probably should be our best two riders."

Gideon furrowed his brow as Joe turned to Liz.

"How 'bout it darl'n?" he asked. "You up for it?"

Without a word Liz grabbed the horn on Pepper's saddle and swung herself into the seat. Joe followed her lead in a far less graceful manner. When he was properly back in the saddle, he smiled over at Liz and she nodded back to him.

"Angel Basin is about a half mile or so that way," Joe said and pointed up the rocky crevasse. "There's a fork in the canyon before ya get out. The one to the right loops around toward Cimarron. We'll want to explore both forks, so two of you take Hercules to the right and the other two go to the Basin on foot."

"Dibs on Herc," Todd called. He leapt to the brown horse and threw himself up into the saddle. With a big grin, he extended a hand down to Tara. "You wanna ride?"

"Yeah man," Tara said as he took his hand and stepped into the open stirrup.

Gideon watched helplessly as the search parties were formed without him.

"Remember, keep a sharp eye out, we're looking for any clue Glenn may have left or some sign of a mine or a cave or anything," Joe said. "If you run across the hooded hombre keep your distance, we don't know who he is or what he wants."

"Or she," Liz added with exasperation.

"Or she," Joe correct with an apologetic nod. "Just holler if you find anything and we'll all come to ya. Otherwise we'll meet at Angel Basin by nightfall and make camp."

With a snap on the reigns Joe and Liz galloped away, across the creek and around a large rocky bend out of sight. Todd similarly spurred Hercules into a slow walk up the canyon. He tossed Gideon a hard plastic water bottle as they moved past him.

"You take care of him, Juan Carlos," Todd said. "We'll see you at the basin."

Gideon placed the extra water bottle in the small day pack he had been shouldering. He looked over at Juan Carlos and tried to piece together how he had come to be paired with this silent stranger. He took his first up close look at Juan Carlos. There was a faint wisp of a mustache growing on his upper lip. His thick black hair lay in waves on top of his head. He had brown eyes, just a shade darker than his complexion and wore a black and white flannel shirt and a baggy pair of blue jeans. He did not wear a back pack or carry anything in his hands and Gideon assumed that his supplies were held within his oversized pant pockets.

"You ready?" Gideon asked.

Juan Carlos nodded and Gideon led the way down the canyon. The sun sat just above the western wall of the canyon and although it was only late afternoon, the depth of the crevasse meant they would lose direct sunlight far sooner than the desert plains above them.

Gideon was in no rush to make time and felt the need to thoroughly explore every nook and cranny to ensure they did not miss a clue Glenn may have left for them. Juan Carlos seemed to be onboard with this approach as he was diligent in pursing any point of intrigue they happened upon. He had raced back toward a small opening between two boulders on the east side of the ravine only to return a moment later with a shake of his head. Gideon was glad to have such a willing and eager companion although he felt obligated to try and engage him in conversation.

"So, do you like treasure hunting," Gideon asked.

"Yeah," Juan Carlos replied.

"Have you been doing it long?"

"No."

"How do you know Joe?"

"My mom," Juan Carlos answered as he looked behind a group of knee high bushes.

"Oh," Gideon replied. He considered it a victory that he had elicited more than a one-word answer and ceased his attempts at small talk, quite satisfied with his efforts.

They continued to search for what felt like hours, although they had no way of telling since neither of them was wearing a watch. From Gideon's estimation, they had traveled far more than a half mile even at their deliberately slow pace, and the sun now touched the upper ledge of the canyon. He chalked it up once more to Joe's imprecise measure of time and distance. Still, he felt they should be getting close to Angel Basin, as the canyon had widened significantly. However, that made their end to end search take all the more time. Juan Carlos kept to the east side of the canyon, and Gideon found himself covering the opposite end as he combed the rocks and nooks for some clue. The more ground they covered the more Gideon began to doubt whether their search was in vain. A football card and a statue was not much to go on. Even if the clues had come from Glenn, and even if they had been properly deciphered, it still left them with a huge area to cover and little idea what they were looking for. A scorpion crawled out of the oval hole in the side of a rock that Gideon was about to stick his hand in and made him reevaluate his search methods.

"Gideon," Juan Carlos called from the far side of the canyon.

Startled at hearing his name come from his largely silent companion, he spun around to see Juan Carlos waving his arm above his head and beckoning him over. Gideon jogged over to where he stood and Juan Carlos directed his attention to three rocks, set down in the earth in a natural row. On top of the rocks were three faint markings of arrows that pointed toward the canyon wall. The markings had horizontal gaps which cut through them, giving the impression that someone had attempted to erase them. Gideon turned to face the direction the arrows indicated and found himself staring at his long shadow where it touched the convergence of two large boulders. As he drew closer Gideon saw that the boulders did not actually connect, but there was a small gap between them. Without hesitation, he shimmied sideways and moved into the narrow passageway.

In just a few yards he stepped into a clearing on the other side and his mouth fell open as he looked on a broken down old wagon next to a patch of cottonwood trees. Juan Carlos joined him inside the clearing and they both looked around at the small haven in the desert. A tributary from the creek ran through the clearing and fed the trees and vegetation on the ground. He had only taken a few steps toward the old wagon when a shack or a shed, tucked back behind the trees, came into view. His first thought was of Glenn living out here in the wilderness waiting for him to arrive. All at once he was filled with excitement, confusion, anxiety, and anger. Without a second thought, he marched straight for the shack with Juan Carlos hurrying along behind him. Just as they cleared the final cottonwood, between them and the shack, a gun shot rang out in the clearing and a bullet ricocheted off the tree beside them. As a self-preserving reflex, they drove behind the cover of the rusty old wagon.

"Hey!" Gideon shouted. "We're friends! Don't shoot!"

Other than the flutter of birds fleeing in the distance, everything was silent. Gideon waited a moment or two for a response and then peered around the wagon toward the shack. A second shot fired from the tiny window next to the front door and impacted the jumper seat in front of him.

"Judas Priest!" Gideon exclaimed as he fell backwards. "We're unarmed! Stop shooting!"

"I wouldn't say that," Juan Carlos said as he pulled a gun from his pocket.

"What the heck is that?" asked Gideon.

"It's my Glock," Juan Carlos replied. He squatted down and peeked through the slats in the rotting wood. "Stay down, I got this."

"What are you going to do?" Gideon's voice jumped an octave in a moment of hysteria.

"Shock and awe," Juan Carlos replied calmly.

He leapt out from behind the wagon and walked in a straight line toward the shack. With each step, he fired a shot in rapid succession. The volley of bullets hit the front door of the shack throwing splinters in every direction. His onslaught continued until he was just a few feet from the door. The shots stopped abruptly and were replaced by the click, click, click of the hammer hitting an empty chamber. The front door flew open and the barrel of a gun emerged from the dark interior of the shack. Juan Carlos dropped his weapon and threw his hands in the air. Still crouched behind the wagon, Gideon looked around and considered his options.

"Come out or I'll plug this feller full of holes," a raspy voice called from inside the shack.

"Cuss," Gideon muttered and peered through the cracks of the old carriage.

"1, 2..." the raspy voice began to count.

"A'right, all right," Gideon popped up from behind the wagon with his arms in the air. "Just be cool."

"Git over here and keep your hands where I can see 'em," ordered the man inside the shack.

Gideon obediently walked out from behind the wagon and slowly made his way toward the spot where his impetuous partner had surrendered. He stood next to Juan Carlos, who did not appear to be shaken in the least. A rope shot out from the dark doorway and landed at their feet.

"You tie up your trigger-happy friend over there," the voice instructed. "And be sure ya make it tight."

"Trigger happy?" Gideon questioned. "You're the one who fired first."

"And I'll be the one who fires last, now hush up and git to tying."

Gideon bent over and picked up the rope. Juan Carlos still stood, rather impatiently, with his hands over his head as he stared into the shack.

"Turn yourself around Sancho Ponza," the voice beyond the doorway ordered. "And put your hands behind your back. And no funny business."

Juan Carlos spun around on the spot and dutifully placed his hands behind his back. Gideon moved around to stand behind him with both their backs facing the shack. He began to tie his wrists together and considered the consequences of not making the knots too tight. With a gun pointed at his back he decided that the wise course was to comply with his demands and not give him any cause to shoot one or both of them.

"His name is Juan Carlos," Gideon replied as he cinched the bowline tightly around his wrists. "And my name is Gideon. What's yours?"

"Betty Crocker," the man replied. "Now you just hush an' make them knots good an' tight."

He looped the rope around the knot he had already tied and pulled down hard to prove the honor of his efforts. The sound of footsteps in the loose gravel drew nearer. With eyes down on his handy work Gideon could see a pair of dusty leather boots come into his field of vision and come to a stop in line with his tennis shoes. He raised his hands above his head again and just as he began to turn his head there was a crack and an intense pain exploded across the back of his skull and, in an instant, all was black.

THE COWBOY WAY

Glenn banged in rhythmic fashion on a tin pot. The blackened coffee pot had been tied to Bernice until they decided it was an ideal noise maker. He had already tried clanking the pot against a rock and rattling a stick around inside. After those failed to produce sufficient noise, he settled on knocking the stick into the side with the mouth pointing toward the opening of the dark shaft. The reverberations reached all the way up to the top of the canyon wall where Jeddediah pressed the brim of his hat against his ears to dull the percussion of Glenn's pot-banging.

Next to Jeddediah was a tire sized boulder with a thick rope tied around it like a Christmas ribbon. The rope ran along the ledge of the canyon over to a large rock formation almost directly above the entrance to the manmade opening near the canyon floor. Jeddediah stood at the ready for almost an hour weary old legs. They worked tirelessly for most of the day to find a suitable boulder and lift, pull, push, and roll it into place. Jeddediah tied one end of the rope to the boulder while Glenn tied the other to the rock formation. Much to the old miner's chagrin, Glenn had inspected his work to ensure the knots were tied to his satisfaction. In retaliation he hobbled over to the rock formation to give similar scrutiny to the work of his young accomplice. When they were both satisfied, Glenn removed the charred coffee pot from around Bernice's neck and carefully made his way down the canyon to entice the beast from its den.

"Maybe he's nocturnal," Glenn shouted back up to Jeddediah.

"Why did'ya stop?" Jeddediah said as he removed his hands from his ears. "Keep beat'n that pot."

"You know, nocturnal," Glenn said. "Like he's only awake at night."

"I know what nocturnal means, you ninny," Jeddediah said. "That means he's up and about in the night, it doesn't mean he can't be woke up in the day time. Besides it's gonna be dark 'fore too long."

The sun dipped low in the blue sky, although there was still plenty of daylight left. Shadows had begun to stretch toward the east, but the shade from the canyon wall had only just reached Glenn. Jeddediah was still set upon by the blazing summer heat of the Arizona afternoon. Even from his elevated position he could see Glenn tremble as he stood directly in harm's way, at the entrance of the menacing shaft.

"Don't ya think if he was gonna hear it, he'd have heard it by now?" Glenn asked.

"That's the trouble with yer generation," Jeddediah shouted back down to him. "Ya ain't got the stamina for real work."

"Real work?" Glenn replied. "I'm banging a stick against a pot. Real work was moving that boulder."

"Hesh!" chided Jeddediah. "It'll hear ya."

"This is dumb," Glenn said as he threw the stick to the ground. "I'm not doing this anymore. You come down here and beat on your own pot."

"Quitter," Jeddediah taunted.

"It's not gonna work," Glenn said.

A stocky dog with charcoal fur trotted up the canyon from the south. Glenn took several steps away from the animal and raised the pot in front of him. At the sight of a pot leveled at its nose the dog dug in his heels and bore his teeth with a threatening growl.

"Dog!" a shout echoed through the canyon as a white Stetson came into view. "Come!"

The dog turned and ran back to a tall cowboy who rode a grey spotted horse. With the dog at his side the cowboy continued to gallop toward Glenn, coming to a stop within arm's reach. He sat back in the saddle and studied the awestruck redheaded. Jeddediah could not hear what was being said but they appeared to exchange greetings.

"Hells Bells," Jeddediah muttered.

Glenn turned around and pointed up to the top of the ledge where Jeddediah stood. The cowboy looked up at him and smiled.

"This here's a marked improvement over your last partner," the cowboy shouted up to him. "That old nag finally leave you?"

On cue, Bernice stepped toward the ledge and brayed down at the cowboy.

"Well I'll be," the cowboy replied. "Guess what she lacks in smarts she makes up for in loyalty. So, ya found the Dutchman yet, old timer?"

"Ya think I'd tell ya if I did?" Jeddediah shouted back.

"Nope, I don't suppose ya would," the cowboy replied. "This wouldn't be it though, would it?"

The cowboy was visibly amused as he pointed toward the opening in the canyon wall and chuckled. Jeddediah rolled his eyes and ran his tongue along the inside of his cheek. Glenn looked back and forth between Jeddediah and the cowboy with some apprehension.

"Why do ya got this kid beating on that pot?" asked the cowboy. "Ya trying to wake the dead?"

"What if I am?" Jeddediah replied. "What's it to ya?"

"You can go about your business any way ya like," said the cowboy. "But it ain't a good idea to be call'n attention to yourself way out here. No tell'n what kind of unsavory folks might be about."

"I reckon we was just found by one," Jeddediah said.

"Well, that's a fine how do ya do when I just come to see if I could be any help," the cowboy said.

"Don't you have some city slickers to play cowboy with?" Jeddediah asked, his voice echoed off the canyon walls. Glenn looked anxiously into the dark tunnel beside him. The cowboy dismounted from his horse and began to survey the opening on the east side of the canyon.

"Doggone it," Jeddediah said. He quickly slipped over the lip of the canyon and followed the course Glenn had taken to the bottom. Twice he slipped and fell on his backside, each time looking up to find the cowboy observing his descent with delight. When he reached the bottom, he hobbled directly to where the cowboy stood.

"Pretty spry for an old polecat," the cowboy laughed.

"We don't need no help and we don't want ya 'round these parts," Jeddediah said with a wave of his arms. "You git back on your horse and head back the way ya come."

"Ya hear that Pepper?" the cowboy said to the gray spotted horse. "Ya try and be a good neighbor and this is the thanks ya get."

His horse chewed on a branch that stuck out from between two rocks and did not seemed concerned with their conversation. Dog had been merrily dancing around the gray spotted horse but settled on a good spot of sand to spread out and lay down.

"I ain't gonna thank ya for stick'n your nose where it don't belong," replied Jeddediah. "Now you git on out of here 'fore something unfortunate happens to ya."

"Well, you would know all about unfortunate wouldn't ya?" the cowboy said. "But it's a free country, old timer, and I was thinking about poking around in this here cave to see what I see."

"Don't," Glenn blurted out and jumped to block the cowboy's way.

"And why not?" asked the cowboy. "What's in there? Whatcha hiding boy?"

"Nothing," Glenn said. "It's just..."

Jeddediah caught his eye and shook his head. Glenn hung his head and stared at the ground, as if it might have the answer he sought. The cowboy walked casually over to the red haired young man and took the charred pot from his hand. He held it up and examined the inside.

"I doubt you're invit'n whatever's in there out for a tea party," the cowboy said as he scrutinized Glenn.

"There's noth'n in the cave," Jeddediah argued.

"Then why're ya beat'n on the pot?" the cowboy asked.

"We just like the acoustics of the canyon," Jeddediah said.

"Bull pucky," said the cowboy. "Then what's the rope for?"

He pointed up to the line that hung over the wall of the canyon.

"Ain't none of your concern," Jeddediah replied.

"Fine," the cowboy said. He swept Glenn to the side with his arm and stepped to the threshold of the tunnel. "I'll just have a look around and see for myself."

"No," Glenn protested. "Stop. Please."

"How 'bout you give me a reason," the cowboy said with a sideways look at Jeddediah.

The trio stood in silence for a moment. Glenn turned his back to the cowboy and raised an inquisitive eyebrow toward Jeddediah. The shade from the western wall had nearly reached the top of the east side of the canyon. A warm breeze blew down the ravine and brought with it an unpleasant aroma. Jeddediah could not decide if it came from the horse or if it was his own body odor being pushed back upon him. In any case, his nose scrunched up, involuntarily, and he fought off a sneeze. Unable to think of a way to rid himself of the persistent cowboy, he conceded defeat.

He quickly calculated how much information he could give that would satisfy his curiosity without revealing what they were after.

"There's a monster in there," Glenn said before Jeddediah could answer.

"Horse crap," the cowboy replied as he placed his head on his hips.

"It's true," Glenn said. "Tell him Jed."

"You let him call you Jed?" asked the cowboy.

"No, I do not," Jeddediah enunciated each syllable in Glenn's direction. "But he ain't lying."

"There's a monster in there?" the cowboy asked as he extended his arm and pointed into the darkness. His dog leapt up onto all four and growled at the hole in the wall.

"I don't know what it is," Jeddediah explained. "If it's a monster or a man or a demon, but there's something in there that ya don't want to mess with."

"Then why are you mess'n with it?" he held up the tin pot and shook it in Glenn's face.

"We're trying to draw it out so we can kill it," Glenn mumbled as he averted his eyes and shifted his weight from side to side.

The cowboy looked back and forth between Glenn and Jeddediah. He glanced back over his shoulder into the cave. Jeddediah brushed at a gnat that had been buzzing around his beard. He could almost see the wheels turning in the cowboy's head, more questions were coming and every answer would bring him closer to the truth.

"What'd it do to you?" the cowboy finally asked as he remove his white hat and swatted at his own pestering swarm of gnats.

"Nothing," Glenn answered.

"Then why not leave it be?" asked the cowboy. "If ain't doing ya no harm, why kill it?"

Glenn looked over at Jeddediah for a response. The look on his face was somewhere between knowing where he wanted to start and not knowing where to stop. Jeddediah shook his head and sighed deeply.

"Unless it's sitting between you and something ya want," the cowboy said almost to himself. "That's it, isn't it? What else is in that cave?"

"A key," Glenn said.

"You fool!" Jeddediah shouted.

"He was going to get at it eventually," Glenn argued.

"A key to what?" the cowboy asked.

"A key to your mother's house," Jeddediah snapped.

"My mother's dead, and I live in her house," the cowboy shot back. "Now what kind of key could be worth facing a monster over?"

Jeddediah walked past Glenn and shot him an irritated glare. He took his pot from the cowboy and strode over to the far side of the canyon. It only took a minute to cross the narrow ravine floor. He could still see the markings on the side of the wall where he and his demon pursuer had clawed their way up to the top. A chill shot up his spine as he turned back around to face the cave that nearly became his tomb. He sat down on a rock and set the pot on the ground beside him as Glenn and the cowboy approached him cautiously. After taking a moment to collect himself, he took in a deep breath and looked up into the cowboy's steely blue eyes.

"I begun to doubt if I'd ever find it," he began. "I searched day and night for months. I started at Cletus's hideout and widened the search pattern each day. I combed every inch of ground and looked over every nook and cranny. I had nothing to go on, but figured from the state he was in he couldn't have gotten far from where he saw it."

"Saw what? The key?" the cowboy asked. "Who's Cletus?"

"Shhh," Glenn hushed him and leaned forward eagerly.

"I didn't have a clue but I knew it was out here," Jeddediah continued. "I could feel it. "Then one evening I was searching through this here canyon and there it was, like a sign from God."

"There what was?" asked Glenn. "The shaft?"

"Just wait," Jeddediah said and he pointed to the opening.

The three of them stared back toward the dark hole and it seemed an unnatural quiet fell over the desert. The shadow's progress up the canyon wall was the only movement. Just as it disappeared over the top, a beam of light shot back over the canyon and a glowing cross appeared on the western wall with the base buried right into the entrance to the shaft.

"Ho-ly crap," an astonished Glenn whispered.

"Well I'll be," the cowboy muttered as he removed his hat.

"They hid it good behind some bush and rocks, but there it was," Jeddediah said. "The sign I'd been looking for."

As quickly as the cross appeared it was gone without a trace. The sun dipped below the horizon and dusk had come. Jeddediah fiddled with the pot beside him, while Glenn and the cowboy stood silently in the last light of day.

"I come back the next evening and sat right here, just to be sure I hadn't imagined it," Jeddediah continued. "I was so excited I couldn't wait until morning. I come with all my gear, fired up my headlamp and set to explor'n. I laid out rope so I could find my way back but that rope run out before too long. I shoulda stopped when I reached that rabbit hole. But I could almost hear it calling to me."

"The key?" asked the cowboy.

Jeddediah nodded.

"A narrow trench run up into a big room on the other side of the rabbit hole," he said. "And there it was, lying there on a rock like it'd been waiting for me. I picked it up and had barely begun to look it over when a terrible stench filled the room. Next thing I knew, I was runn'n for my life."

Another breeze swept down the ravine, only this one felt cooler than the last. Dog lifted his head and looked up and down the canyon while the gray spotted horse shuffled to the side. The cowboy hurried to his horse and took hold of the reigns.

"Easy girl," he soothed her. "Easy Pepper."

Jeddediah looked up into the evening sky. Scattered stars were already visible in the dark blue blanket over head. Glenn had not taken his eyes off of the entrance to the shaft that led deep into the earth, deep into the monster's den. The cowboy appeared to study the tops of his boots as he moseyed back over to them. He took off his Stetson and gently beat it against his leg.

"So ya left it in the cave?" he asked.

"No," Jeddediah replied emphatically. "I come out with it. But it's been reclaimed."

Glenn glanced over his shoulder back at Jeddediah who had laid an accusing eye on him. The old miner was not certain he could be seen in the fading light of dusk but he made every effort so the young man might feel his stare. If Glenn had not happened along when he did Jeddediah would have already killed the monstrous creature and would have his prize all to himself. He imagined that he would have probably found the treasure by now and be well on his way to fame and fortune. Instead, he found himself sitting on a rock staring straight down the barrel of his worst nightmare with a nosey cowboy and a wounded ginger.

"So ya want to go back in there and get it?" asked the cowboy.

"Not as long as that thing is liv'n," Jeddediah replied.

"I can take care of that," the cowboy said as he pulled his sidearm from the hostler.

"If ya want to go and get yourself killed, be my guest," Jeddediah said, struggling to his feet.

"Anybody have a light?" the cowboy asked.

"I do," Glenn said. "It's in my pack. Hold on a second, I'll go with ya."

"Are ya crazy, boy?" Jeddediah said. "Let him go. We've got a plan."

Glenn walked over to where he left his backpack, near the opening. He returned with a flashlight and switched it on. Dog turned his attention to the new circle of light that shone on the ground.

"The plan's not working, Jeddediah," Glenn said. "Sooner or later we're gonna have to go into that cave. I'd rather do it with Wyatt Earp, here, than do it alone."

"My name is Glenn," he turned and extended his hand toward the cowboy.

"Cal," the cowboy replied as he shook his hand.

Glenn turned back to Jeddediah who had his arms folded across his chest in protest. The light cast eerie shadows across his young friend's freckled face. He knew what he was saying was right but did not want to face the inevitability of their destiny. His jaw began to quiver at the thought of descending back into the dark confines of the monster's lair.

"Listen," Glenn said. "You climb back up on the ledge. We'll go in and get the key. If that thing follows us you be ready to drop that rock and take him out. We'll call it plan B."

Jeddediah was relieved he would not be expected to return, and ashamed at how willing he was to allow them to venture into danger without him. Before he even realized what was happening he nodded in agreement and Glenn turned and led the way into the cave, followed by the gun toting cowboy. Dog jumped up and followed after them.

"Stay here, Dog," Cal said. "Look after Pepper. I'll be right back."

With that they disappeared into the mouth of the cave, leaving only a remnant of the glow from Glenn's flashlight. Jeddediah hobbled back over to the west side of the canyon and began his climb up to the top. He listened carefully for some sound from the cave, but heard only the faint whisper of the breeze that blew down the ravine. His old lungs burned as he reached the top. He struggled to draw in a full breath, with a needle like pain in his side. Bernice walked up to him and nestled her large head into his chest. As a reflex, he reached up and patted her head, as his thoughts and attention were turned fully to the shaft of terror beneath them.

The only light that remained was from the setting sun as the flashlight had disappeared over the ledge deep into the cave. The desert had already begun to cool, freed from the solar onslaught of day, and the moon now ruled the sky and shone down on him in all her glory. Although he had fully recovered from the climb out of the canyon, his heart beat at an elevated rate as he looked helplessly down at the opening. With each moment that passed in silence his mind filled in the unknown with fresh horror and tragedy. If they succumbed to the monster, how long would he wait before he did something, and what would he do? The questions stacked up on each other with no answers to be found. Beads of sweat formed on his forehead despite the slightly cooler temperatures. It became nearly unbearable to hold his position any longer but he could not decide whether to pursue them into the darkness or flee into the night.

Before he could come to any conclusion a shot rang out from inside the cave followed by another and then another. He leaned over as far as he dare but it did not improve his vantage point. The shots were followed immediately by a bone chilling scream and slightly softer shouts of panic. Two more shots were fired in rapid succession accompanied by more screams and shouts. Jeddediah nearly lost his balance and fell over the cliff when he had leaned out too far. He quickly steadied himself and stepped back from the edge. The shouts and shots stopped and all was silent again. Although he had no better idea what was happening, whether it was quiet or not, he almost preferred the shouting and shooting because at least he knew they were still alive. One more shot exploded from the shaft only this time it was much louder. A few seconds later Cal came stumbling out of the cave without his cowboy hat. Dog ran to his side and began barking furiously at the darkness, and Pepper had already bolted down the ravine to the south. Cal raised his gun and pointed it toward the shaft.

"Get ready!" he shouted up at him.

"Where's the boy?" Jeddediah shouted back.

"He's com'n," Cal replied. "Get ready."

The moonlight illuminated the scene and Jeddediah could see Cal's wide eyes staring back down the tunnel. A deafening roar exploded from the cave and made them both jump back in fright. Glenn tumbled out of the hole and fell at Cal's feet.

"Now!" Cal yelled.

Jeddediah took a second to see if his young friend was moving. Glenn scurried away from the cave on his hands and knees as another roar bellowed into the canyon.

"Now!" Cal repeated. "Let it loose! Now, man, now!"

In a panic, Jeddediah hobbled to the far end of the boulder and pushed it with both hands. When it barely moved he put his shoulder into it and dug in his heels. The boulder rocked forward several inches before it stopped. He slid lower on the boulder and pushed again but it did not budge.

"Do it, Jed!" Glenn yelled as his voice cracked with terror. "Now!"

With all the strength he had left he drove his shoulder into the massive rock and screamed. He felt a fuzzy hide slide up next to him and all at once the boulder tipped forward and fell over the ledge. Bernice stood beside him and whinnied loudly as the rock and rope disappeared into the canyon. Jeddediah raced to the edge of the cliff and looked to see the boulder careening off the wall as it bounced its way downward. The rope suddenly tightened and the boulder was pulled toward the opening just as they had planned. At that moment, a dark shadow burst through the hole and laid hold on Glenn. Dog barked ferociously and jumped back and forth.

"Ah!" Glenn shouted.

Cal leapt forward and grabbed his arm just as the boulder made a sickening impact with the monster, like a wrecking ball smashing through a brick wall. There was another ear-splitting roar that echoed up and down the canyon as the dark shadow was throw to the side. Cal pulled Glenn to his feet, and they both ran up the canyon with Dog right on their heels. The boulder swung back and rolled across the wall until its momentum failed and it was pulled back in the opposite direction. As Glenn, Cal, and Dog made their way up the side of the west canyon the monster staggered to its feet. The boulder settled to a stop at the end of the rope just next to the opening to the cave. Jeddediah's heart was in his throat as he watched helplessly from his elevated position. Although his concern was with his partners, his eyes were fixed on their pursuer. On unsteady legs, the hairy beast leaned against the wall for support. It took several tentative steps forward and paused to balance itself again. He could not believe the boulder had not killed it but was at least relieved, in part, that the blow had severely hindered it.

"Come on," Jeddediah beckoned to Cal and Glenn. "Hurry."

The monstrous cave dweller looked up at him and all Jeddediah could see was the moonlight reflecting of the white of its one good eye. Jeddediah swallowed hard and waited for it to make a move. Its eye narrowed into an angry glowing slit and it seethed hatred up at him with a shrieking scream. Glenn and Cal spun around in alarm as tremors shook the earth and waves of terror washed over Jeddediah. None of them moved, even Dog remained silent and still. The wounded beast limped around the boulder, which was suspended off the ground by the taught rope. It did not take its eye off the group at the top of the ledge until it disappeared back into the dark shaft in the side of the canyon. Jeddediah was the first to regain his voice.

"What are ya wait'n for?" he said. "Git a move on."

The old miner turned around to find that Bernice was nowhere to be seen. He did not fault her, as he too would have fled if not for the paralyzing fear. Glenn, Cal and Dog finally made it up to where Jeddediah waited.

"Ya weren't lying," Cal said. "What in the blue hell was that?"

"Did ya get it?" asked Jeddediah.

Between heaving breaths Glenn proudly held up a burlap sack. He and Jeddediah smiled at each other. Another ear-splitting roar cut short their revelry as their attention was drawn back to the dark opening at the bottom of the canyon.

"Let's get far away from here before we throw a party," Cal said. "Pepper run off and I see your old mule did the same, so it looks like we're on foot."

"We've got a place," Glenn said.

Jeddediah shot him a disapproving look. He was not keen to share his hideout with yet another unwelcome guest. Glenn gestured to him with an encouraging nod and Jeddediah relented without raising an objection.

"How far is it?" Cal asked with a worried look back down into the canyon.

"Far enough," Jeddediah said as he followed the cowboy's gaze down toward the monster's lair. "Let's get going."

They put the canyon behind them and headed due north. The moon bathed the desert in its light and allowed them to see clearly enough to move through the rocks, bushes and cacti without a trail or flashlight. With fresher legs, Cal led out in front with Glenn and Jeddediah hobbling along behind him. After having to stop several times to allow them to catch up he fell back and walked beside them. When they had put a good deal of distance between themselves and their harrowing trials of the canyon, Cal looked down at the sack in Glenn's hand.

"So, let's see it then," he said.

Glenn hesitated and looked over to Jeddediah.

"Come on," Cal insisted. "I wanna see what I risked my neck for."

Jeddediah nodded and Glenn quickly stopped, set the burlap sack on the ground and anxiously uncovered the prize. From the burlap bag, he pulled the hefty iron head of a pick ax and laid it gently back on top of the burlap.

"That's it?" Cal said with a quizzical look. "We were nearly killed for that?"

Glenn stood up straight and placed his hands on his hips. He knocked his hat to the ground as he ran his hands through his red locks. Jeddediah bent down and picked up the pick ax as if he were laying hold on a delicate egg. With outstretched arms, he presented it to his comrades.

"Shine your light right here," Jeddediah instructed.

There was a moment of hesitation, as Glenn studied the old miner, before he slowly reached into his pocket and produced the flashlight. It flicked on and illuminated an unremarkable piece of iron. The light did not improve the looks on his partner's faces as all it revealed were the dents, dings and chunks missing from the ancient pick ax. Jeddediah turned it over slowly with deliberate showmanship and watched for their displeasing expressions to change. A wide gap-toothed grin broke across Glenn's face first, while Cal's skeptical expression only softened slightly. On the back of the pick ax was the unmistakable engraving of a cross skeleton key, like the one he had seen in Cletus's Spanish journal.

"The key," Glenn said.

"The key," Jeddediah agreed.

"I still don't get it," Cal said.

"I'll explain it to you once we put some miles between us and the canyon of doom back there," Glenn said as he lifted the burlap sack under the pick ax. Jeddediah placed the pick ax carefully back in its holder and took the sack from Glenn. He threw it over his shoulder and marched forward with his chest out and his head held high. All the years of toiling and suffering and all his own missteps and mistakes ran through his head, but they no longer plagued him like they had before. He was the victor, free from all ridicule and regret; at last he had a piece of redemption.

Cautiously, Dog led the way forward with wary looks on all directions. Glenn kept glancing back over his shoulder which disturbed Jeddediah's revelry and prompted him to grunt at the young redhead.

"Do you think it will be all right?" Glenn asked.

"What?" Cal asked. "The monster? Who cares?"

"It looked hurt," Glenn replied. "I hate to see suffering."

"We'd be do'n the suffer'n if it had its way," Jeddediah answered.

"Well, we did bust into its home," Glenn argued.

"Home?" Jeddediah spat incredulously. "Didya see a din'n room table in there? That ain't no home. It's a cave, a monster's lair."

"Okay, then we busted in to its lair," Glenn said. "I'm just saying it had every right to…"

"Right?" Jeddediah interrupted. "There ya go again with the law. When Sasquatch, back there, wants to get a lawyer and take me to court I'll consider its rights."

"Fine," Glenn conceded. "All I'm saying is I feel bad. That's all."

"Ya can send it flowers and a gift basket for all I care," Jeddediah said. "I ain't gonna feel guilty winn'n. Don't ya understand? This here is the key to riches. That thing wouldn't know what to do with it."

Jeddediah held up the burlap sack and shook it in his face. Glenn bowed his head without another word. The three of them stood quietly with the only the wind and Dog's panting breaking the uncomfortable silence. The cowboy removed his hat and beat it pensively against the side of his leg. When Jeddediah was sure the subject was exhausted, he turned and continued toward the safety of his mountain sanctuary. Glenn lagged behind as the cowboy hustled up next to Jeddediah and matched his hobbled stride.

"So we have a key" Cal said. "What do we do now?"

"We go find the door," Jeddediah said as he smiled straight ahead into the dark of night.

HATS AND HOODS

A rush of cold water exploded across his face and left him gasping for air. All at once Gideon's heart was racing from the shock to his system. There was a dull throbbing sensation at the back of his skull that pulsed in concert with the water that dripped over his eyelids. He strained to look around the darkened room. A soft purple light bled into the room through the window to his right but it offered little insight into what lie within the walls that surrounded him. Only when he leaned forward did he feel the ropes that bound him. Gideon squirmed from side to side and tested the restraints wrapped around his chest. His arms were tied behind his back and his feet were bound at the ankles.

"What are ya do'n here?" a raspy voice asked from the darkness.

Gideon looked to where the voice had come from but saw only a dark corner. He heard rapid breathing behind him and felt the quivering body he was tied to. The water that soaked his head and shirt amplified the cold winter air. He craned his head behind him and could just make out Juan Carlos's profile in the muted light of dusk. Gideon turned toward the light and saw a towering shadow on the distant black horizon. A single mighty saguaro rose up from the hilltop; its silhouette looked like a giant monk praying over them, with its two limbs drawn close to its tall trunk.

"I said, what are ya do'n here?" the raspy voice repeated.

"Some lunatic hit me over the head and tied me up," Gideon replied.

Juan Carlos shifted and sat forward which pulled the ropes tighter against Gideon's chest and drew him back slightly.

"You're trespass'n," the man in the dark corner said. "This lunatic has the right to protect what's his."

"Isn't this federal land?" Gideon asked. "I can't be trespassing if it's not your property."

"You hesh up an' quit playing dumb," the agitated voice ordered. "What brought ya here?"

"Do you want me to hush up or answer your question?" Gideon asked. "I can't do both."

A silver pistol emerged from the shadows with the barrel pointed right at Gideon's forehead. He stared down the cylinder as a lump formed in his throat.

"I ain't got the patience for foolishness," the voice threatened from behind the pistol.

"All right," Gideon said. "We'll answer your questions, but it feels absurd to be talking to the darkness. Can you turn on a light?"

The revolver withdrew back into the black, and Gideon heard a metallic clanking noise as something drug across the floor. A moment later, there was a tiny combustion from a matchstick and the flame on a stick illuminated the corners of a gray beard. At the turn of a knob and the touch of a match, the kerosene lantern filled the cramped quarters with light. An old bearded man stood by the lantern and shook the smoking match stick until the flame went out. The man wore a dusty wide brim hat with the bill pressed back against his head, his thick scraggily beard almost completely covered his gaunt wrinkled face. He wore blue jeans and a canvas overcoat with dusty old boots that matched his dusty old hat.

"Ya got your light," the old man said. "Now talk."

"Thank you," Gideon said. "Now how 'bout you untie us and we'll chat like civilized people."

"No deal," the man barked, with his pistol leveled at Gideon. "You ain't go'n nowhere 'til ya tell me who ya are and whatcha do'n here."

"Fine," Gideon said. "As I said before you clubbed me over the head, I'm Gideon and this is Juan Carlos. What was your name again?"

"Don't make no difference what my name is" the old man said. "We ain't never met."

"I make it a rule to always learn who kidnapped me and tied me up," Gideon said. "That way we can keep in touch."

"That's enough sass outta you," the man said as he pulled the hammer back on his revolver. "The name's Jeddediah, now you git to talk'n."

"Pleased to meet you Jed," Gideon said. "Can I call you Jed?"

"No," Jeddediah seethed as his crooked teeth grinded together.

"Okay," Gideon said, as he quickly recognized a line he had crossed. "We're looking for a man in a gray cloak. He disappeared back up the canyon and we think he might have come this way."

"A hooded feller?" Jeddediah asked.

"Yes!" Gideon exclaimed. He felt Juan Carlos shift and twist behind him as he tried to look at the old man by the lantern. Gideon slid to his left, a couple of inches, to allow Juan Carlos a better vantage point but still keep his eyes on the old man. "You've seen him then?"

"I seen him," Jeddediah confirmed. "Skulk'n about like a vulture. Who is he to you?"

"Nobody," Gideon said. "He's been following us and we want to know why."

"Following ya where?" Jeddediah asked. "Why are ya out here?"

Gideon did not want to share the purpose of their quest with this stranger, at the same time he did not wish to anger him and get shot. He looked around the ill-kempt room for a viable distraction. To his left were several tattered blankets spread in the corner with a stained old pillow. There was a charred coffee pot and a cast iron skillet with several boxes covered by a pile of burlap sacks, next to a rusty lantern with cracked glass. There was a single door behind the old man, barely clinging to its hinges as the frame leaned back toward the boxes and bedding. He scanned the wall to his right and found a modern looking red backpack and a stack of assorted clothes beneath the window. On top of the stack was a white canvas hat with a flap on the back. The flap was tarnished on the bottom edges and all at once Gideon recognized it.

His eyes widened as he studied the hat. Glenn wore an identical hat on all their campouts. He called it his Lawrence of Arabia hat, only he did not quite pull off the Humphrey Bogart look. The black marks on the bottom edge of the neck flap were from when Todd had briefly tossed the hat into the campfire during one of their frequent quarrels over who would prevail in a fight between Batman or Superman. Glenn sided firmly with the Caped Crusader while Todd argued for the Man of Steel. There was not a doubt in Gideon's mind that he was looking at his friend's old hat.

"We are looking for our friend Glenn Bicklesby," Gideon said. "Red hair, round face, gap-toothed smile. Have you seen him?"

The old man's eyes narrowed as he studied Gideon. Juan Carlos fidgeted behind him which pulled at the ropes. Gideon simply stared back at their captor and waited patiently.

"You say he's a friend of yours?" Jeddediah asked.

"That's right," Gideon said. "We've been friends since we were kids."

"And it took ya all this time to come look'n for him?" Jeddediah questioned. "That boy went miss'n over a year ago."

"And how would you know that?" asked Gideon.

"It was in the papers," responded Jeddediah.

"You get the paper way out here, do ya?" Gideon replied and laid a deadly look on the old man. Jeddediah returned his glare and the conversation halted. Gideon had thrown his line in the water and now he waited like a patient fisherman for a bite. Beyond the window, nearly all the daylight had vanished leaving only a thin blue line above the horizon. Gideon's wrists and arms became irritated from the twine rope that dug into his skin. He stayed still like a statue and refused to blink as he attempted to break his opponent down with his eyes.

"You're ly'n," Jeddediah finally said. "Ya ain't look'n for that boy."

"Tell me then," Gideon said. "What are we look'n for?"

"You're in cahoots with the hood," Jeddediah accused. "Come to drive me out."

"First of all, no one says cahoots," Gideon replied. "Second, I told you the truth. The man in the hood has been following us, we're looking for our friend and I think you're the one who's lying."

"What makes ya think that?" Jeddediah asked.

"Because that's Glenn's hat over there," Gideon said, with a nod to the stack beneath the window. "How 'bout you tell me what ya did to him?"

"It was him that did to me!" Jeddediah exploded in a fit of rage and waved his pistol in the air. "That dirty no good thief took what he had no right to take!"

The old man's eyes filled with anger, the corners glistening with tears. Gideon swallowed hard against the lump in his throat and tried to process this revelation. Glenn had indeed encountered this bearded lunatic and had somehow crossed him.

The thought of Glenn meeting a grizzly end had always been a possibility that Gideon had pushed to the back of his mind. To be faced with such a reality was almost more than he could bear. His pain was amplified by being powerless to do anything about it. He struggled against the ropes and leaned toward the old man. Jeddediah walked over to him and kicked both he and Juan Carlos onto their side.

"Where do ya think you're go'n?" Jeddediah taunted.

"Gideon!" a distant shout was heard from outside the shack. "Juan Carlos!"

Jeddediah dashed to the lamp and dimmed it until it was nearly out. Gideon noticed the old man was hobbled by some sort of injury and moved with a pronounced limp. Jeddediah ducked down low and peered through the window.

"Gideon!" the distant voice repeated and echoed around the rock walls. "JC! Where you at?"

"Ya keep your mouth shut or I'll plug ya both," Jeddediah turned back to them and whispered his threat into the darkness.

From down on the floor, Gideon could only see the grey sky through the window. It was difficult to judge just where the voice came from, but there was no doubt the voice belonged to Todd. Even if Gideon were to call out, he did not know whether to shout a warning or cry for help.

"How many are with ya?" the old man asked in a low voice.

"Twenty," Gideon lied. "And they're all highly trained mercenaries who don't suffer fools."

"Like Quick Draw MaGraw over there," Jeddediah said with a wave toward Juan Carlos. "I ain't worried. If they come look'n for trouble, trouble's what they're gonna get."

Jeddediah moved to the front of the shack and slowly pulled open the door. Still crouched behind the shelter of the shack, the old man leaned his head around the corner and looked from one side to the other. Juan Carlos lay motionless on his side, making it nearly impossible for Gideon to sit up properly. The dim light, from the lantern in the corner, cast a yellow haze over everything inside the shack but offered no clue as to what lie beyond the doorway.

"Wait," Gideon whispered to the old man, as he was about to step outside. "They don't want any trouble. Please, just let 'em be."

"I didn't bring 'em here," Jeddediah said. "You did."

With that, he stepped beyond the threshold, with gun in hand, and vanished into the night. The only sound inside the dilapidated shack was the sound of kerosene burning and Juan Carlos breathing.

"Sit up," Gideon ordered. They both struggled and squirmed up and down to no avail. Gideon tried to pry his wrists free from the ropes that bound him, but found the knots far too tight. When that failed he attempted to muscle his arms up toward his left pocket but they barely budged. He brushed across Juan Carlos's sweaty knuckles and felt his clenched fists.

"Hey, can you reach into my pocket?" Gideon asked. "I've got a pocket knife."

"Hold up," Juan Carlos said. He naturally gravitated toward the pocket that was off of the ground.

"No," Gideon said. "The other one."

"Oh," Juan Carlos strained to force his hands through the ropes while Gideon craned his neck behind him, but could only get far enough to stare directly down at the dark dirt floor. The ground was cold, even colder than the crisp winter air. It quickly became apparent that Juan Carlos was similarly unable to reach Gideon's pocket.

When Gideon turned back to the doorway and he found his view blocked by a pair of black boots. Before he could even attempt to look up, the figure knelt down and brandished a long bowie knife. The polished metal reflected the dim yellow light and shone prominently against the darkness of the room. Gideon lay helpless and breathless on the ground entirely at the mercy of this silent assassin. The knife moved beyond his field of vision and Gideon began to fear it was intended for Juan Carlos. No sooner as the blade disappeared than Gideon felt his bands being loosed one by one, beginning by his elbows and working its way toward his shoulders. In moments, he was freed from the ties that had bound him to Juan Carlos. He rolled over onto his stomach and felt his mystery rescuer step over him toward his fellow captor. No one spoke and Gideon was left to wonder who this person was and how he had found them. He felt a tug on the rope around his ankles and then, like before, the ropes were loosed one by one. When at last his hands were freed, he rolled over onto his back and looked up at his rescuer. A hooded figure in a flowing cloak stepped away from him toward the open doorway.

"Hey," Gideon called, as he quickly scrabbled to his feet.

The hooded figure crouched down beside the door, turned around to face him and removed his hood. Even in the diminished glow of the lantern, Gideon could see his face clearly. The man had a broad nose and wide round eyes with dark circles around them. He had shaggy black hair and looked as if he had not shaved in weeks. The man in the cloak held his index finger over his mouth to silence any further outburst.

Juan Carlos had come to his feet and stood next to Gideon. They looked at one another and then back to the man in the cloak, who once again turned to the open door. After he briefly scanned the way ahead, their hooded rescuer beckoned them forward with a wave of his arm and then led the way into the dark night. Juan Carlos obediently followed, while Gideon paused for a moment until his flight impulse kicked in. He struggled against the pull to the world outside. While he wanted answers from the old man, he also wanted to be free of this dingy old shack. Two shadows passed by the window sill to his right. As he turned toward the window, the pile of clothing beneath it caught his eye. He rushed to the pile and snatched Glenn's hat off the top and stuffed it in the front pocket of his hoodie before quickly exiting his termite riddled cell.

With only the moonlight to guide them, they hurried around the back side of the broken down old structure. Gideon kept turning to look behind them to ensure they were not being followed or that the old man had not seen their escape. In less than a hundred feet, they reached a small stream that glistened amongst the shadows. The man in the cloak stepped gently into the water and moved swiftly and silently downstream. Juan Carlos followed, with less success in both swiftness and silence. As Gideon's foot hit the cold water, a stinging sensation engulfed his ankle and he began to question the wisdom of the path they were following. Before long, they passed behind an elevated plateau that nearly surrounded the little valley and Gideon could no longer see the shack on his frequent checks for a pursuer. The man in the cloak trudged out of the stream and followed a ridgeline of giant boulders that led away from the plateau between them and the valley.

"Hold up," Gideon called.

The man in the cloak stopped and turned back toward him. Juan Carlos stood in between and glanced back and forth. Gideon stared into his large round eyes, visible even in the shadow of night.

"Who are you?" he asked. "And where are we going?"

The man in the cloak did not answer but simply stared back at Gideon. His facial expression had not changed, and Gideon had no indication that he understood him at all. When Gideon felt he had let more than adequate time pass for an answer he looked at Juan Carlos.

"Maybe he doesn't speak English," Gideon said. "Ask him in Spanish."

"Me?" Juan Carlo replied.

"Yeah you," said Gideon. "Don't you speak Spanish?"

"Why 'cause I'm Mexican?" Juan Carlos asked incredulously. "Man, I'm from Scottsdale."

"Who I am is not important," the man in the cloak finally said. "All you need know is that you are in danger."

"I know danger," Gideon said. "I don't know you."

The man's eyes narrowed and Gideon felt as if he were trying to penetrate his skull with his cold stare. Juan Carlos shrank and stepped back out of the crossfire. Gideon drew in a deep breath and straightened up to his full height. He had no intention of following this stranger any further. A coyote howled in the distance and reminded Gideon of his friends, who were out there somewhere looking for them. He feared they might run into a crazy old man instead, and his mind nearly filled with scenarios of harm and death. With all the turmoil in his soul he did not allow himself to break eye contact with the man in the cloak. The standoff had drawn on long enough that his heels began to feel sore from the resolute posture he was holding. If someone was going to relent, however, he knew it would not be him.

"My name is Miguel," the man in the cloak said. "And where we are heading is to a safe distance from here."

A voice echoed off the boulders from somewhere behind them. Gideon could not immediately understand what was being said but he spun around and listened.

"Gideon!" the distant voice called out into the night. Several hundred yards away he could see small beams from flashlights shining out in different directions. His heart leapt and fell all at once. The joy at hearing his friend's call was cut short by the thought of the pistol toting old man lurking someone in the darkness. Instinctually, he moved toward the flashlights.

"Wait!" Miguel ordered.

"Those are my friends," Gideon pointed toward the beams of light. "They are looking for us."

He turned again to leave when Miguel grabbed hold of his arm and spun him around.

"The old man," Miguel blurted out. "What did he want with you?"

"What?" Gideon furrowed his brow. "Nothing. He's a crazy old man. Said we were trespassing."

"Did he say why he's still out here?" asked Miguel. "What he's after?"

"No," Gideon said as he ripped his arm away from his cloaked rescuer. "Look, I need to get to them before he does."

He took several steps down the incline, away from the boulders and the man in the cloak. A crisp winter breeze blew up from the basin and cut through his wet clothes. He cursed the old man and every moment since he encountered him. Though he still had many questions for his cloaked stalker, his primary concern was reuniting with his friends.

"Did he say anything unusual?" Miguel called after him.

"He said cahoots," Gideon called back over his shoulder. "That's pretty unusual."

Juan Carlos followed after Gideon and the two of them strode lockstep toward the search party in the basin below. Gideon glanced back over his shoulder at the spot where Miguel had been standing but no one was there. He stopped abruptly, nearly causing Juan Carlos to collide into him. They both turned back and looked at the spot where the cloak figure had disappeared. With mouth agape, Gideon shook his head and wondered who this man, able to vanish like a ghost, was and what he wanted with them. He heard the shout of his name echo from the distant group behind him, but when he turned around he was startled to find Miguel standing in his way.

"Holy geez!" Gideon shouted as he stumbled backwards.

"Did he mention a key?" Miguel asked.

"How in the world...?" Gideon wondered aloud.

"A key," Miguel repeated.

"No, he didn't mention a key," Gideon replied. "If it's so important to you, ya know where he lives. Go back in there and ask him yourself."

Miguel stood silent, with a stone-faced expression and his arms folded in contempt. Gideon simply stepped around him and once again walked away from the hooded man of mystery. His mind whirled with questions. How did he move so swiftly and silently? Why was he lurking around in the desert? What did he want with them? What was this key he was after? Did the old man have it? At the moment those questions were less important than the safety and wellbeing of his friends. He closed the distance between them than as fast as he could move through the uneven and dark terrain. When he was within a few hundred feet he called out to them.

"Hey!" he shouted.

"Gideon?" Todd's voice shouted back. All at once four beams of light pointed in his direction. The lights bobbed up and down as they danced toward him. He shielded his eyes with one hand and waved a greeting with the other. Liz was the first one to him. She threw her arms around his neck and squeezed him tightly. Gideon wrapped his arms around her as tingles shot throughout his body.

"Oh my gosh, Gideon," she whispered. "I thought you might..."

Her voice trailed off as the rest of the group arrived. She released her grip on him and he held on for one more second before he too released her. They did not move apart though, as Gideon gazed down into her shadowed face. He thought he could see the reflection of tear streams on her cheeks in the passing glow of the flashlights.

"You're alive," Todd said. "We heard gun shots and when we couldn't find you we started to worry."

"Yeah, that was Pistol Pedro over here trading gunshots with a crazy old miner," Gideon said with a nod over his shoulder. Juan Carlos shrugged his shoulders with a sheepish grin. Todd moved beside Liz and Gideon and put his arm around him.

"Everybody okay?" Joe asked.

"We're fine," Gideon replied. "It has been a crazy couple of hours though."

He sent a reassuring nod over to Tara who stood at the back of the group with her arms folded and her lips pursed. She looked uneasy standing back in the darkness and Gideon felt guilty for once again dragging her out into the wilderness on an ill-conceived quest.

"And the miner?" asked Joe. "Is he fine?"

"As far as I know," said Gideon. "But he's armed and he's look'n for trouble so we need to be careful."

"Is he an old fella with a thick grey beard?" asked Joe.

"Yeah," Juan Carlos replied. "It's the same guy as before."

"Wait, you know this guy?" Gideon asked as he looked back and forth between Joe and Juan Carlos. "You failed to mention that when we were tied up on his floor."

"You were tied up?" Liz asked. She reached out and grabbed his forearm. Gideon considered briefly going all in and playing all his sympathy cards but was not certain the timing was appropriate.

"Yeah, but we were saved by the hooded dude," Juan Carlos said.

"The guy in the cloak?" Todd asked.

"Or girl," Liz said.

"Nope it's a guy," said Gideon. "His name is Miguel."

Gideon turned and looked back up toward the base of the boulders, where they left Miguel, and saw only rocks bathed in moonlight. He wondered where this mysterious man might be at the moment and then remembered the threats of the old miner.

"We need to find cover," Gideon said. "It's not safe out in the open. He's out here somewhere."

"The hood?" asked Todd.

"The miner," Gideon clarified.

"Jeddediah's harmless," said Joe. "He's got quite a bark but it's just the bluster of a dejected old hermit."

"You know him?" asked Gideon.

"We've had a couple run-ins with him, yeah," Joe replied. "Saw him last a couple weeks back, down in a canyon. He chased us out of a canyon babbl'n something about a monster and it being for our own good. We left just to get away from his fuss'n."

"He's not harmless Joe," Gideon said. "He shot at and kidnapped us."

"We can talk later about how a crippled seventy year old got the drop on you," Joe said with a smirk. "How did you get away from the hood?"

"We saw your lights and told him what's up," Gideon replied. "He was more concerned with what the old man wanted."

"Did you find out what he's doing out here?" Todd asked. "Why he's following us?"

"We didn't get to all that," Gideon said. He felt foolish at how quickly he had abandoned the curiosity that led them all into danger. Although the man in the hood now had a name and a face there were still more questions about his motives and intentions than ever. Gideon was angry at himself for not compelling him to come with them, for not even inviting him.

"Either 'im afta somet'ing or 'im protecting somet'ing," Tara spoke up from the periphery.

The key, Gideon thought. The truth of Tara's words penetrated his chest and seemed to grab him by the heart. Only then did he remember Glenn's message 'To get to me you must find the key'. The words echoed into his consciousness as he squeezed Glenn's hat. Like a giant jigsaw puzzle the pieces fell into place right before him. The crazy old miner claimed that Glenn had taken something from him. Glenn told Todd that he found the key. His letter said to find him they would need a key. The man in the cloak and hood was after a key. It all fit and suddenly Gideon knew exactly what he had to do.

"We need to go back and find that old man," Gideon said.

"What? Why?" Todd asked.

"Because he knows what happened to Glenn," he replied.

"Gideon," Joe said softly. "Jeddediah is a hermit, a loner. Even if they had met, it's not likely he knew him."

"He knew him," Gideon said. He held the canvas hat over his head. "He's got his stuff back in that old shack."

"Is that Glenn's hat?" Todd asked.

Gideon nodded and Todd reached up and took it from him. He gazed down on it with wide eyes and his mouth hanging open. Liz folded her arms and bit her lower lip. They stood in complete silence and it seemed as if the entire desert had gone still. Todd clenched his fists over the hat and his arms trembled.

"Let's go get that son of a b...."

"Todd!" Liz exclaimed before he could utter another syllable.

"He's got a gun," Gideon said. "And if he's holdup in that shack again it won't be easy to get at him."

"Maybe I can go talk with him," Joe suggested.

"I don't think he's in the talking mood, Joe," Gideon replied. "Let's find a safe place for the girls to lay low and then..." "Oh no you don't," Liz interrupted. "Glenn was my friend too. I'm not going to go hide under a rock because I'm a girl."

"Me neither," Tara said as she refolded her arms defiantly.

"I don't want you to get hurt," Gideon said.

"So I'm just supposed to wait and worry," Liz said. "No way. Besides are you saying you want Todd or Joe or Juan Carlos to get hurt?"

"Yeah," Todd chimed in with a furrowed-up brow. "That's sexist."

"Fine," Gideon relented. "We'll all go with an equal chance of getting shot. Are you happy?"

"Very," Liz replied.

The group formed a circle and closed in shoulder to shoulder. They all looked at Gideon as if awaiting instructions. He smiled and nodded at each of them individually. His grandfather used to say that many hands make light work and Gideon was grateful for the willing hands all around him.

"Okay, does anybody besides Juan Carlos have a gun?" Gideon asked.

"The old man took my gun," Juan Carlos said.

"I have a revolver," Joe said.

"Anybody else?"

Tara, Todd and Liz all shook their heads.

"Good," said Gideon. "We don't need anybody getting shot in the crossfire. Joe don't even take it out unless it's a matter of life and death. Now, where are the horses?"

"We tied them up back near the edge of the basin," Todd said.

"All right," Gideon continued. "We'll need 'em."

"What's the plan?" asked Joe.

"We're going to get nice and neighborly with a grumpy old hermit," Gideon replied with a wink. He turned toward Juan Carlos. "Shock and awe."

JUDAS

Beads of sweat pooled and dripped down his forehead. Jeddediah drew in a deep breath and rolled unto his side. The midmorning summer sun bled in through the cracks in the old shack and heated it like an oven. Two new bedrolls lay on the dirt floor next to him. He sat up with a start when he found both the bedrolls were empty. A quick check to his left confirmed his biggest fear. The burlap sack, tucked between himself and the wall, was also empty. He scrambled to his feet and frantically searched from end to end of the tiny shack.

"No," he muttered.

He threw bedding from one side of the room to the other and cleared the floor. The more he searched the more desperate he became. His head spun and his heart pounded in his chest. He had slept like a rock as sleep visited him like a long-lost friend. Now he awoke to a nightmare of panic and betrayal. He stumbled out the front door, and his eyelids blinked rapidly as he attempted to force a prompt adjustment to the daylight. There was no sign of either of his partners. His private desert oasis had been vacated except for a lone cactus wren perched in the cottonwood tree nearest the shack. In a brief exchange, he looked at the wren with pleading eyes hoping that the bird could help him. His vain hope literally flew away as the wren hopped from the branch and took flight.

"Ahhhhh!" Jeddediah screamed at the sky.

With his fists clenched tightly, he returned to the shack with murder on his mind. He rooted around his belongings for his sidearm. At last he found his pistol beneath his overturned bedding in the corner. He checked to see it was still loaded and stormed back outside to look for some clue as to which way they had headed. There was no way of knowing how much of a head start they had on him, but he did not care. If it took the rest of his life he would not stop until he found them and reclaimed his prize.

In the soft dirt in front of the shack there were several sets of footprints going in and out of the doorway. His boot prints and those of the cowboy were nearly indistinguishable so he focused on Glenn's sneakers. They had a large N stamped in the middle of the size 10 print and he followed several tracks with his eyes until he found one that broke off from the group and headed north around the side of the shack. He followed the trail until it reached the little stream of water at the far end of his little valley. The trail disappeared into the water and Jeddediah fell to his knees and plunged his fists into the muddy banks.

"Cotton pick'n thieves!" he shouted.

Tears filled his eyes until one dripped on the ground. He remained motionless on all fours and cursed his miserable existence. When snot began to run from his nose he wiped at it with the back of the hand that held fast to his pistol. The cold steel barrel brushed across his cheek and he knelt back on his heels and looked down at his firearm. All he could think of was the many disappointments he had suffered in life and his labors that had only brought him pain and toil. Overhead, the heat of the desert sun seemed to beat down as if it had a personal grudge against him. At the moment of agony, it was beyond his capacity to formulate a plan or even see a way forward. The thought of starting over was too much to bear. He could not even lay hold on the fleeting hope that he would find those who had betrayed him and visit them with his vengeance. The only thing he could see was his old revolver and an end to his suffering. He raised the pistol to his head and pressed it to his temple.

"Jed!" Glenn shouted. "Uh, Jeddediah."

He spun around to find Glenn standing back by the shack with his floppy canvas hat in his hand. There was a genuine look of concern on his round freckled face. Jeddediah got to his feet and wiped at the tears that pooled in his eyes.

"Where were ya?" he seethed.

"We need to talk," Glenn said.

"Where's the key?" Jeddediah shouted and pointed the pistol at him.

"Come inside and we'll talk," Glenn placed his hands in the air.

"Where's the cowboy?" Jeddediah stepped forward slowly with his gun still leveled at Glenn.

"He went to find his horse," Glenn said, with a slight quiver in his voice. "Just point that thing somewhere else, and we can sit down and talk."

"I want the key. Now!" Jeddediah demanded. "I ain't got noth'n else to say. Now you start talk'n or I'll start shoot'n."

"The key is safe," Glenn said.

"Safe, where?" Jeddediah asked. He was just a few feet away from him and could see the young man trembling.

"Put the gun down and we'll talk," Glenn said.

"I ain't play'n with ya, boy," Jeddediah said as he pressed the barrel to the young man's forehead.

"You shoot me and you'll never find it!" Glenn shouted as he closed his eyes.

"You gall dang Judas!"

Jeddediah raised his arm and stuck Glenn on the forehead with the pistol's handle. Glenn fell to a knee and placed his hand on his head. With great heaving breaths Jeddediah loomed over him and poured all his hatred down on him. What right did he have to take it? What game was he playing? A tiny whisper of logic told him Glenn spoke the truth, if he were to shoot him the key would be lost, however, his rage and anger did not care. He pulled the hammer back on his side arm and placed the barrel to the back of his skull.

"Listen," Glenn said. "I have to go home. If I don't check in people will come looking for me. Is that what you want?"

"They ain't never gonna to find ya," Jeddediah said. "Out here people disappear all the time."

"Maybe," Glenn said. "But do you really want a posse stomping through your world?"

He raised the pistol again to strike him but paused as Glenn flinched and prepared for the blow. His raged diminished as the young man cowered beneath him. This was not anything he wanted. All his life he had been pushed around, bullied, and ridiculed, forced and cajoled to submit to the whims and wishes of those who had the power. Now, at last when he found himself in a position of power he hated himself for it. Jeddediah lowered his weapon and staggered back away from Glenn as if an invisible force repulsed him. Glenn looked up and slowly came to his feet with his eyes locked on the old miner. Too ashamed to meet his gaze, Jeddediah looked down at a patch of dried up reeds near the stream.

"I'm gonna come back," Glenn spoke softly. "I just need to check in. My mom will worry if I don't. One day is all I ask. I'll be back tomorrow morning."

"Leave the key an' ya can go," Jeddediah pleaded, as he once again took aim at the redhead with much less zeal and contempt.

"No deal," Glenn said as he stood up straight and tall. "If you have the key you can go after the treasure without me."

"Ya have no right."

"I risked my life to go get it," Glenn argued. "I'd say that gives me some right. Besides, what if you run into the monster, or something worse. You need me. This guarantees you won't try and go it alone."

"And what guarantee do I have you'll come back?" Jeddediah asked.

"I'll leave all my stuff," Glenn said. "You know, as collateral."

"I don't want your junk," Jeddediah replied, his ire returning. "That ain't good enough."

"I swear on my life I'll come back," Glenn said.

"And what if you don't make it back?" Jeddediah asked. "What if ya run into the monster, or something worse?"

The sound of galloping hoofs drew their attention back to the stream at the back of the valley. Cal rode in on his gray spotted horse, splashing through the water with Bernice in tow. Dog led the way with his tongue hanging out of his mouth. Cal pulled the caravan to a stop next to the shack and dismounted. Jeddediah still had his pistol pointed at Glenn.

"Hells bells," the cowboy exclaimed. "What are you two on about?"

"He took the key an' hid it," Jeddediah said.

Immediately Cal drew his side arm and pointed it at Glenn. Dog hunched down and growled menacingly, out of loyalty more than malice.

"What's your play hombre?" Cal demanded.

"Oh my heck," Glenn blurted out as he once again raised his hand in surrender. "Why is everyone so quick to throw down out here? I need to go see my mom. I just need to check in and then I'll be back."

"Give us the key and you can go," Cal said.

"We've been through this," Glenn replied. "If I give you the key you'll leave without me."

"And if ya leave we might never see you or the key again," Jeddediah responded.

"Please just put your guns down," Glenn said. "I have a plan."

From the corner of his eye Jeddediah saw Cal glancing over at him. He briefly considered their options and a way out of the standoff. The least violent way forward was to listen to what Glenn had to say. With the cowboy on his side he doubted a chubby young man with a wounded leg would be able to overpower or outrun them even without their weapons. He nodded to the cowboy and lowered his gun. Cal did the same and tucked it back in his hostler.

"Thank you," Glenn said, lowering his arms.

"This better be good," Cal warned. Dog barked his concurrence.

"I don't want to leave you with the key and you don't want me to leave without giving it up," Glenn said. "I get that. So here's the deal. I've hidden the key where no one will simply stumble across it. I will leave Jeddediah with part of a clue to find it. I'll give the other part to Cal once he gives me a ride out of here. If I don't turn up in the morning he'll just join up with you and together you can find the key."

"Suppose I don't trust either of ya?" Jeddediah said.

"Jed...," Glenn began. "...dediah, you've got to trust somebody some time. We've all got a vested interest in finding the treasure and our odds are better together."

"The kid's right," Cal said. "It's a good plan."

"I don't give two hoots what you think. Ya stumbled into this thing last night," Jeddediah turned and waved his pistol at Glenn. "And you, you're only here 'cause I saved your life. Ya ain't got no right. I'm the one who put in all the blood, sweat and tears. I ain't hav'n no Johnny-come-lately call'n the shots, that's for dang sure."

The three of them stood in awkward silence. Cal spit on the ground near Glenn's feet and Glenn stared down at the spot where it landed. The uncaring sun bathed them in its heat. Jeddediah removed his hat and wiped the sweat from his brow. He tried to think of a peaceful way out of this situation, other than the idea already proposed. Besides cursing Glenn for putting them in this position and a myriad of unspeakable ways he could coerce him into giving up the key, Jeddediah could not lay hold on a single rational thought. He looked from Glenn to Cal and then back to the redheaded betrayer.

"I got no way of know'n if you two are in cahoots," Jeddediah said.

"First of all, no one says cahoots anymore," Glenn said. "And second, if we were in cahoots we'd be long gone. Why would either of us have come back here? We have nothing to gain. I'm not trying to wrong you, Jeddediah. I'm just trying to make sure I don't get left behind."

"What if I swear I won't leave without ya?" Jeddediah asked.

"No good, I got trust issues too," Glenn said as his lips turned up in a faint grin. "Probably from being shot."

"There ya go again," Jeddediah flailed his arms in the air. "How long ya gonna sing that song?"

"It was two days ago!" Glenn replied.

"Hold up," Cal said. "You already shot him?"

"You stay outta this, Slick," Jeddediah warned and turned his attention back to Glenn. "I can't have ya leave me with only one piece of the puzzle. I trust him less than I trust you. What if ya don't come back and he don't come back neither? I need assurances."

Glenn scrunched up his forehead and rubbed at his rosy cheeks. He looked over at the old mule and his face lit up.

"Bernice!" he shouted.

She raised her gray head on cue and stared over at the young man. Uncertain of what Glenn was suggesting, Jeddediah looked over at his mule and turned back to Glenn with a tilt of the head.

"You said she always finds her way home, eventually," Glenn said. "We'll take Bernice with us and I'll tie a copy of the other half of the clue to her, at the same time I give it to Cal, and turn her loose. If something happens to either of us she'll find her way back to you and you'll have the whole clue. In the meantime, it will give me a chance to check in and get back out here."

The only thing in his world that Jeddediah knew he could count on was that old mule. His plan sounded a whole lot better than it did a few minutes ago. Still, he did not like that Glenn had forced his hand in such a way and did not want to let him win. He racked his brain for a better compromise but could only think of how he wished this stubborn thief would relent and return his prize. Unable to divine a nonviolent solution to his forced predicament, his shoulders slumped down and he let out an exasperated sigh.

"A'right," he conceded. "We'll do it your way."

"Thank you," Glenn said. "I promise I'll come right back."

"Don't ya dare thank me," Jeddediah said. "I blame ya for this whole mess. I wish I never met ya. Ya been noth'n but trouble. If ya don't come back I'll hunt ya down like a dog. Understand?"

"Understand," Glenn replied timidly.

Dog's ears perked up and he eyeballed the old miner. Jeddediah walked over to Bernice, placed both hands on the sides of her face and touched his forehead to hers. He leaned back and looked right into her deep brown eyes.

"I'm count'n on ya girl," he said. "Don't let me down."

Glenn shifted anxiously from side to side and Jeddediah glared back at him over his shoulder. Cal took hold of the reigns and swung himself back on top of the gray spotted horse while Dog danced around under foot.

"I'll be back as quick as I can," Glenn promised.

"Empty your pockets," Jeddediah said.

"What?" Glenn replied.

"Empty your pockets," he repeated. "Leave all your stuff with me. I want ya to have every incentive to come back."

Glenn removed his hat and stuck his hands into the pockets of his shorts. He dumped the contents of his right hand into the upside down hat, which consisted of a Swiss army knife and an old gum wrapper. In the left hand he held a folded up slip of paper, which he handed to Jeddediah.

"This is your part of the clue," Glenn said.

He walked away from Jeddediah without looking back. Cal reached down and helped him swing into the saddle behind him, with Dog nipping playful at his heels. The old miner took hold of the rope around Bernice and led her over to the duo on top of the horse. His stomach was twisted in knots at the thought of their departure. If all went according to plan he would only have to wait a day to once again be in possession of his long-sought prize. But in his experience things rarely went according to plan, at least not with his luck. He handed the rope to Cal and looked back at Glenn.

"Ya do what ya said ya'd do," Jeddediah warned. "Ya hear?"

Glenn nodded and appeared to struggle with a lump in his throat. From the expression on his freckled face Jeddediah was satisfied that his threatening tone had conveyed his message properly.

Cal steered his horse around and headed back toward the way he had entered the tiny valley. Helplessly, Jeddediah watched as they entered the stream and headed beyond the large boulders that surround the little valley. He looked down at the hat in his hand and the folded up slip of paper that sat on top of it. With a trembling finger, he brushed over the top of paper before quickly withdrawing it. His nerves would not allow him to open it and he said a silent prayer that he would never need to.

HOLY SENTINEL

He sat on the dirt floor of the broken down old shack staring out the doorway and grinding his teeth. In one hand he smashed the taunting slip of paper over and over again as if he were trying to wring the answer out of it. In the other, he held fast to his pistol and gently stroked at the hammer with his callused thumb. His warm breath turned to steam as it hit the cold winter air and he muttered threats and curses out into the lonely dark night.

The worn and tattered slip of paper was the only thing that had kept him company these many months. He could not be without it and yet he hated it and wished he had never seen it. A piece of rope lay at his feet, the only sign of the visit from his unwelcomed guests. Jeddediah was not surprised to return and find his prisoners gone, as he seemed destined to be left alone in his misery. Everyone he had ever known had left him, never to return, it seemed to be the way of things. So he sat and waited for morning when he could resume his fruitless search for the prize which had been stolen from him.

A shadow moved between the trees beyond the doorway, and Jeddediah's heart began to pound wildly. He struggled to his feet as fast, as his creaky bones would allow, and squinted his old eyes to peer into the darkness. All at once a blinding light exploded in through the doorway. He lifted his arms to shield his eyes when another light poured in from the window to his right. With a blind lunge forward, he smacked his face against the door and several splinters cut into his nose. He staggered back, took hold of the door and forced it closed. Tiny streams of light seeped in through the cracks of the drafty old shack. A second stream of light burst in through the window and the crossed streams, which lit up the entire shack and left only a small triangular shadow in the far corner.

He backed into the corner between the door and the window with his pistol pointed into the center of the empty room. The sound of thundering hoofs grew from the distance, and he strained to listen in a vain attempt to discern the size of the herd. A dark shadow shot by, briefly blotting out the streams of light that assaulted the front of the shack. Jeddediah took aim and tracked it with the barrel of his gun as it crossed around the side of the shack. A pillar of smoke shot through the window, just as the shadow passed, and landed with a thud in the corner. Quickly, he jumped over to the smoke-filled corner. He reached down and laid his hands on a red-hot saddlebag that had white smoke billowing out from the leather flaps.

Another shadow followed the first and a second smoky saddlebag was heaved over the window sill. A thick layer of white smoke had already filled the shack up to his shoulders and threatened to engulf the entire room. Jeddediah heaved the first saddle bomb toward the window, but it hit the ledge and fell back into the smoky pool. The lights that poured through the window seemed to turn the white vapor into an impenetrable wall. His eyes began to burn as a third galloping shadow was followed by yet another smoking saddlebag.

Unable to see anything through the blinding light and smoke, Jeddediah stumbled around the room coughing. Each time he tried to draw in a breath he sucked down only the suffocating white smoke. Desperately, he felt around for an escape. When he finally found the wall to his left he followed it down to the corner. He knocked against one of the smoldering saddlebags with his foot and gave it a contemptuous kick. From the corner, he felt his way to the door and pulled it open without a second thought.

He stumbled forward through the threshold, with smoke pouring out all around him. Eyes burning and chest heaving with every painful cough he staggered away from the smoky shack and collapsed on the ground. A tremendous pressure bore down on his right hand as the heel of a boot smashed his fingers, which were wrapped around his pistol. As a reflex, he released his weapon and pulled his hand away from the boot.

"Ah!" Jeddediah screamed in agony.

As he opened his eyes he saw the lights all around him bouncing about as they closed in. Multiple shadows encircled him. However, from his hands and knees all he could see were their shoes.

"No," a voice said. "No guns."

Jeddediah heard a faint thud as his pistol hit the ground over by the old cottonwood trees. He tried to stand up but was immediately shoved back to the ground.

"No man," a feminine voice commanded. "Ya stay down d'ere."

"Easy Tara," the first voice said. "He's not going anywhere."

"Should we tie him up, like he tied you up?" a third voice asked.

"No," the first voice said. "But search him for weapons."

Two hands grabbed him under the arms and lifted him to his feet. He coughed uncontrollably as his body tried to clear his smoke-filled lungs. With the bright lights still shining on him and his eyes still burning, he blinked rapidly and attempted to look around at his captors. The hands that had lifted him began to pat around his waist. Jeddediah slapped at the hands and pushed away from them but immediately ran into someone else.

"Hold still old man," a blonde-haired man ordered. "We can do this the easy way or the hard way."

"Jeddediah," the first voice said from behind him. "I don't want to tie you up but I will if I have to."

Reluctantly, Jeddediah submitted to the unwelcome pat down. When the hands were satisfied he was not hiding anything from his armpits down to his toes, the assault on his person ceased and the circle of shadows widened slightly. Jeddediah looked around through tear filled eyes at the motley crew who had laid siege to the old shack.

A bearded man with wild dark hair held a large circular light on his shoulder and, thankfully, had finally pointed it to the ground. Its light illuminated the rest of the group. Next to the bearded man was the blonde young man who had patted him down. Two young ladies stood beside him in stark contrast to one another, with one being dark like coffee and the other as white as cream. As he turned to his left he laid eyes on Gideon and Juan Carlos, the two escaped trespassers. He was taken aback by the smile on Gideon's face while Juan Carlos held a flashlight like a sword and wore a scowl that Jeddediah would have expected from his former prisoner.

"Dude, Gideon," the blonde man said. "That was awesome! Just like you drew it up. Without firing a shot."

"Yeah, but I burned my hand pretty good throwing that last fireball," Gideon replied.

A violent and painful cough exploded from Jeddediah's mouth. He doubled over and drew in heaving breaths between convulsions. The older man with a dark beard stepped forward and patted him gently on the back.

"Easy there, old timer," the bearded man said. "Just relax, there's plenty of air out here, you'll find it. Just breathe."

When his coughing fit subsided, Jeddediah looked over at the man with the dark scraggily beard. In his eyes he saw a tinkle, like that of a child, which did not match his weathered and callused exterior. He nodded in appreciation for the kind gesture and the man smiled back from behind his thick beard.

"Do I know ya?" Jeddediah asked.

"You chased me out of a canyon a while back," the man said as he stuck out his hand. "Name's Joe."

"Jeddediah," he replied as he shook his hand.

"Pops, you're not supposed to get all friendly," the blonde haired young man chided.

"What's the golden rule, Todd?" Joe responded.

"Treat others the way you want to be treated," Todd recited quickly, before wagging an accusing finger at Jeddediah. "But this Jacob Waltz wannabe killed Glenn."

"I did no such thing," Jeddediah yelled.

"All right," Gideon said, stepping between him and Todd. "Then explain to me why you've got his stuff."

Gideon held up the floppy canvas hat and dangled it in front of his face. Jeddediah looked away and closed his eyes. He had stared at that hat for over a year as it haunted him. With no one else to blame for his current plight, he heaped all his hatred on that hat and wished he had never seen it. Long shadows spread out in all directions from the posse surrounding him. There was no conceivable route of escape and, even if there was, he was in no condition to fight or run. His only choice was to submit to their questioning.

"He left them things with me," Jeddediah answered.

"How did you and Glenn meet?" Gideon asked.

"I shot him," Jeddediah replied in the matter of fact tone.

"There!" Todd shouted. "He admitted it."

"I said I shot him, I didn't kill'd him," Jeddediah argued. "It was an accident, and I patched him up afterwards."

"When did you last see him?" Gideon asked.

"July before last," Jeddediah replied.

"And he was alive?" Gideon questioned.

Jeddediah answered with a slow solemn nod. He could not say what happened after the red headed thief rode out of sight, but the one thing he was certain of was that the last time he had seen Glenn he was alive and well. Jeddediah had just as many questions about what had become of him as the mob that surrounded him. Another round of involuntary coughs attacked his lungs and he raised his arm and hacked into his sleeve. When the coughs subsided, he looked back into the shadowed face of his primary interrogator.

"You said he took something from you," Gideon said. "Was it a key?"

With squinted eyes Jeddediah studied Gideon. He searched his clouded memory through his brief encounter with this young man for a reference he may have made to the key. He was sure he had not made mention of his precious prize, as he would never have willingly alluded to its secret.

"What key?" he feigned ignorance in an attempt to draw out what he knew.

"Glenn said he found a key," Gideon said. "He wrote me a letter saying we would need to find a key to get to him. He left us clues that led us here. If he took something from you I'm betting it has something to do with this key. Please, we just want to find out what happened to our friend."

In his voice was a tenderness that softened Jeddediah's uncaring heart. There was a sincerity in his pleading that completely disarmed his crusty old soul. He did not want to feel for them or trust them, but could not help but believe him. His lip began to quiver uncontrollably as all the bottled-up feelings of a lifetime of regret and disappointment bubbled up to the surface.

"I found the key and lost it, he helped me get it back," Jeddediah began as his raspy voice cracked like a pre-pubescent teen. "Then he hid it so I wouldn't leave him when he went home to see his mother. He left me with noth'n but a worthless old piece of paper an' a torment'n clue."

"What's the key to?" Joe asked.

"Treasure," he replied.

"The Dutchman?" asked Todd.

"No," Jeddediah shook his head. "Ya ever hear of the Black Robes?"

"You're talking about the Jesuit gold?" Joe replied.

Jeddediah nodded to him.

"What's Jesuit gold?" asked Gideon.

"It's one of the legends of the Superstitions," Todd answered. "Supposedly, priests hid their riches up here in the mountains before they returned to Spain. It's said to still be out here somewhere."

Distant thunder rolled across the mountain tops. It was an ominous overture that echoed through their earnest conversation. Jeddediah's hip began to ache, which was a sure sign that a storm was coming. He looked up into the sky and took note of a few gray clouds that were threatening to block out the moon.

"You said he left you a clue?" Gideon asked him.

The old miner turned around and looked back at the dark shack. The smoke had diminished a bit, but white vapors still rose up into the starry sky. In the frenzy of the moment he was certain he had dropped the piece of paper somewhere in the smoke-filled room, not that he needed it as the enigmatic message was burned into his consciousness.

"A holy sentinel watches over you..." Jeddediah recited as his voice trailed off.

"That's it?" Todd questioned. "That's not much of a clue."

"He left the other piece with the cowboy and Bernice," Jeddediah explained. "An' I ain't seen neither of them since."

"Bernice?" the brunette girl asked.

"She was my mule," Jeddediah replied.

"Right," she responded with a raised eyebrow and a slow head nod.

"Holy sentinel!" Gideon blurted out.

Jeddediah cocked his head and studied the excited young man. He looked on with both hope and disdain. He hoped the young man had some insight into the partial clue, but the idea that he had solved so quickly a puzzle that plagued him for these many months was more than irritating.

"Sentinel," Gideon repeated to his blonde friend. Todd shook his head with a blank expression on his face that told Jeddediah he was just as clueless as the rest of them.

"Glenn liked to imagine that the saguaros were really mighty warriors who stood to protect their home," Gideon explained. "He called them the sentinels of the desert."

"Okay, but there's thousands of saguaros around here," Todd said.

"Right, but how many are watching over you?" Gideon said. "Jed, where were you when Glenn gave you this clue?"

"We was right 'round the side of the shack over there," Jeddediah replied, resisting the urge to admonish him again about abbreviating his name.

"I knew it!" Gideon shouted. "When I was tied up in the shack, I saw a huge saguaro up on that butte there. In the light from the setting sun it looked like a silhouette of a priest or an angel praying. A holy sentinel watching over you!"

"Oh my heck, Gideon," the brunette girl said. "You're like Sherlock Holmes."

With an ear to ear grin, Gideon grabbed the large deer spotter from Juan Carlos and shined it up to the top of the ridge, northwest of the shack. A tall saguaro stood alone with two arms close to the trunk, like arms drawn together in prayer. Jeddediah would have been overjoyed if he was not being held against his will outside of his smoldering abode.

"The angel, the angel statue," Todd said. "Maybe it had a double meaning. Maybe it wasn't just Angel Basin, maybe it was the angel *of* the basin."

"That sounds like something Glenn would do, even though there's no way we would have ever found it without Jed's clue," Gideon said. "Glenn would have thought it was so clever, even if his little Easter egg was entirely useless to us."

"The name's Jeddediah," he finally corrected him. "Quit call'n me Jed."

"Sorry," Gideon replied. "Jeddediah is a mouthful though."

"Then just take my name off your lips if ya can't say it," Jeddediah replied.

"Fair enough," Gideon said as he turned back to Joe. "Let's get the horses and head up there."

"The horses will have a terrible time gett'n up there," Jeddediah said. "I know a better way."

"All right, tell us," Gideon replied.

"I'll show ya," Jeddediah replied.

"I don't know," Gideon shook his head.

"Ya ain't leav'n me," Jeddediah said. "I'll die before I let ya claim what's mine."

"If you try anything I'll tie you up out here and leave you for the buzzards," Gideon threatened.

"That won't be necessary, Gideon," Joe spoke from the shadows. "This is his clue and his key. He has every right to come along."

"Joe," Gideon protested. "He had me and Juan Carlos tied up just a few hours ago. And we still don't know if he had anything to do with Glenn's disappearance. I'm sorry, but I'm not ready to put him on the roster just yet. If he comes he's gonna come under our terms."

"Young man you haven't been here long enough to start barking orders," Joe replied. "You don't trust him? That's fine, but you aren't the only say here."

"You just feel sorry for him 'cause he's just like you," Gideon replied.

"What are you talk'n about?" Joe asked.

"Gideon don't," Todd pleaded.

"You're worried you're never gonna find your pot of gold either," Gideon said. "Well this isn't about that. I want to know what happened to Glenn. I don't give two drops of monkey crap about this treasure, he can have it. But I'm not putting my friends in danger because you've found a crazy kindred spirit."

"Gideon!" Todd shouted.

"That was not cool, Gideon," the brunette girl said as Joe lowered his head and turned away from the circle.

The group fell silent as they all watched Joe. Jeddediah looked at each of his captors and saw that their attentions were trained on their wild haired patriarch. He quickly glanced around to the horses beneath the cottonwood trees and began to calculate how long it would take him to hobble his old bones over to them. His scheming was cut short, however, when the swarthy girl in the blue jeans slid between him and the horses. She quietly folded her muscular arms across her chest and shook her head menacingly at him. Jeddediah spat on the ground and turned back to the standoff between Joe and Gideon.

"I say we put it to a vote," Joe said as he turned back to the group and gently scratched at the side of his head. "We can continue to treat this man like a pariah and tie him up and leave him here, guaranteeing that we make an enemy. Or we can choose to trust him and bring him along to help us find answers. Regardless of how we're treated we still have a choice how we'll respond. I choose to trust, who's with me?"

Joe raised his hand high above his head. Todd immediately joined him, followed by Juan Carlos. Gideon turned around just as the brunette girl raised her hand and finally the swarthy warrior woman uncrossed her arms and raised a hand with her eyes still fixed firmly on Jeddediah. Gideon tilted his head to the side and cast a discriminating look in his direction. Jeddediah glared back and raised his hand, just as another wave of thunder rolled across the mountain tops, as if it too had a vote.

"Fine," Gideon said. "He can come along but for the record I'm against it."

"Noted," Joe replied. "Would it be wise to wait until morning before heading up there?"

"Nah," Jeddediah said. "It's a piece of cake if ya know what your do'n."

The truth was it would have been much easier in the light of day but Jeddediah could not wait to see if this young man had indeed solved the long vexing puzzle. He stepped tentatively forward, out of the center of the group. When no objections were offered and no one attempted to stop him, Jeddediah limped ahead at his full stride. The rest of the company filed in behind him as he led the way into the thin crevasse of the entryway to his secret holdup. Once into the breach he stopped and pointed upward. Todd shined his bright light up the wall where Jeddediah pointed. Shadows of ridges and handholds dotted the vertical rock formation.

Not wanting to be the first to attempt the arduous climb, Jeddediah stepped to the side and gestured for Gideon to go first. Gideon eyed the old miner up and down before he scaled the wall without a word. Jeddediah stood and watched as one by one the group followed after their friend. While he was anxious to get to the top and examine the tall cactus, he was wary of making the climb. He hacked through another round of coughs just as Joe brought up the rear.

"After you," Joe said as he shined his light on the wall.

Jeddediah nodded at his fellow treasure hunter. He reached up and searched for a handhold when Joe caught him gently by the shoulder.

"Between the two of us," Joe whispered. "If you do anything that puts these kids in danger, I'll kill you."

"Fair enough," Jeddediah replied.

The wall was less than twenty feet high but that did not stop Jeddediah from huffing and puffing his way to the top. When he reached the rocky shelf, his old lungs wheezed as he struggled to draw in a deep breath. Todd shined a light on the opposite end of the entry to give light to Joe on his ascent. As Joe clawed his way over the edge and came to his feet he exchanged a knowing look with Jeddediah.

"This way," Gideon declared and pointed his light straight at the mighty saguaro.

"No," Jeddediah said. "That way's full of loose shale and a steep drop off just the other side. Ya want to come 'round this way."

He walked past Gideon and took the lead position. There was a row of waist-high cacti that formed a natural fence and blocked their way. The path to the right, where Gideon had headed did appear wider and more welcoming but as they slipped through a narrow break in the poky fence their flashlight shone down on a solid rocky ridge that led all the way to the monolithic cactus near the center of the butte.

They moved forward with prudence as Jeddediah made sure they stayed far away from the edge. He was not overly concerned with their safety but would not allow a mishap to derail his single-minded desire to reach his long sought holy sentinel. With each step, they drew nearer to their destination, however, it did not appear to Jeddediah that they were any closer to the mighty saguaro and he had to fight the impulse to run. At last he stood at the feet of the desert guardian and an unexpected feeling of reverence fell over him. The group gathered around as all lights pointed to the top of the domed saguaro.

"Now what?" the girl with the chocolate complexion asked.

"Look for some sign or marking," Gideon replied.

They spread out and surrounded the sentinel with their flashlights scanning up and down the prickly trunk. When they had made of full rotation Jeddediah's heart sank. There did not appear to be anything special about this cactus and they found no signs or markings of any kind. His hope in the young man's theory quickly evaporated. Gideon turned away from the saguaro and shined his light back down into the secreted valley. Scattered rain drops began to fall from the heavens, and Jeddediah felt the sky mourned with him.

"This isn't it," Gideon said.

"What?" Jeddediah asked. "What do ya mean?"

"Look," Gideon replied and pointed down at the shack. "We're looking down at the front corner, I saw the praying saguaro through the window around the side. This isn't it."

All at once the company turned in unison and the lights all pointed further up the ridge. Nearly fifty yards away was another saguaro cactus, not as tall or grand as the one they surrounded but its limbs grew close to the trunk. They needed no prodding or instruction. Each of them set off on their own accord toward their new hope as the rain began to fall. There was a small saddle in the ridge, full of loose slag stones, that quickly became slick from the moisture. Jeddediah lost his footing as two stones slipped under the pressure of his step. He saw Gideon and the brunette similarly flail their arms to catch their balance and the pace of their race slowed noticeably.

"Look!" Todd exclaimed when they were all still some distance away. "Look!"

On the ground, tiny flashes sparkled from the reflection of their lights near the base of the saguaro. They climbed out of the saddle and unto more solid ground. Todd was the first to reach the reflected light and stooped down to pick one up. He held it up with a bright smile on his face. Jeddediah looked at the hand carved black stone in Todd's hand, being pelted by rain drops. It had been molded down to a fine point at one end and spread back evenly to form a perfectly balanced arrow.

"It's an Apache tear arrowhead," Todd said.

"That's Glenn," Gideon replied.

The lights were turned back to the ground where they found two more arrowheads placed back to back atop the volcanic rock and pointed directly at the saguaro. Once again, they fanned out and surrounded the tree. Jeddediah followed Gideon's light up to the nearest limb which had a hole in the side. The two of them looked over at each other with wide eyes and Gideon handed Jeddediah his light. He stepped forward and reached up to the hole. Despite his height he had to stand on his tippy toes, and stretch his long arms as far as they could reach in order to stick his hand through the hole.

"There's something in here," Gideon proclaimed as his hand disappeared into the limb.

"What? What is it?" questioned Jeddediah. His hands started to tremble and heart beat as rapidly as the rhythmic rain drops that drummed along the brim of his hat.

"Ouch!" Gideon recoiled from the saguaro and rubbed at his wrist. "Flipp'n needles. It's heavy, whatever it is."

"Well what are ya wait'n for?" Jeddediah asked. "Pull it out."

Gideon stretched his arm back up to the poky limb and stuck his hand in the hole. With a grunt and a heave, he pulled a burlap sack out of the cactus. Jeddediah rushed forward and ripped it out of his hands. The group gathered around and all the lights shone down on the sack. Jeddediah knelt down, laid it on the muddy ground and hastily removed the burlap covering.

Tears welled up in his eyes as he once again held his coveted prize. Although he had not given up the search it was a desperate search with little hope. Now, with the pick axe in his hand, he felt a vindication of all his fruitless efforts even though they had not led him anywhere near its hiding place. For that he needed the friends of the riddler to stumble into his lonely existence.

"Thank you," Jeddediah whispered to his prize.

"You're welcome," Gideon answered.

"I wasn't talk'n to you," Jeddediah said without taking his eyes off the pick axe.

"So is that the key then?" Todd asked. "Because it looks like an old rusty head of a pick."

Jeddediah stood up and cradled the pick in his hands like an infant. He held it under the light and his inquisitive followers all leaned in for a proper look.

"Here," Jeddediah said and pointed to the symbol etched in to the blade. "This is the marking of the Black Robes. The four hoops all bonded together and branching out to form a cross."

"With a key at the base," Gideon added excitedly.

"That's right," Jeddediah said.

"So, what does it mean?" the brunette asked.

"It means this will lead me to their cache," Jeddediah said.

"Us," Gideon corrected.

Jeddediah grimaced. He had not yet come to terms with the unwelcome additions to his quest. In his many long dormant dreams over the lonely years he had always won his victory alone and he was not enthusiast about sharing the glory with a group of strangers.

"But how?" she asked.

"Look here, little miss," Jeddediah began.

"Liz," she quickly interjected.

"Well Liz, it has several markings besides that," Jeddediah explained. "Look here."

He turned the pick axe over and pointed to an N and an S etched in to opposite ends on the bottom. Then he turned it on its side and pointed to a marking of a towering mountain.

"That's Weaver's Needle!" Gideon shouted.

"Yep," Jeddediah said. "That's what we figured too."

"When you say 'we' you mean you and Glenn?" Gideon asked.

Jeddediah nodded and swallowed at the lump in his throat. They had excitedly examined the pick the night they found it. Glenn was the one who was certain that marking had to be Weaver's Needle. The towering rock formation had been there for centuries and could be seen for miles. It made sense if the Black Robes were going to use a landmark from the area as a guide to their hiding place that they would use the most prominent one they could find. When Glenn did not return, Jeddediah made the trek to Weaver's Needle and searched for some time but it proved useless without the key.

"If they hid it at Weaver's Needle it's long gone," Joe said. "That place has been gone over with a fine-tooth comb for over a hundred years."

"They wouldn't go through all this trouble just to hide it in such an obvious place," Jeddediah argued. "It might be there, it might not, but this key is leading us to Weaver's Needle."

"There's only one way to find out," Gideon said.

Jeddediah nodded. He struggled within himself as he both hated adding these strangers to his expedition and took comfort in having company and support. If he was ever going to find the treasure, he knew he would need help or perhaps a sacrificial lamb or two. In any case he was stuck with them for the time being and intended to keep both eyes open for ways in which he could either use them to his advantage or ditch them the first chance he got.

"So we're going to Weaver's Needle then?" asked Liz.

"Sounds like it," Todd said.

"We leave at first light," Jeddediah replied with a long look down at his prize. The pick axe seemed to vibrate in his hands, as if it were endorsing their decision. With his callused thumb, he brushed gently at the precipitation that pooled on top of the key-cross symbol. He felt an excitement he had not felt in years, and those long-forgotten fantasies of gold and victory returned as he had cause to dream once more.

EYE OF THE NEEDLE

A strong tail wind blew the smell coming from behind him and assaulted his nostrils. Gideon could not decide if it was coming from Hercules or the dirty old miner wrapped around his waist. Somehow he had once again drawn the short straw and ended up sharing the mighty Hercules with Juan Carlos and Jeddediah. Joe and Todd led the caravan from the always steady Moses with Tara and Liz paired up on the jittery gray spotted horse. Gideon could not remember exactly how the riding arrangements were decided but he blamed Todd by default.

They spent the last several hours riding through the wet canyon bedrock of Needle Canyon that led them to Weaver's Needle. Gideon was sandwiched between a scrawny Mexican he barely knew and the crazy old man who had tied them together the previous evening. He could not help but smile when he considered the obscured nature of his life. As they came around one final bend the giant monolith rose into view. Weaver's Needle looked like an enormous thumb jutting up out of the earth and it dominated the surrounding landscape. A wave of excitement washed over Gideon and he wished he could prod Hercules into a trot.

"There she is," Todd proudly proclaimed as if he had fashioned the great stone high-rise with his own hands.

Jeddediah sneezed on the back of Gideon's neck and he felt as if he had just been infected with some incurable disease.

"Bless you," Juan Carlos called back over his shoulder.

"Thanks," Jeddediah responded as he wiped at his nose with the sleeve of his dirty flannel shirt.

Gideon set his sights on their destination ahead and looked forward to being free from this overburdened saddle and unpleasant stink. Rain had threatened all morning but so far the gloomy gray clouds hovered harmlessly overhead. Weaver's Needle rose up out of a wispy white fog scattered among the desert canvas. The soft gray light made the entire scene look like it was painted by an artist with a giant-sized brush.

"Scientists believe that millions of years ago fissions exploded from pressure and dumped heat, ash and lava all over this area," Gideon said to no one in particular. "Erosion carved out the valleys and canyons with only the strongest foundations able to resist. Weaver's Needle has got to have deep roots to still be standing."

Juan Carlos looked back at Gideon and nodded along while Jeddediah simply grunted behind him. Each hoof that beat into the ground drew them closer to this rock beacon at the middle of the wilderness.

Weaver's Needle had been a point of interest for travelers, explorers, geologists, artists, and treasure hunters alike. Gideon knew if a treasure had been hidden there it would have certainly been discovered by now. His only hope was that this key would allow them to piece together some previously unsolvable puzzle and lead them to the hidden legend. However, Gideon still held to his private hope they would find some idea of what had become of their friend and possibly bring some closure for those who cared for him.

"The last time you saw him," Gideon began as he turned around as far as he could to look into Jeddediah's gray eyes. "What did he say to you?"

"The redhead?" Jeddediah asked.

"Yes, Glenn," Gideon clarified. "What was the last thing he said?"

"He told me he'd come back," Jeddediah answered. "He gave me my part of the clue."

"Your part?" Gideon asked. "Who got the other part?"

"Supposedly, he gave the other to Bernice an' the cowboy," he replied.

"Bernice was your mule?" Gideon asked.

"That's right," Jeddediah said. "She still is, if she's still liv'n."

"And the cowboy?" Gideon asked. "Who's the cowboy?"

"Don't recall his name," Jeddediah said. "He was a slick talk'n pretty boy who somehow horned his way into my life an' made a mess of things."

"Did you ever go looking for them?" Gideon asked.

"I looked all over for 'em," Jeddediah said. "They just disappeared. That's what happens out here."

"Yeah," Gideon agreed mindlessly.

"Ranger Rick turned up a few weeks after," Jeddediah continued with a far-off look. "Said there was a search party look'n for the boy. Figured he must've got lost or hurt someways."

Gideon stared up at the approaching peak and thought of all the people who had lost their lives or disappeared in this harsh desert wilderness. Dozens and dozens of treasure hunters had gone missing and hundreds of men and women had combed the Superstitions in search of remains to bring home to mourning loved ones. However, it was just one who missing person who weighed heavily on Gideon's mind at the moment.

"Is that what you think?" Gideon asked.

"Could've been any number of things I suppose," Jeddediah replied.

"And the cowboy?" Gideon asked.

"Dunno," Jeddediah said. "I reckon he either shared his fate, buggered off like a coward, or set out on his own. Whatever the case, I ain't seen hide nor hair of him since."

They dropped down a steep decline toward the expansive base of the needle. The angle of their descent forced them forward and smashed Gideon between his riding partners like a smelly sandwich. At last they reached a labyrinth of car sized boulders, and Gideon was finally liberated from the overcrowded horseback as they halted and dismounted. His legs trembled as they hit the ground and he shook them rapidly to regain the feeling in them.

"How's everyone doing on water?" Joe asked.

"Good," Tara replied as she shook her canteen.

"I've got plenty," Todd replied.

"Yeah," Juan Carlos agreed.

Gideon checked the charred and smoky saddlebag where he had placed his canteen. It was nearly full as he had not touched it since they filled up at the creek behind the shack earlier that morning. He removed it and took a drink while everyone stretched their legs and looked around. Jeddediah pulled the pick out of the saddlebag opposite him and began to walk with purpose to a cluster of large boulders. Gideon locked eyes on him and watched closely for any suspicious behavior. The old miner addressed the boulder head on and unbuckled his pants with his legs spread slightly apart.

"You still don't trust him, do you?" Liz asked as she had quietly sidled up beside him.

Gideon turned and looked into her soft brown eyes. In so many ways this had not been the reunion he intended, but at the moment he could not think of any place he would rather be and was grateful to have her with him.

"I don't," Gideon replied.

"You think he knows what happened to Glenn?"

"I don't know," said Gideon. "He might, or he might be telling the truth. Either way I'm not taking my eyes off him until this is over."

He turned his attention back to the old miner who was relieving himself near the base of a large beige boulder. Gideon cast his eyes down to afford Jeddediah some privacy.

"Gideon?" Liz said.

"Yeah," he replied while staring intently at the horn on the saddle.

"Why did you come back?"

Her direct question took him aback and he turned again to face her. He had been unable to answer the first time she asked and did not think he would be given another opportunity. Now as it had once again unexpectedly presented itself he struggled to find the words.

"Uh," he began. "Well, actually…I came back to see you."

His eyes grew big and his expression stiffened involuntarily as he braced for her reaction.

"Me?" she replied with a smile. "Really?"

"Liz, I like you," Gideon finally admitted out loud. "I always have. I think I love you. I needed to know if you might feel the same."

She opened her mouth but no words escaped. The look on her face was just as warm and welcoming as it had ever been but the silence tore into Gideon's soul. He felt the tingling of tears begin to well up in the corner of his eyes as he braced for what he was sure would be the sweetest and kindest rejection of all time.

"Gideon," she began. "I…"

"Hey where'd he go?" Todd shouted from the other side of Moses.

Gideon quickly spun back toward the boulder and, to his horror, Jeddediah had disappeared. He sprinted around the horses with the rest of the group right on his heels. When he reached the spot he had last seen the old miner, Gideon surveyed potential escape routes. Mounds of rolling dirt sprawled out to either side with hundreds of boulders nestled together. The gaps between them formed tiny passageways like a maze. Todd and Juan Carlos had already headed around the far side of the boulder they had last seen the old man at and Gideon instinctually followed them.

"Mi a go dis way," Tara said as she doubled back in the opposite direction.

"Good idea," Joe said as he stopped to catch his breath. "I'll stay here in case he gets by either of ya."

"I'm with you," Gideon said as he reversed direction and followed Tara.

Liz fell in line with them as they raced through the gap to the left. All the legendary stories of Jacob Waltz ran through Gideon's mind. Dozens of people had tried to follow him into the Superstitions and time after time he lost them or led them into a dead end and vanished. Jeddediah had spent years in the mountains and the wily old timer likely knew of nooks and crannies where he could disappear or escape. Gideon was upset he had taken his eyes off of him and disappointed his conversation with Liz had been interrupted. Tara sailed forward like a bobcat, with grace and ease, while Gideon plodded forward huffing and puffing like a buffalo with asthma. He checked over his shoulder to see Liz, effortlessly jogging behind him. When he turned back Tara had come to an abrupt stop and, unable to put on the brakes, Gideon spun sideways in an attempt to avoid a collision. He clipped her side and careened helplessly to the ground. Tara stepped over and helped him to his feet.

"Sorry," Tara said.

"No," said Gideon. "My bad."

"Look," Tara said. She pointed back into a large crack between two boulders where Jeddediah had wedged himself into the crevasse and stood stiff and silent.

"Come out from there," Gideon demanded.

Tara stepped forward and took him by the shirt sleeves and dragged him out into the open.

"Take your hands off me," Jeddediah said as he wriggled free from her grasp.

"What was your plan, old man?" Gideon asked. "Where did you think you were going?"

"As far away from my kidnappers as I could get," he replied.

"We didn't kidnap you," Liz said. "You are free to go whenever you like."

"Yep," Gideon said. "Just leave the key and you can go."

"This here is mine," Jeddediah complained as he tucked the pick under his arm.

"Fair enough," Gideon replied. "Let's see where it leads us then. Together."

Todd and Juan Carlos came charging around the bend. When they caught sight of the group they halted and drew heaving breaths with their hands on their knees.

"Flipp'n old man," Todd said. "What's your deal?"

"I ain't with ya," Jeddediah replied. "Ya want a part in this then ya better keep up."

The old miner turned and hobbled back toward the horses where Joe waited calmly. He and Jeddediah greeted each other with a nod before Joe lightly shook his head. Gideon could not decide how to feel about this unspoken mutual respect they had for one another. In some ways Gideon admired Joe for his cool calm demeanor, but it did not change the mistrust which he felt he justifiably harbored for the old stranger. They all congregated back by the horses and formed an uneasy circle around their gray haired flight risk.

"So what now?" Todd asked.

"To the Needle I suppose," Jeddediah said.

"Fine, but no more funny business," Gideon warned.

"Ain't noth'n 'bout this business that's funny," the old miner grumbled.

Joe covered his mouth to hide a grin as he looked over at Todd. Gideon shook his head and escorted Jeddediah back to their horse and waited for him to mount up with Juan Carlos. He looked over to Liz who had already taken her place atop Pepper and helped Tara into the saddle. She smiled at Gideon and his heart leapt in his chest. He laid his heart bare and now was completely at her mercy. Once he had squeezed himself onto the back of Hercules, the group made their way through the boulders and headed up the long incline to the bottom of Weaver's Needle. A gentle roll of thunder followed them up the hill and Gideon checked the ominous gray sky for signs of rain.

Without any further drama, they reached the top of the hill where the ground met with the towering rock formation. As they dismounted, Gideon took special care to stay close to the old miner. Jeddediah held up the pick and they all looked down at it. From where Gideon stood he could see the golden N and S engraved on the bottom and the etching of Weaver's Needle carved into the side. There was a straight line cut in the bottom connecting the N and S. Jeddediah turned it over and Gideon noticed that the top, where the interlocking cross was carved, was much smoother than the well beaten under carriage.

"Maybe we need to hold it with the N pointing north and the S pointing south," Gideon suggested.

"Great idea," Todd agreed. "Who's got a compass?"

Simultaneously Gideon, Joe, and Juan Carlos reached into their pockets and pulled out three unique compasses. Gideon had a small bubble domed compass that fit in the palm of his hand, while Joe had a round sturdy casing from his military compass and

Juan Carlos held a dial that sat atop a plastic rectangle with a fleur-de-lei imprinted on the top.

"Be prepared," Gideon said to Juan Carlos who grinned and nodded back. "Eagle Scout, troop 354."

"Life scout," Juan Carlos replied. "Troop 872."

"Sergeant Major, Hundred and first infantry division," Joe chimed in with a wink.

"Wha dem a chat 'bout?" Tara asked.

"I think their compasses are bonding," Todd replied. "Unless you're gonna exchange decoder rings and secret handshakes, can one of you highly trained and accomplished boy scouts please find north?"

"All right, relax," Gideon said as he held out his compass and took a bearing.

"Hang on, Gideon," Liz said. "You are too close to the pick. It's going to affect the reading."

"The girl's right," Jeddediah said. "Ya need to stand a ways off."

Without argument Gideon, Joe and Juan Carlos shifted away from the pick in Jeddediah's hand and let their compasses adjust. Gideon stooped down in the ground and drew a line with his finger in the dirt. Then he gestured to Jeddediah to step to the line. Juan Carlos and Joe did the same marking their line on either side of Gideon's to form a back to back to back lines that pointed north and south. Jeddediah walked up to the lines and held the pick parallel to them. They all looked back and forth from north to south and back at the pick.

"Okay, now what?" Todd asked again.

"Maybe the treasure is buried along the line," Gideon suggested.

"Nah," Joe replied. "We got no way to know which side of the Needle we should be on. It's too broad to give us a sure direction."

Jeddediah placed the pick on the ground right on top of the line and took several steps back. Gideon mirrored his movements and stepped away to get a different perspective. From their position, the marking of Weaver's Needle on the side of the pick pointed back at the real thing. Gideon and Jeddediah each turned around and faced toward the towering rock behind them.

"There's got to be another clue," Gideon said.

He turned back and walked closer to the pick. The gold symbol on the top with the interlocking loops shone brightly against the dark metal pick. It was etched into the side that tapered down to a fine point, while the opposite side was broader and looked rough and beaten. Jeddediah walked up and stood next to him as the group closed in the circle and stood shoulder to shoulder over the mysterious key. Gideon stooped down and looked back up at Jeddediah.

"May I?" he asked with his hands outstretched toward the pick.

Jeddediah nodded and Gideon gently rocked the pick forward and scooped it up. It was the first time he had held it since retrieving it from the saguaro. Somehow it was heavier than he remembered. His fingers slid across the uneven ridges on the bottom of the pick as he lifted it up and examined it. He turned it over and over in his hands but could not find any other markings besides the four that had led them to this point. The etching of Weaver's Needle was rudimentary but undeniable what it represented. Gideon was certain the N and S stood for north and south but was unsure what it was supposed to tell them. The cross with the interlocking loops at its center was interesting, because the loops were not symmetrical even though the trunk and arms were perfectly straight lines perpendicular to one another. Matter of fact, all the marking on the pick were made with precision and made Gideon wonder why these loops were shaped the way they were.

While he contemplated this irregularity, his fingers rubbed the uneven grooves underneath the pick. He lifted it over his head and examined the grooves. They ran the width of the pick from end to end, although at first, he had thought these grooves were perhaps dents from use or abuse, he now saw that they had been smoothed out and looked to be made intentionally. He furrowed his brow and squinted slightly as he tried to discern the meaning of these grooves, which did not appear to have a pattern or clear indication of why they were there.

"Whatcha doing?" Liz asked.

"These grooves, somebody made them," Gideon replied. "But they look totally random. I can't figure what they're supposed to be."

All eyes were on him, and the group waited and watched as Gideon studied the grooves closely. He raised the pick to eye level and turned it right side up. From the side, the grooves had the appearance of an inverted skyline with the dark metal as the sky while the negative space below acted as the mountain peaks and ridges. With a slow meticulous motion, Gideon aligned the bottom of the pick axe with the distant horizon. He held it as far as his arms would allow him and closed one eye while he moved from left to right.

"Ho-ly crap," Gideon said as the grooves in the bottom of the pick lined up perfectly with the skyline to the east. "Look at this."

Jeddediah excitedly stepped forward and took the key from his hand. He held it to his eye line, just as Gideon had done, and slowly adjusted it. His old eyes grew wider.

"Ho-ly crap," Jeddediah repeated.

"Let me see," Todd said as he took the pick from Jeddediah.

Gideon could not help but smile as he and Jeddediah exchanged astonished looks. For him this was confirmation that someone had indeed fashioned and left this pick as a guide and possible a key to find what they left behind. The prospect of hidden treasure had never seemed so real or so close.

"It's like *Goonies*," Todd exclaimed as he handed the key to Joe. "This is amazing! Remember how they used the medallion to find the lighthouse?"

"What lighthouse?" Jeddediah asked. "What's a goonie?"

"It's a movie," Todd replied. "You've never seen Goonies?"

"What's with ya doggone kids and movies?" Jeddediah asked with a scrunched up face. "Ya ever heard of books?"

"Whatever, Goonies is awesome," Todd rebutted. "So where does it lead us?"

"There's a tiny hole in the side," Joe replied with one eye closed.

"Let me see," Gideon said. He took back the pick axe and looked closely at the side. There was a spot of rust colored build up on the side just next to the etching of Weaver's Needle with a tiny pin hole in it. Gideon had to hold it at just the right angle to see light streaming through from the other side. He quickly got out his Swiss Army knife, extended the metal file from its slot and began to pick at the hole. It gradually expanded as the corrosive build up flaked away and soon he could see properly through to the other side.

"I'll bet that hole indicates which way we should go next," said Joe.

"Maybe, but we'd have to know exactly where to stand otherwise, just a few degrees and we could get way off course," replied Gideon.

"It's right there," Joe said as he pointed to the side of the pick. "The hole is at the base of the Needle. It's on the side with the S carved into the pick axe. We just need to line this baby up north to south right over there at the southern base of the peak."

Gideon could not argue with the logic as it seemed sound. He was slightly disappointed he had not gotten there first, but was mostly grateful for Joe's incomparable puzzle solving skills. Jeddediah took the pick from Gideon and headed back toward the southern end of the Needle. They all hurriedly followed after the hobbling old man.

"Look for some indication of where we should put it," Gideon said.

They all fanned out and searched the ground for some clue as to where they should place the key. Gideon was sure to stay close to Jeddediah and kept one eye on him while they surveyed the rocky ground.

"This might be something," Liz called from the head of the group.

Gideon and Jeddediah hurried to her side and looked down at two rocks laid side by side in the earth. Between them, right in the center where the stones touched, was an unnaturally symmetrical circle filled with dirt. Gideon knelt down on the ground and began to scoop the dirt from the fist sized hole. It was several inches deep and reminded him of the old flag postings at Camp Geronimo.

"Do you see that?" Todd exclaimed as he pointed to the rock closest to the Needle.

A faint etching in the gray stone was barely discernible but looked like a cross with four interlocking loops at the center. Juan Carlos was the first to recover from his astonishment as he oriented his compass and drew a north south line right through the center of the two stones. Gideon jumped up and looked around for some type of mount or stand that would fit in the hole.

"We need to find a stick," he instructed.

"This is like Raiders of the Lost Ark!" Todd exclaimed.

"I've seen that one," Jeddediah excitedly pointed to Todd.

"How 'bout this?" Joe said as he hustled over to Moses and dug in his backpack. He pulled out two collapsible walking sticks and extended them with a flick of his wrists.

"Perfect!" Gideon beamed.

Joe stepped up and planted them upside down in the ground where Juan Carlos' line and the circle met. Jeddediah wedged the head of the pick axe atop the walking sticks and lined up the grooves with the horizon.

After several anxious moments, his expression fell and he slowly stepped away from the key. Gideon stepped in as Jeddediah gave way, with his eyes still trained on the horizon. Gideon bent down and peered through the hole in the side of the pick. He looked at a depression between two distant peaks at the dead center of the hole.

DEATH MARKS THE SPOT

"Get out a map," Gideon ordered.

Juan Carlos ran back to the horses while Joe and Gideon switched places. Jeddediah stood to the side and stared straight ahead. Gideon watched him for a moment and wondered what caused him to act that way. By the time Juan Carlos returned with the map Todd, Tara and Liz had all taken turns looking through the peep hole in the side of the pick axe. He spread out the large topographical map at Joe's feet. The group anxiously gathered around, all except for Jeddediah who stood transfixed on some distant point.

"All right, we're here," Joe said. He oriented the map and pointed to a group of tightly formed circular lines. "This is north, but the key is pointing us in this direction."

Joe made a mark on the map with a stubby little pencil he pulled from his shirt pocket. He scooted over in front of the key and made certain it was still aligned with the mark Juan Carlos had made on the ground. When he was certain he was lined up properly, he put his forehead right on the pick axe to look through the hole and double check his direction. Gideon watched him for a moment before he trained his eyes on the map. Joe made another marking between a pair of loosely grouped lines.

"This right here is Bluff Springs Mountain," Joe explained, pointing to the group to the left. "And beyond that is…"

"Herman Mountain," Jeddediah interjected as a clap of thunder punctuated his words. He still had his eyes set dead ahead.

The excitement of the group vanished in a moment from the tone of his voice. Gideon felt as if the old miner's words had sucked up their glee like a Hoover. Tara looked around with a quizzical expression. Liz answered her expression with a shrug of her shoulders.

"Is that a bad thing?" Liz asked Jeddediah.

"Death and disappointment marks this path," Jeddediah replied. "It didn't end well for ol' Adolf and the Petrasch brothers."

"Adolf?" Liz asked. "Like Hitler?"

"Adolf Ruth was a prospector who died in the early nineteen hundreds," Joe explained. "They found his head six months after he went missing near Bluff Springs Mountain."

"His head?" Liz asked with a horrified look. Joe nodded.

"A month later and nearly a mile away, they found his body on the east slope of Black Top Mesa," Joe continued. "The skull had a hole in the side. Left most to believe he was murdered but the sheriff didn't pursue an investigation. Adolf was seventy years old. It was written off as an old man meeting a tragic end in the Superstitions."

"But 'ow did 'e get separated from 'is 'ead?" Tara asked.

"That's a good question," Joe replied. "Nobody knows. There are more than a few stories of prospectors being separated from their heads out here. It goes all the way back to the first explorers that came through these mountains. Some blame the Apache. Some believe this land is cursed."

"He was as old as I am now," Jeddediah again found his voice as he finally turned and faced the group. "Ol' Adolf an' me share a birthday too."

"And the Petrasch brothers?" asked Liz.

"I got this one," Gideon replied. "Reinhart Petrasch was with Julie Thomas when Jacob Waltz died. Supposedly, Waltz whispered the location of the mine on his deathbed to Julie and Reinhart. Reinhart enlisted his brother Herman to help them search for the mine."

"Herman Mountain," Liz affirmed.

"Yep," replied Gideon. "Julie Thomas spent her last dime looking for the mine before she gave it up. Reinhart and Herman never did. After decades of searching, Reinhart blew his brains out but Herman continued to search until he died, he even lived out here for years."

"I thought we were looking for the Black Robes treasure," Todd said.

"We are," Jeddediah replied.

"Really?" Todd questioned. "Cause it sounds like we're back talking about the Dutchman."

"Are we sure they are two different things?" Gideon asked.

"What do you mean?" Liz asked.

"There's a theory that there was never any Lost Dutchman Mine," Joe said. "Some believe Waltz found an old cache from the Peralta massacre, but it could have been that he stumbled onto the hiding place of the Black Robes."

"Massacre?" Tara asked.

"The Peralta's, a family of Mexican miners, operated in the Superstitions until they were wiped out by the Apache, who did not appreciate uninvited guests," Joe replied.

Gideon looked down at the three marks Joe had made on the map. They formed a straight line that headed to the east. He looked out of the distant landscape and shook his head.

"There's got to be thousands of places along this line that it could be," Gideon said. "How do we know where to start?"

Joe picked up the key from its resting place, atop the walking sticks, and turned it over in his hands. Gideon peered over his shoulder and carefully studied the pick axe as it rotated slowly in Joe's callused hands. He could not see any other distinguishing marks on the black metal pick, besides those they had already identified. There were no more clues or any indication how far they would need to go. On Joe's second rotation the rough end opposite the cross caught Gideon's eye. It too appeared to be formed intentionally into what looked like the back end of a boat. Gideon turned his attention back to the map that lay on the ground.   Another thunder clap directly overhead was accompanied by a distant streak of lightning that danced across the sky. Seconds later, scattered drops of rain began to land on the dirt all around them. A single drop impacted the map to the left of the markings Joe had made. Juan Carlos quickly reached down to protect the map until Gideon grabbed his arm.

"Wait," Gideon stared in wide-eyed astonishment at the spot where the rain drop fell. It was in line with the markings Joe had made and equidistant from the two markings over Weaver's Needle and Herman Mountain. He pointed to the rain drop at the left side of the map.

"Kakatak Tamai," Gideon whispered.

"What?" Juan Carlos asked.

"Look at that," Gideon said as his bent down and put his finger on the lone rain drop. "Crooked Top Mountain. Flatiron is lined up perfectly with Herman Mountain with Weaver's Needle smack dab in the middle!"

"Whoa!" Todd exclaimed.

"And look," he continued and pointed to the pick. "Doesn't that look just like Flatiron?"

"Good work," a voice called from behind them. "I'll take it from here."

Gideon turned around to see Cal with his pistol drawn and pointed at him. To his right, Jeddediah had turned to face the cowboy as well. His face hardened and his lips clenched together.

"You," Jeddediah seethed at him.

"You know him?" Gideon asked. "Wait, that's "the cowboy"?"

"Cal, what are you doing?" Joe questioned. "Put that gun down."

"No sir," Cal replied as he waved his sidearm in the threatening motion. "I ain't lett'n it outta my sight again. Now hand it over."

"All right," Gideon said as he raised both over his head. He reached over blindly and took the key from Joe. "Nobody needs to get hurt. It's just a hunk of metal."

"Bull squat," Cal said. "Accord'n to that old codger that's the key to a whole heap of gold."

"And ya know what to do with it, do ya?" Jeddediah questioned. "Ya couldn't find your butt with both hands, ya empty headed animal."

Cal drew the hammer back on his pistol and pointed it directly at Jeddediah's head.

"Easy," Todd said as he stepped between the miner and the cowboy. "Cal, come on. You don't want to shoot anybody. Let's talk this out."

"Maybe he already has," Gideon said.

"What?" Cal and Todd asked in unison.

"Maybe he's already shot somebody," Gideon accused. "What happened to Glenn, Cal?"

"I didn't shoot 'im, if that's what you're ask'n," Cal said.

"He left with you," Gideon said. "You were the last person to be seen with him."

"He was alive, last I saw him," Cal said.

"Then why didn't ya come back?" Jeddediah asked.

Cal lowered his gun to his hip but still kept it trained on the old miner. He sighed deeply and removed his white Stetson as the rain fell now in steady sheets. The cowboy wiped at his brow and placed his hat back on his head while the anxious group watched and waited.

"When we got back to the ranch I tried to get him to give me the other half of the clue," Cal began. "He refused and said he was gonna stick to the plan. Well, I drew down on him to try and scare him. I wasn't gonna shoot him, I swear."

"You double cross'n snake," Jeddediah shouted.

"I didn't know if he was ever com'n back or if it was some kinda plan ya'll cooked up to cut me out of my share," Cal said.

"Your share!" Jeddediah yelled. "Ya hadn't done diddly squat 'cept show up an' shoot the place up."

"You and that pudgy ginger wouldn't have had a prayer without me," Cal yelled back.

"Enough," Joe said. "Cal, put that gun down."

"I'm call'n the shot here," Cal said. "Now give me the key or I swear someone's gonna get shot."

Gideon looked back at his friends. To his right Joe and Todd stood defiantly next to Jeddediah with Liz, Tara and Juan Carlos just behind them. Liz turned and looked over at Gideon, and he forced a smile in an attempt to set her at ease. She fought the corners of her mouth upwards but it somehow made Gideon more fearful that someone could get hurt. He resolved to take control of the situation.

"I knew we couldn't trust you," Gideon said.

"Jealously ain't the same thing as intuition, kid," Cal replied. "Now I'm gonna count to three."

"Hold up," Gideon said as he lowered the key to his side. "You tell me what you did with Glenn and I'll give you the key."

"I didn't do noth'n with him," Cal said. "That blasted mule kicked me in the leg and the kid hit me in the head with a rock. By the time my head cleared he had jumped in his old jalopy and cut out."

"Where's Bernice?" Jeddediah asked.

"I was angry and I wasn't think'n straight," Cal replied. "I shot that old girl in the head."

"Ya monster!" Jeddediah shouted. He lurched toward the cowboy but Joe stuck his arm out to stop his assault. In the struggle Joe's other hand flailed in the air to steady himself and brushed against the hostler that held his pistol. Gideon took a step toward them to help restrain the furious miner when a gunshot echoed off the rock tower beside them. Joe grabbed his gut and collapsed to the ground.

It all happened in an instant and yet the whole world seemed to move in slow motion. Gideon heard Todd scream, from what sounded like a mile away. He turned back to see white heat vapors floating off the barrel of the revolver. Cal's mouth had fallen open and he stared down at Joe with a horrified expression. Todd fell to his knees at his father's side and pulled at his arms to try and get a look at the wound. Gideon and Juan Carlos both rushed toward the stunned cowboy but he quickly wheeled the smoking gun in their direction.

"Don't," Cal warned.

They both halted and put the arms up in surrender. Gideon immediately looked back around to check Joe's condition. Blood had already begun to soak through his flannel shirt and Todd was applying pressure to the wound. Liz had knelt down over him and cradled Joe's head. Jeddediah stepped into view with his fists and jaw clenched tightly.

"Get the first aid kit," Todd pleaded.

"Nobody move," Cal ordered when Juan Carlos and Tara started toward the horses.

"We need to stop the bleeding," Gideon said.

"Everybody just shut up," Cal shouted. "This wasn't s'ppose to go like this."

"He needs help," Gideon said.

"He needs a doctor," Liz added.

"I said shut up," Cal threatened as he waved his gun from side to side. "I need to think."

He paced back and forth as his eyes darted in all directions. Gideon stood still as not to agitate the situation further. He studied the cowboy earnestly and worried for his friends. Behind him, Joe grunted in pain as Gideon tried to remember the statistics he had read about gunshot wounds to the stomach. He could not remember if it was a matter of hours or days that a body could survive and he prayed it was closer to days.

"A'right," Cal finally said. "Pick one of ya to go get help. The rest of ya are staying put."

"I'll go," Juan Carlos said. "I know the fastest way out."

"Okay," Gideon said. "But don't go alone. Take Liz."

"Gideon…" Liz began to protest.

"I said one," Cal repeated.

"It's a dangerous ride," Gideon said. "It's safer if two go."

The cowboy grimaced and stared back at Gideon.

"Fine," Cal said. "He can take the brown girl."

"But…" Gideon started to argue.

"Or we could all just stand here while he bleeds to death," Cal interrupted.

"I'll go," Tara said as she reached up and put her hand on Gideon's shoulder.

"Good," Cal said. "Now git 'fore I change my mind."

"Take Pepper," Liz said. "She's the fastest."

Juan Carlos nodded and he and Tara jogged over to the gray spotted horse and climbed up in the saddle. Before they rode away, Juan Carlos pulled a white pouch with a red cross out of the saddlebag and tossed it at Joe's feet. He prodded Pepper forward with a kick of his heels and they disappeared around the corner.

"They ain't just com'n back with a doctor," Jeddediah said. "They'll be bring'n the law too."

"Well then, it's a good thing we won't be anywhere near here," Cal responded.

"What do you mean?" Gideon asked.

"You and the old timer are gonna go fetch me my treasure," Cal said.

"What about Joe?" asked Gideon.

"His boy'll take care of him 'til your friends get back," Cal replied.

"No way," Gideon said. "We're not leaving him."

"Well then," Cal began coolly. "Your girlfriend is gonna meet an abrupt end."

He pointed his revolver at Liz and closed one eye to take aim. Gideon jumped between them and raised his arms again.

"Hold up," he said. "You don't have to do that. I'll go. We'll go."

"That's a good boy," Cal said.

Gideon turned around and looked down at Joe whose face was contorted from the pain. Todd held on to his father's blood-stained hands, pressed firmly over the hole in his stomach. Liz had already unzipped the first aid kit and was unrolling an ace bandage. Gideon knelt down behind her and Todd.

"We better just do what he wants," Gideon said. "You two stay with Joe and I'll go with Jeddediah to see what we can find."

"Actually the girl's com'n with me," Cal said.

"What?" Gideon said as he shot him a disdainful look. "No way."

"Like the old man said, the law is com'n," said Cal. "I don't plan to be here when they arrive."

"No deal," Gideon said as he stood up as straight and tall as he could.

"You don't get it," Cal replied. "You ain't in charge here."

Gideon's shoulders slumped and he looked back down at Liz. She looked as if she were about to cry. A pool of tears began to gather in the corners of Gideon's eyes and he looked away quickly and wiped them dry with the sleeve of his hoodie.

"Don't cry, darl'n," Cal said to Liz. "I'll take good care of ya."

"If you hurt her I'll…" Gideon began.

"You'll what?" Cal interrupted. "You just bring me a big ol' pile of gold and you won't have to worry 'bout it. Ain't nothing gonna happen to her unless I don't get what I want."

"What if we can't find it?" Gideon asked.

"We'll burn that bridge when we get there," Cal said. "Besides you're a bright fella and you sound like you're unto something. Have faith."

"If you aren't going to stay put, then where will we find you?" Gideon asked.

"Well I ain't gonna share that with Abraham and Isaac down there," Cal said as he gestured to Joe and Todd. "We'll ride out a ways, then I'll tell you where to meet. That way these two can't point a posse in my direction."

Gideon stepped closer to Liz and took her by the hand. He looked into her brown eyes and this time managed a genuine smile. Streams of rain fell down her face and glittered against her cheek.

"I won't let anything happen to you," he said. "One way or another, I'm coming for you."

She nodded and squeezed his hand. Gideon knelt down next to Todd and they exchanged a solemn look.

"How long will it take Juan Carlos to get help?" he asked.

"It's about a four hour ride if he rides hard," Todd said. "The only thing getting in here besides a horse is a helicopter so…"

Todd's voice trailed off as he looked down on his father. Gideon studied the anguish on his face and said a prayer that God would watch over his friends and keep Joe alive. Just after he said a silent amen Gideon noticed Joe's pistol still holstered to his side. Before he could formulate a plan, however, Cal stepped forward.

"I'll take that," Cal demanded with a gesture toward Joe's side. "Nice and easy."

With his eyes trained on the cowboy, Gideon reached across Joe's body and slowly removed his gun from the hostler. He kept the butt of the gun upward with the barrel pointed toward the ground and surrendered it to Cal. The cowboy immediately tucked it into the front of his pants.

"Now, time is ticking so ya'll better get a move on," Cal said. "Come on over here little missy."

On her way toward him, Liz stopped in front of Gideon. She leaned in and kissed him on the cheek and Gideon bowed his head as her warmth radiated against the cold winter air.

"Don't worry about me," she whispered. "You just be safe. There's no treasure in the world worth a life. No matter what, you come back. You understand?"

"Understand," Gideon replied.

"A'right love birds," Cal interrupted. "Mount up."

Jeddediah had already begun to pull himself up on top of Moses when Gideon turned around. Liz reluctantly joined Cal while Gideon swung up into Hercules's saddle. Cal put his thumb and index finger in his mouth and let loose an ear-splitting whistle. From around the corner a black horse trotted toward him as the rain fell in bunches now. He motioned for Liz to climb up and immediately followed her into the saddle, much too close for Gideon's liking. Cal prodded his horse ahead passing very close to Todd and Joe.

"This weren't the way I planned it," Cal said. "Just want you to know that."

Deep creases formed between Todd's eyebrows as he could not contain his contempt for the cowboy. Gideon had never seen such a look on the face of his usually happy go lucky friend. He wished he could take his pain and anger from him or exact a measure of revenge. Since he knew the former was impossible he focused on the latter and allowed the seeds of vengeance to take hold in his mind. Cal trotted by, with Liz held tightly in his arms. Gideon boiled with rage until Joe's grunt reached his ears.

"Hold on, Joe," Gideon said. "Help's on the way."

"Gideon," Joe called out. "There's always a way out. Remember that. There's always a way out."

He nodded to Joe although he was not completely sure what he meant. With a look over his shoulder, he barely caught sight of Moses tail as it disappeared around the corner. He looked back to Todd who gestured with his head for him to follow after the cowboy and the old miner. Gideon spurred Hercules forward and galloped after two men he could not care less for and the girl who he cared for above all others.

They descended down from the summit and traversed through the boulder labyrinth at the bottom until they were several hundred yards away from the Needle. Cal swung his horse sideways across their path to block the way. Gideon pulled Hercules to a stop next to Moses and stared straight into the cowboy's cold blue eyes, as they were all bathed in rain.

"Here's the deal," Cal began. "This little lady and I are gonna enjoy the sunset at the top of the Superstitions this evening. We'll hold up there for the night. Come sunrise if you don't turn up you're gonna read a tragic story in the papers about a girl who got lost in the mountains and fell from the top of Flatiron. If I see any lawmen, over she goes. If a helicopter comes buzz'n around, over she goes. If I so much as smell your breath on the breeze, over she goes. Do you understand?"

"That's not a lot of time," Gideon argued.

"Then you'd better get go'n," replied Cal.

"What if we don't find anything?" asked Gideon.

"Then you know how this ends," Cal said.

The cowboy did not wait for any further questions or protests; he swung his horse around and trotted west into the gloomy gray morning. Gideon watched them for a moment until Jeddediah glided into view.

"Come on," the old miner said. "We've got eight miles and no time. Heeyah!"

At that, both horses broke into a gallop and they slogged forward into a headwind as they were pelted mercilessly with giant raindrops. Low clouds hung in the sky in front of them, between the hills and mountains. Normally this would have inspired awe and appreciation for Gideon. This morning, however, all this grand scene represented were the millions of potential hiding places that would prove deadly for him and his friends.

CLOAKED IN DARKNESS

The rain subsided for the moment but there was a bitter chill to the air. Gideon's clothes were soaked through and he lamented his total lack of preparedness for the elements. Gray clouds still hung ominously overhead and the rolling thunder threatened from the distance. Jeddediah pawed at a group of rocks while Gideon stood by with his arms folded tightly across his chest. He looked up to the top of the mountain above them, at a cave that rested on the steep cliff face.

"Why don't we try that cave?" Gideon suggested as his body trembled.

"Nah," Jeddediah said, as he momentarily halted his examination of the small cluster of rocks. "All sorts of folks have been over and over Herman's Cave. There ain't nothing up there but disappointment and despair. Besides that's a heck of a climb even when it ain't wet."

"Well what are we looking for down here?" Gideon demanded.

"Dunno," Jeddediah said. "This was your idea to come here."

Gideon spun around and kicked at the rocks behind him. He had not been able to stop thinking about Liz, in the arms of that monster, or Joe bleeding to death at the foot of Weaver's Needle. He did not expect the treasure to present itself to them, but hoped for some clue to go on or sign they were on the right track. The lack of either, combined with his wet clothes and the unrelenting cold, he could not imagine a more miserable state.

"There has to be something," Gideon argued. "Get out the key."

"Help yourself," Jeddediah said with a nod back toward the horses. "Ain't nothing there we ain't already seen."

He shuffled over to Moses, pulled open the damp leather flap and removed the pick axe from the saddlebag. Again, it seemed even heavier than the last time he held it and Gideon felt its burden mounting. Over and over again he turned it every which way in search of some previously overlooked clue or sign. When at last he had exhausted his hope, he flung the key down into the mud.

"Take it easy," Jeddediah said. He hobbled over with a grimace and plucked the key from the ground.

"Take it easy?" Gideon shouted. "Joe is lying back there on the ground dying and Liz is a hostage! And we're piddl'n around with nothing to go on! I will not take it easy!"

"Gett'n all worked up ain't gonna help your friends," Jeddediah said. "You can't do noth'n for Joe and if ya want to help the girl we need to find something to give the cowboy."

"How?" he yelled with his arms spread wide. "How are we gonna find anything out here?"

"I believe I can help with that," a voice said from behind him.

They both turned back toward the horses and saw the man in the gray cloak standing beside Hercules. His cloak was covered in beads of rain that dotted the coarse fabric. He peeled off his hood and stepped toward them.

"You?" Jeddediah questioned.

"You know him too?" Gideon asked.

"He's the priest from San Xavier," Jeddediah replied.

"What?" Gideon asked. "What are you talking about?"

"I'm not a priest," Miguel said. "But I am the caretaker of San Xavier Del Bac. My name is Miguel Velasquez and I can help you find what you're looking for."

"You two know each other?" Gideon asked.

"I brought him Cletus's old Spanish journal," Jeddediah said.

"Journal?" Gideon said. "You've got to be kidding me."

"The journal is why I'm here," Miguel said.

"You're after the same treasure," Gideon asserted. Miguel nodded. A knot formed in the pit of Gideon's stomach. The last thing he needed right now was competition. He had no idea what the intentions of this stranger were, was he there to help them or hinder them?

"The journal told ya to come here?" Jeddediah asked.

"No," Miguel said. "I followed you. The journal is just one part of the puzzle. You have the key."

He removed the journal from under his cloak and presented it to Gideon. A cross symbol identical to the one on the pick axe was etched into the cover. Gideon gently took the journal from Miguel and opened it. Inside the cover, the handwritten text was entirely in Spanish and Gideon could do little more than pick out a word or two from the decorative writing.

"You've read this?" Gideon asked.

"I have," replied Miguel. "It says to follow the key."

"We've done that," Jeddediah replied. "The key leads here."

"May I?" Miguel asked with a gesture toward the pick.

Jeddediah looked down at the pick and then over to Gideon who nodded back at him. He handed over the pick gently and Miguel turned it in his hands. Gideon leafed through the journal and found several drawings interspersed between the text. The cross with interlocking loops was drawn multiple times throughout the journal and there was one drawing Gideon recognized as the face of San Xavier Del Bac.

"This led you here?" Miguel asked.

"Yeah," Gideon said. "How long have you been following us?"

"I have been following you, Gideon, since you arrived in the Superstitions," Miguel said.

"Me?" Gideon questioned. "Why me?"

"Because Glenn put his faith in you," Miguel replied.

"What did you say?" Gideon squinted his eyes together as his mouth fell open. He could not reconcile the words that came out of the mouth of the man in the cloak. How was it possible that he knew of Glenn or his faith? Question after question sprang to his mind in a dizzying array.

"Would you like an explanation or would you like to find the treasure?" Miguel asked.

All at once Gideon remembered Liz in the arms of his enemy and he peered up into the cloudy sky, unable to find the sun for a point of reference. His best guess was that it was late afternoon and the alarms on his internal clock rang loud and clear.

"If we find the treasure we need it as a ransom for my friend," Gideon stated.

"For the girl," Miguel clarified.

Gideon nodded and tilted his head sideways to scrutinize this mysterious man who seemed nearly omniscient.

"Very well," Miguel said. He extended the pick to Gideon and motioned for the journal with his free hand. They made a simultaneous exchange as Jeddediah came and stood next to Gideon. The rain had done little to tap down the aroma that emanated from the old miner, if anything it just made him smell dank on top of everything else. Miguel flipped through the journal and opened to a page near the back. He turned it around and Gideon saw a drawing at the bottom of what appeared to be a four hump mountain.

"Is that Four Peaks?" Gideon asked.

"That is what I thought originally," Miguel said. "But no. According to the journal this is located near the entrance that will lead to the treasure. Until now I did not know where to begin my search. I think we should split up, to cover more ground.”

“Not on your life,” Jeddediah said. “I’m not lett’n either one of ya out of my sight.”

“Jed,” Gideon began before Jeddediah’s deathly stare gave him pause. “...dediah, he’s right. We have a better chance of finding it if we split up.”

“And what if he finds it first?” Jeddediah argued. “Ya trust him to holler for ya? Ya don’t know this man from Adam.”

“I don’t have time for mistrust,” Gideon said. “We’ve got till morning to solve a two hundred year old mystery and deliver a legendary treasure that may or may not even be out here to a psychopathic cowboy who shot my friend and kidnapped the woman I love. Now you can get on board or get out of the way.”

Jeddediah folded his arms gruffly across his chest and grimaced at the ground. Gideon felt as if he were channeling Todd who had a talent for summing up a predicament like no other. His mind shifted to the father and son lying helpless beneath Weaver’s Needle waiting desperately for help. He said a silent prayer that Juan Carlos and Tara would be carried swiftly and safely on their rescue mission as he turned back toward Miguel and took a deep breath.

“Does the journal give any other clues where we should look?” Gideon asked calmly.

“The journal says that its shadow touches the entrance at sunset,” Miguel said as he tapped on the picture of the four humps.

Gideon looked over his shoulder to the top of Herman Mountain. The peak was far too high for the setting sun to shine on anything in the ravine where they stood, and a glance to the west showed only dirt, rocks and shrubs, nothing that could be the entrance to a treasure hold.

“Okay, we need to get clear of the mountain” Gideon began. “You two head south and I’ll head north. Once you have a good east-west view of the area start looking for something with four humps. Make your way east first and we'll meet up on the other side of the mountain."

Without waiting for objection or agreement, Gideon jogged over to Hercules and swung up into the saddle. He used the reigns to swing the powerful horse around and they moved forward, with purpose, northward. His eyes scanned the ground thoroughly although he had not yet cleared the mountain, he was afraid he would miss something. They had approached Herman Mountain from the north side and Gideon knew the terrain was more open, with a large wash that cut down the side of colliding declines. He led Hercules in a zigzag pattern in and out of the wash. Gideon briefly abandoned this tactic and climbed down out of the saddle in an effort to better search the brush and rocks on the ground. It only took a few minutes for him to decide that he had a much better vantage point from the top of his muscular steed and that the search would go much faster.

Thoughts of Joe, Todd and Liz whirled through his mind and he struggled to focus. He wondered how Juan Carlos and Tara were doing and if help was on the way. His mind was also pulled to the opposite side of the mountain. He imagined Jeddediah and Miguel had already located the treasure and were busy divvying up the spoils with no thought of the consequences he and his friends would suffer. As he continued his lonely search, he sought for a peace of mind he knew he could not find alone.

"Heavenly Father," he prayed aloud. "Please bless Joe to survive and endure until help arrives. Bless Todd to be comforted and watch over Liz and keep her safe until I get to her. Father if thou would have mercy on me and help guide me to the landmark I am seeking, I would be grateful. I would in no way misuse this blessing. I only want to rescue Liz. Please Father, I know with you I can do all things. I ask for these blessings in the name of Jesus Christ, amen."

Although he concluded his vocal prayer he did not cease to pray in his heart. He thought back to the many times God had answered his prayers and remembered his earliest recollection of God's tender mercies. He was eight years old and had misplaced his Chuck Norris action figure. After he had searched high and low, young Gideon recalled a primary lesson on prayer and he dropped to his knees and offered a brief but sincere prayer. When he opened his eyes, he noticed something white sticking out of the orange couch cushions. He reached in and pulled out his missing action figure. Gideon did not expect for the treasure to manifest itself that easily or for his friends to miraculously be delivered, but he knew that God does answer prayers.

It began to sprinkle again as he slowly bent his way south back to where he expected to meet up with Jeddediah and Miguel. The search area broadened significantly as the terrain flattened and sprawled out toward the west. He mostly kept his attention toward the base of the mountain as that was the most likely place he would find the treasure hold. With each passing moment his anticipation faded and the questions and cold returned. His clothes were still damp and frozen to his shivering body. He thought of the cloaked stranger who was now helping them and somehow knew Glenn. His jaw quivered and he tried to push the questions aside and focus on his search.

"Gideon," he heard his name called from around the bend.

He stood up tall in the stirrups and listened to his name echo off the canyon walls ahead of him.

"Gideon. We found it!"

A rush of energy grew from inside him and almost seemed to warm his cold body. He spurred Hercules into a gallop and raced around the corner. As he cleared a set of boulders near the base of the mountain, he found Jeddediah and Miguel standing in front of Moses looking at the ground. He rode right up next to them and leapt out of the saddle as soon as his horse came to a stop.

"You found it?" Gideon asked.

Miguel pointed to a solid rock with four humps on the top of it. Gideon quickly surveyed the area east of the four hump rock and expected to see a cave or shaft or at least a hill or a mountain. To his great disappointment there was nothing but a series of large flat boulders that lay side by side on the ground.

"This is it?" he asked. "Where's the entrance?"

"I do not know," Miguel answered as he too scanned their surroundings.

"This can't be it," Gideon said. "We must be missing something. What else does the journal say?"

Miguel pulled the journal from under his cloak and opened to the page where the four hump rock was drawn. He scanned the page with his finger and furrowed his brow.

"It just says its shadow touches the entrance at sunset," Miguel translated. He turned to the next page and continued reading. "Time is your foe, you must push back time to enter."

"Push back time?" Gideon questioned. "What does that even mean?"

"It's a riddle," Jeddediah said.

"No kidding," Gideon replied with an eye roll.

"Boy, I will slap the sass out your mouth," Jeddediah threatened.

"Enough," Miguel said. "This is not helping."

The trio stared back at the four hump rock in silent contemplation with the sporadic rain drops beating in random patterns on the ground all around them. Gideon tried to clear his mind of the worry, fear, frustration, and doubt that pervaded his thoughts like a thick cloud. He concentrated on only two things, the rock and the riddle.

"Glenn would love this," he muttered to himself.

Out of the corner of his eye he saw Miguel briefly turn to look at him and his previous curiosities returned. Solving the riddle slowly slid from the top spot as his many question rose up his internal list of priorities.

"How did you know Glenn?" Gideon turned and questioned the man in the cloak.

Miguel faced Gideon straight on and his brown eyes widened slightly.

"We met out here," he began. "After the old man came to San Xavier I became intrigued by the journal and began to read. It tells of a hidden treasure and the clues necessary to find it. I came here in search of Jeddediah but instead found Glenn."

"Where did you find him?" Gideon asked.

"He was not far from here," Miguel replied.

Gideon waited for him to elaborate but he stayed aggravatingly silent. Just as he was about to continue his interrogation Jeddediah spoke up.

"What did he tell ya?" the old miner asked.

"He told me you had found a key and that his life was in danger," Miguel answered.

"The key," Gideon said. "That's it!"

Miguel and Jeddediah both turned an inquisitive eye on Gideon. He jogged over to Moses and pulled the pick axe from the nearest saddlebag. With the key held in front of him like a compass, he methodically walked back toward the four hump rock. First, he tried to place the pick at the center of the humps with no success. Next, he attempted to hold it at varied angles and fit the two together like pieces of a jigsaw puzzle. When that too failed, he walked slowly around the rock in search of a place to insert the key.

"What are ya up to boy?" asked Jeddediah.

"Of course," Miguel exclaimed. "Why didn't I see it earlier?"

He threw off his cloak to reveal a thick piece of twine around his neck. In one fluid motion, he reached behind his back, took hold of the rope and flung it over his shoulder. As he did so a cross with interlocking loops swung into view tethered to the end of the rope.

"What in Sam Hill?" Jeddediah exclaimed.

"You had that the whole time?" Gideon yelled.

Without a word, Miguel removed the twine from around his neck and stepped toward the rock. He held the cross over the rock and turned it until the loops lined up perfectly with the four humps on top. Carefully, he lowered the cross down onto the rock until the fit neatly together.

"Ho-ly crap," Gideon muttered. "Where did you get that?"

"It was secreted beneath San Xavier," Miguel answered.

"You've been carrying that around your neck the whole time," Gideon stated in disbelief. "Who does that?"

"Now what?" Jeddediah asked bringing their attention quickly back to the cross, fit snuggly between the humps in the rock.

"Perhaps it points in the direction of the treasure," Miguel suggested.

"But the journal said the shadow of the rock touches the entrance at sunset," Gideon reminded him. "This cross is pointing north and south."

"It could've meant the shadow of the cross," Jeddediah said.

"The cross only sticks out a foot or so from the rock," Gideon shook his head. "Both shadows will still point east."

Jeddediah removed his damp hat and beat it pensively against his leg before he returned it to his shaggy gray head. Unconsciously, Gideon wiped across the bill of his cap while he considered the clues before them.

"What did the journal say about time?" Gideon asked.

Miguel opened the journal again and read aloud, "Time is your foe, you must push back time to enter."

"Brilliant," Gideon smiled. "Push back time. Look!"

He pointed to the longest part of the cross at the bottom and then made a whirling circular motion around the rock with his arm.

"Time," Gideon repeated. "A clock. Time is our foe, we have to push back time."

Miguel and Jeddediah exchanged bewildered expressions and turned back to Gideon. The old miner's mouth hung open and Miguel simply shook his head.

"Counterclockwise," Gideon sighed. "This is like a clock. We have to turn it counterclockwise. Push back time."

He waited for the recognition to register on their face. When they began to smile, Gideon strode confidently around to the side of the rock on the west side of the cross. He bent down and placed both hands on the lengthiest part of the cross and pushed with all his might. For several seconds he did not breathe in or out but struggled against the metal cross. At last his lungs failed him, and he was forced to draw in a desperate gulp of air and momentarily ceased his futile struggle with the cross. He stepped back and looked at the base of the rock which was clearly buried in the muddy earth.

"It's probably been covered over," Gideon said. "We need to dig it out."

Miguel fell right to his knees and began to claw at the damp dirt with his hands. Gideon joined him while Jeddediah walked around the far side of the rock and began to use the pick axe to excavate the four hump rock. They were aided by the rainy day and night through the first couple of inches of soil, but the ground quickly turned to hard clay.

The rock was as wide as a trash can and appeared to go straight down into the earth. When Gideon noticed Jeddediah had tired, he extended his hand and beckoned for the pick. Jeddediah handed it over without argument and sat down on the wet ground. Gideon rolled up his sleeves and began to pound the hard ground with the pointed end. He quickly dug down to nearly a foot before he spotted a crease in the rock. Miguel cleared away the loose clods of dirt and they examined the nearly straight line, between the rock and the ground beneath it. They smiled as they continued their dig. Gideon broke up the ground with the pick and Miguel scooped the pieces away. Jeddediah joined them once they made it around to his side of the rock.

Despite his labored breathing Gideon did not feel tired at all. He felt as if he grew stronger the more they uncovered. The break in the rock went all the way around and connected in a straight line back where they started. Gideon tossed the pick aside and laid hold on the cross once more. This time Miguel was by his side and they pushed together. The rock budged slightly and Gideon thought he saw one of the large flat boulders in his periphery move along with it.

"Did you see that?" he asked excitedly.

"See what?" Miguel asked.

"I saw it," Jeddediah replied with matched enthusiasm. "That big old rock shifted. Keep push'n."

With renewed effort, Gideon and Miguel leaned into the cross and pushed like a pair of oxen yoked to a plow. The four hump rock lurched forward ever so slightly but it was enough to confirm to Gideon that his theory was correct. He dug into the mud on the balls of his feet and leaned on the cross like he was driving the football sleds back in high school. Inch by precious inch they moved the rock and Gideon could see there was a definite crack opening between the large flat boulders in front of them. Jeddediah had moved over next to them and stared at the tiny new opening as if he were willing the boulder to move.

"Open up, ya blasted stone," he chided. "Open. We're com'n in."

The progress they were making did not diminish the pain that surged through Gideon's shoulder. Though Miguel labored next to him with one hand on the cross and the other on Gideon's back there was no question who bore the lion's share of the load. Just as Gideon began to fear he lacked the strength to continue much longer, there was a distinct click and a pop as the cross gave way and sent him hurdling to the ground with Miguel crashing down to his side. They landed in a thud as Jeddediah swore from back above them, where he stood anxiously waiting for the flat boulder to open. Gideon picked himself up and brushed at the fresh mud on his pants and sweatshirt. He and Miguel walked over and stood next to Jeddediah.

They looked down at the small opening that had formed between the flat boulders as the long stone in the middle had dipped into the earth. The gap spanned the length of the boulder that was at least ten feet long and the opening could not have been more than two feet wide, which would prove challenging for someone of Gideon's stature.

"Well?" Jeddediah said, allowing his vague question to hang in the cold winter air.

Gideon looked back at the cross that was still wedged between the four humps on top of the rock. He walked over to it, laid hold with one hand and gave it a push. It almost spun freely with the weight of the rock and the cross as the only resistance. Clearly, they had broken whatever mechanism had been designed to lower the boulder and open the entrance to the treasure hold.

"We can fit," he heard Miguel say to Jeddediah. Gideon walked back toward them.

"I'm sure we can," Gideon answered. "But how do we know there's not a trap that will spring the door shut the minute we slip through?"

Miguel looked around at the ground for a moment and calmly sidled over to a nearby bush. He bent down, picked up a large rock and wedged it in the opening between the flat boulders. With a sweeping gesture toward his stone doorstop he answered Gideon's concern.

"Fine," Gideon said. He walked with purpose over to the horses as the rain began to fall in steady sheets. With a silent prayer, he gave thanks for Todd's preparation as he opened the saddlebags full of flashlights and batteries. He could not help but smile as he thought of the irony of him benefiting from Todd's preparation for once. The sky had significantly darkened in the past few minutes and, although the sun could still not be seen, Gideon knew it must be near dusk. His anxiety grew as the window to rescue Liz shrank.

"Let's get going then," Gideon said as he handed out the lights to the motley band of treasure hunters.

Jeddediah climbed down first, an honor Gideon did not begrudge, as this was his life's work. His interest in what lied beneath was now strictly for Liz's sake. When the old miner's wide brim hat disappeared beyond the opening, all Gideon could see was the beam from his flashlight jostling around against the blackness.

"What do you see?" asked Miguel.

"Just a bunch of rock," Jeddediah replied. "But it goes back a good ways. I'm gonna check it out."

"Wait for us," Gideon said as he kicked against Miguel's rock wedge to make sure it was nice and secure. Then he gestured for Miguel to go first. "After you."

Miguel nodded and sat down on his rear end to slide himself through the narrow opening between the flat boulders. Gideon waited for the man in the gray cloak to clear the entrance before he bent down and slid his legs beneath the ledge. He was anxious to get his body through the gap without being snapped in half, if and when the entrance slammed shut. His progress was only stopped for a few seconds as he wriggled his backside through a space not designed to accommodate a full sized man. Gideon decided that if he survived he would dramatically reduce his intake of chicken, rice, and peas going forward.

Gideon flipped on his light as soon as his feet hit the floor. He shined it from side to side and found the floor and walls were formed by tightly compacted dirt. Overhead was the bottom end of the flat boulders that were visible topside. The rock ceiling only carried forward for a few feet before it too vanished into the earth. There was not room enough for Gideon to stand upright. The three of them filled the space and immediately he felt as if the walls were closing in on them. A lump formed in his throat and he suppressed the urge to climb back out the way he came.

"Let's get going," he urged.

Jeddediah led the way, followed by Miguel with Gideon lagging behind at a comfortable distance. There was a decided downward grade to the shaft that almost seemed to propel them forward. As they progressed, much to Gideon's relief, the space between the top and bottom of the shaft widened and he could stand upright again. Though he gained more head room the narrow passage did not widen, in fact he felt as if it was growing increasingly narrower. Just as he began to wonder how far the shaft went, it opened into a much wider hallway a few steps ahead.

He could see quite a bit forward now and did not have to walk behind Miguel and Jeddediah. Up ahead was a break in the wall and they all hurried over to it. They discovered a nearly identical break in the other side of the wall which appeared to have been cut by erosion, as the manmade tunnel cut through an old volcanic heat shaft. The shaft was lined from top to bottom by jagged dark rocks. Gideon shined his light over head on what appeared to be a massive red hand print.

"Would you look at that?" he said.

They each shined their light up on the handprint, and Gideon reached up as high as he could and his fingers barely touched the bottom of the palm print. There was another print on the other side of the break in the wall. A look to the opposite wall showed an identical pair of prints near the top of the perpendicular break through the tunnel.

"The Black Legion," Gideon muttered.

"What did you say?" asked Miguel.

"The Black Legion," Gideon repeated. "Legend says that an ancient band of Apache warriors have guarded this region for centuries. They were said to be seven feet tall and ride like ghosts, leaving no trace. They left their mark on stone as a warning to those who might venture into their territory."

"That ain't no Apache," Jeddediah said.

"How do you know?" Gideon questioned defensively.

"Trust me," Jeddediah said. "In any case, we don't want to go mess'n with whatever left that. Let's keep mov'n."

The tunnel turned slightly upward after it crossed beyond the volcanic breaks in the wall. They moved from walking on their heels to treading on their toes, up the barely perceptible incline. Gideon's eyes were trained on the back of Jeddediah's head, but his mind was back in the dark crevasse marked by the ominous handprints. Who put them there? Was it the Black Legion or something else? Whoever and whatever it was, their handprint was at least twice the size of Gideon's and they had stretched to lengths he could barely reach. He imagined that the volcanic crevasse must have pre-dated the tunnel as there had not been volcanic activity in that area for several millennia. Before he could formulate a theory, the group came to an abrupt stop and Gideon had to pull up to avoid running into the smelly old miner.

"What's the deal?" he asked.

"It just stops," replied Miguel.

Gideon peaked over his shoulder into what appeared to be a closet carved out of the earth. In front of them were shelves dug out of the dirt with matching dirt shelves on the side walls. The shelves were empty except for scattered fragments of wood and cloth that lay haphazardly on the floor. Jeddediah stepped forward toward the most prominent shelf in front of them as he solemnly laid the pick axe on the empty flat surface and placed his palm face down next to it. Gideon's heart sank as he realized this was the end of the line and whatever had been left here was long gone.

"No," Gideon said as he pushed his way past Miguel into the empty hold. He turned and looked around at the dejected faces of the miner and the man in the cloak.

"This can't be," Miguel said to no one in particular, with his blank expression trained on the empty shelf in front of him.

"Hells bells!" Jeddediah exclaimed as he threw his hat to the floor. "All this for noth'n."

"No," Miguel said with a suddenly wild-eyed stare. "It's got to be here. We can dig. It's probably hidden somewhere in the tunnel."

"Dig with what?" Gideon said. "And any digging we do could lead to a cave in. Besides Liz doesn't have time for that. We've got hours to make it to the top of Flatiron before sunrise."

"And appease her kidnapper with what?" Miguel said with a gesture around to the empty closet.

"With the truth," Gideon said. "The treasure, if there ever was one, is long gone."

"That won't work," Miguel said.

"Well it's all I've got," Gideon replied. "You can stay and dig your own grave for all I care, I'm going."

Miguel slid to the side and pushed Jeddediah all the way into the room next to Gideon. He pulled a pistol out from under his cloak and leveled it at the two of them.

"Nobody is going anywhere until I say so," he seethed with a dark demeanor that Gideon had not expected. The man in the cloak had been mysterious, certainly, but his actions and speech up until that moment had been far from hostile.

"Everyone has a gun out here but me," Gideon sighed as he raised his hands.

"Well I did, 'til ya took it," Jeddediah said as he too placed his hands over his head. "Bet your wish'n I had it back now."

"Enough," Miguel threatened. "We're going to stay down here until I find the gold or until we've dug out this entire tunnel. Do you understand?"

"Is this what you did to Glenn?" Gideon asked. "Did you shoot him when he wouldn't help you?"

"I didn't have to," Miguel replied. "He was all too willing."

"All right," Gideon said behind squinted eyes. "It's answer time. How do you know Glenn?"

"I met him out here," Miguel replied.

"Out here, when?" Gideon asked.

"After the old man delivered the journal, I read it from cover to cover and discovered there were pages missing," Miguel said. "I came to the Superstitions in search of the missing pieces to the puzzle."

"Was this before or after you last saw Glenn?" Gideon asked Jeddediah.

"After," Jeddediah replied. "I visited San Xavier a couple months before I met Glenn."

"I arrived at a ranch where I was told there was a man who could take me into the mountains," Miguel continued. "There was no one there so I waited all day. Just after nightfall, I heard voices arguing and I took cover in the back of a pickup truck. They spoke of a key, a clue and a treasure. Before I knew it, the truck started up and roared down the dirt road. I thought about leaping out but there was a gunshot back at the ranch, so I stayed put."

"Glenn was driving the truck," Gideon asserted. Miguel nodded and continued his story.

"He drove to a house and parked the truck in the driveway," Miguel said. "After he was inside I climbed out of the back and crouched beneath the lone window with the lights on. I heard him talking but could not make out exactly what was said. He appeared to be having a conversation with himself. Then there was prolonged silence, outside of some shuffling here and there. Then I heard second softer voice and there was an argument. The front door opened and I froze beneath the window. Glenn walked out to the mail box, shoved a letter inside and lifted the flag. I quickly jumped back into the bed of the truck and hid among the shadows and camping supplies. He tore off down the road, back toward the mountains, only not back to the ranch."

"He drove to the face of the mountain," Gideon said.

"Yes," replied Miguel. "He waited in the truck until just before sunrise and then started his hike to the top. I waited several minutes and followed him from a good distance. By the time I reached the top he had already begun to make markings on the rocks with a piece of chalk and frantically moved from place to place. He disappeared behind a large group of boulders and I came out of my hiding place to investigate. I found him placing a canister in the ground and startled him. However, once I showed him the journal and explained who I was he told me everything."

"What everyth'n?" Jeddediah asked.

"He told me of you and the cowboy, the key and the clues he was to leave," Miguel said. "He also told me of the cowboy's betrayal and how he feared for his life. Then he told me he was leaving breadcrumbs for his friend, who he knew would come after him if anything went wrong."

Gideon thought of the faith Glenn had placed in him. He was ashamed it had taken him so long to come looking and that he had initially missed the message altogether. The thought that Glenn had counted on him to come and rescue him, and that he had failed to do so was bore down on him like a boulder on top of his heart. Gideon closed his eyes tightly and tried to push aside the pain. His thoughts turned to Liz and how she too was counting on him. He opened his eyes and set a resolute glare on the man in the cloak.

"And did something go wrong?" he asked. "What did you do to Glenn?"

"I did nothing to Glenn," Miguel said coolly. "I only told him the truth."

"What truth?" Jeddediah asked.

"That by rights that treasure was mine," Miguel said. "I am Don Miguel Velasquez, a descendant of Francisco Noel Velasquez, whose journal this is."

Miguel pulled the journal from beneath the cloak and held it up into the glow of their flashlights. Gideon focused his attention on the bright beam of his own flashlight and all at once a plan so simple came into his mind. He was upset he had not thought of it sooner, he could temporarily blind their captor with the light and wrestle the gun from his hand. No sooner had the thought arrived, however, than it was dismissed as the closed quarters made it more likely that someone might get shot in the scuffle.

The same idea must have dawned on Jeddediah though, because he shined his light into Miguel's eyes and lunged at him. An ear-piercing shot rang out into the tiny hold as Gideon joined the struggle for the weapon. His ears were still ringing when he heard a distant roar from back down the tunnel. The three of them froze and turned to look back into the darkness from where the chilling sound came from.

"What was that?" asked Gideon.

No answer was given as the fight over the gun resumed. Jeddediah released his grasp on the pistol, leaving the conflict between Gideon and Miguel. The old miner disappeared briefly behind Gideon and returned a moment later leveling a thunderous blow to Miguel's skull with the broadside of the pick axe. The man in the cloak immediately collapsed in a heap on the ground. Both he and Jeddediah stood over the fallen man, breathing heavily.

Jeddediah dropped the pick on the ground with a thud. When Miguel did not immediately move Gideon knelt down and placed his ear near his blood-stained face.

"He's still breathing," Gideon stated. "What was that sound?"

"We stand here much longer an' you'll get a personal an' unpleasant answer to that question," Jeddediah replied. "Let's git while we still can."

"What about him?" Gideon asked. "We can't leave him here?"

"Do ya want to save your girl or don't ya?" Jeddediah demanded.

The old miner stepped around Gideon and the unconscious man in the cloak and started back down the tunnel. Gideon shined his light on the pick next to their cloaked assailant and thought of all the time and effort spent to find it.

"You're just going to leave the key?" Gideon asked. Jeddediah stopped and turned back to give it another look.

"Like he said, by rights it's his," the old miner stated with a hint of remorse, as he once more turned his back on Gideon and his long sought prize.

Without another word of protest, Gideon followed after him, with Miguel's pistol still in hand. Jeddediah did not stop when he reached the break in the wall. Gideon paused briefly as he thought he heard what sounded like pebbles dropping back up in the volcanic crevasse beyond the giant red handprints. Whether it was his imagination or not he could not tell and his body trembled all the same, not caring for a distinction. He clenched the pistol tightly as he closed the gap between himself and the old miner.

They reached the opening to the world above and were greeting by a black sky and rain falling through the space between the boulders. Jeddediah slid out first followed closely by Gideon, whose heart and mind were racing with the terrible possibilities that lie behind him. With the rain beating down on his shoulders, he pulled his legs out of the tunnel before anything real or imagined could lay hold on them. He stood up quickly and helped Jeddediah to his feet.

Even beneath the storm clouds and the dark canopy of night there was still a faint perception of light that they had not enjoyed in their journey beneath the earth. Jeddediah nodded to Gideon and they both turned toward the horses.

"We need to decide what we're going to say to Cal," Gideon said.

"Or ya could just give it to me straight," a voice spoke from the darkness to their left.

FINAL RESTING PLACE

A cold chill shot down Gideon's spine as they turned and shined their lights on a slow approaching black horse with two riders. Liz shielded her eyes and Cal raised his gun in their direction.

"Lower them lights," Cal ordered. They complied and aimed the bright beams near the flanks of the dark stead but Gideon had instinctively raised the pistol in his hand to meet Cal's.

"What happened to meeting at the top of Flatiron?" Gideon asked.

"Well that was the plan, wasn't it?" Cal said. "Plans change. A helicopter passed over head a few hours after we broke up. I figured it was on its way to Joe and his boy but when I saw the lights of a second chopper sweep'n up the valley I figured that one was for us, so we made out right quick."

"How did you find us?" Gideon questioned, as he made eye contact with Liz. She looked worried and wet but otherwise unharmed. He realized that, with the cowboy tucked safely back behind her, his gun threatened her more than him.

"We knew you was up here 'round Herman's Mountain," Cal explained. "We was just pok'n 'round seeing what we could see when we heard a distant gunshot and an unholy bellow. We swung 'round the bend just in time to see your lights come out of your little hole there. Seems good fortune has at last smiled down upon me."

"I wouldn't be so sure," Jeddediah said. "There ain't no gold."

"What do ya mean there ain't no gold?" Cal demanded.

"It's a dead end," Gideon said. "If there was gold, it's gone."

"You're ly'n," Cal shouted.

"Go see for yourself," Gideon said as he gestured back to the opening behind them.

"How 'bout ya drop that pea-shooter 'fore we make a mess of this pretty little thing between us," Cal turned his gun and pointed it at the side of Liz's head. Gideon immediately threw the pistol to the side and raised his arms over head. Jeddediah spit to the side in contempt.

"Now back up," Cal ordered. They each took several steps away as Cal maneuvered his horse closer. The cowboy lowered Liz down from the saddle and swung himself off after her, without taking his eyes off the old miner. Liz folded her arms across her chest and bowed her head as Cal pulled her back to him.

"Good call, hombre," Cal said. "No need for a shootout 'tween old friends."

Gideon lamented how briefly he had been armed and wished he had made better use of his weapon while he had it. But he could only dream of a scenario where his discharging the firearm had a happy ending. Cal had one arm wrapped around Liz's neck and the other extended out toward Gideon and Jeddediah with the barrel of his revolver alternating between them. He looked back and forth between his targets and the entrance to the tunnel behind them. All at once, he shoved Liz in Gideon's direction, as he reached down for the gun Gideon had surrendered. She stumbled and Gideon leapt forward and caught her in his arms.

"Show me," Cal ordered and waved both guns toward the opening in the ground.

Gideon looked down at the brown eyed girl and smiled. She smiled back up at him and a warmth grew inside him and fought back the cold wet night. He turned back toward Cal with Liz still in his arms.

"I'm not going back down there," he said. "If you want to see, you're on your own."

"You still don't get it," Cal said. "You ain't in charge here. You're gonna do exactly as I say or you're gonna watch your girl die."

He looked back down at Liz and remembered his previous threats on her life. Although he had not followed through on his original threat, Gideon did not think it was prudent to provoke him.

"If the helicopters are looking for us they'll come here," Gideon warned. "Juan Carlos, Tara, Todd and Joe all knew this is where we were headed."

"That may be true, but it's likely they had to put down when the storm set in," Cal replied with a wave of his pistols toward the opening in the ground.

"All you're gonna find down there is trouble," Gideon said.

"Well, I brought something for that trouble," Cal said as he reached back and removed the saddlebag from his horse. He slipped it over his shoulder and motioned for them to move. "Now hush your mouth and get go'n."

Gideon turned around as Liz moved slowly out from under his arm. She took him by the hand and the two of them made their way, through the rain, toward the entrance to the underworld. Jeddediah followed quietly on their heels with Cal lagging behind like a cattleman herding sheep.

"Are you okay?" Gideon whispered to Liz. "Did he hurt you?"

"No," she replied softly. "He spent most of the time trying to convince me that all this was justified. Gideon, what was that roar we heard?"

"I don't know," said Gideon. "I'm afraid we're about to find out."

They stopped at the ledge that led down to the opening in the boulders. Cal swung around to their left to examine the cross, still embedded atop the four hump rock. When he turned to face the entrance head on an ominous thunderbolt echoed off the mountain to the north and caused Liz and Gideon to flinch. To add to Gideon's shame, he noticed that the miner and the cowboy were not rattled in the least by the unexpected noise. With Liz by his side, he wished he could have remained as steady and unshakable as these two hardened souls.

"A'right," Cal said. "The girl's gonna go first, you two step back and I'll follow after her. When I say so, ya come down one at a time. Understand?"

Gideon knew it was pointless to argue, so he simply nodded and squeezed Liz's hand one last time before he let go. He handed her his flashlight and she accepted it with a forced smile as she moved in front of the entrance. She sat down on the wet rock and slipped through the gap between the boulders. Cal waved Jeddediah and Gideon back further and kept both pistols trained on them as he followed behind her.

"A'right, come down," he shouted over the rain.

"Follow my lead," Jeddediah said as he grabbed hold of Gideon's arm and held him back.

Gideon reluctantly conceded and let the old miner go ahead of him down into the tunnel. A part of him was relieved to be back in the warmer, dryer confines of the shaft but he feared his relief would be short lived. They would shortly be confronted with either an empty treasure hold, an unconscious man in a cloak, or perhaps something louder and scarier. His feet had no sooner hit the ground when Jeddediah set off down the tunnel. Gideon pulled a small backup flashlight from his pocket and turned it on, thankful once more for Todd's preparation. Cal motioned for Liz to go next and then for Gideon to follow her. The cowboy kept his guns so close to Gideon's back that, though they did not touch him, he could almost feel the barrels on his spine.

All at once, it occurred to Gideon that he, Liz and Jeddediah held the only lights in the dark tunnel with Cal's hands full of revolvers. He had only just begun to formulate a way to communicate to his co-captives when they reached the breach in the wall beneath the giant handprints. Jeddediah stopped and shined his light on the prints above the opening to their left.

"These marks show the way," Jeddediah stated. He turned around and with wide eyes gave a subtle nod to Gideon. Only then did he understand what the old miner meant when he told him to follow his lead. Although he was developing a plan of his own, he decided to go along with Jeddediah for the time being.

"Yeah, supposedly this is the mark of the Black Legion," Gideon said. "We figure this was meant to scare off anyone who might stumble onto their hiding place."

"Well, lead the way then," Cal ordered impatiently.

Ultimately, Gideon worried for what awaited them in the ancient volcanic crevasse, but he hoped it would buy them some time. Jeddediah was the first to cross the threshold and stepped on the crumbly black rocks. They followed in the same order, as Gideon was determined to keep between Cal and Liz. He returned his thoughts to how he might communicate their advantage without alerting the gun toting cowboy. His concern was, that even if he could signal them to turn their lights off simultaneously, a couple of erratic shots in the narrow crevasse might hit, harm, or even kill Liz, Jeddediah, or himself. Unless he was certain he could immediately disarm Cal, there was no point in forcing his hand. Still, with each step they took, deeper into the unknown, he worried they would eventually have to face the potential of gunfire anyway. Gideon kept his eyes up, and trained his ears down the shaft for signs of anything beyond the crunching of their feet atop the volcanic surface. The shaft was just wider than his shoulders which he was grateful for. The temperature was cool, but not cold, like it was an ancient ventilation system. Jeddediah led the way forward as if he actually knew where he was headed. They passed a couple of smaller off shoots to their right, which were much narrower and would have been nearly impossible to traverse. But that did not stop Gideon from wondering where they led.

"How much further?" Cal demanded.

"Not far," Jeddediah replied without turning around.

They had already covered a good distance more than they would have if they had continued up the tunnel to the empty closet. Gideon was satisfied he made the right decision going along with Jeddediah. Now, however, he hoped that the old miner had a plan other than aimlessly meandering up the old volcanic passage until they tired or met with the originator of the bone chilling roar. Just then, Jeddediah stopped cold and an impromptu line formed tightly behind them. Gideon peered over the shoulders of Liz and the old miner and saw a distinct fork in the passage with another fork a few feet further beyond the branch to the left. Cal was literally breathing down Gideon's neck.

"Which way?" he asked.

Jeddediah's flashlight went dark and Gideon saw him reach back and take hold of Liz's light.

"My light's out," Jeddediah said just as Liz's light went out too. Before Gideon could react, Cal had raise one pistol to the side of his head and pulled back the hammer.

"Don't even think about it," he threatened. He pointed the other gun toward Liz but kept his eyes set firmly on Gideon. "Turn them lights back on or I'll blow his brains out right here, right now."

Liz quickly obeyed, switched her light on, and pointed it at the side wall. Jeddediah cursed under his breath and turned his light on as well. Cal tucked the revolver in his left hand into the front of his pants, with his sidearm still pinned to Gideon's temple. He then beckoned for Liz to hand over her light. When she did, Cal took several steps back with a flashlight in one hand and a gun in the other.

"Ya thought ya could put one over on me?" he seethed. "I thought we had an understanding. It didn't have to go down like this."

He swung his aim from Gideon to Jeddediah but before he could pull the trigger a dark figure set upon him and laid him out with a single sickening blow. His gun discharged and impacted the rock ceiling above as he collapsed hard to the rocky ground. The man in the cloak stood in the space Cal had vacated, with the pick in his hand. Miguel had a streak of dried blood on the side of his face and breathed heavily as he looked on Gideon with fury and contempt. There was another unholy bellow from up the crevasse, only this time it seemed much louder. Liz turned around to look toward the frightening howl but Gideon and Jeddediah kept their eyes on Miguel.

"Let's get out of here," Liz said.

"You're not going anywhere," Miguel spat.

"Come on Miguel," Gideon protested. "You're in bad shape. Let's get out of here and we'll get you fixed up."

"I'm not leaving here without my birthright," Miguel said as he wielded the pick axe like a knife.

"There's no birthright!" Gideon yelled. "It's gone. We're not going to die down here for some sick obsession, now move!"

Miguel bent down and picked up the revolver, illuminated by the fallen flashlight, lying next to Cal on the ground. He pointed it at Gideon who stopped in his tracks and stepped to the side to shield his friends. The man in the cloak gritted his teeth and spewed hatred at them through his bloodshot eyes. Gideon considered for a moment going with the old light in the eyes trick again but the distance between them was a step too far for him to be sure he could reach him, and lay hold on the gun, before the cloaked maniac could get off a shot.

"Listen, son," Jeddediah spoke up from the back of the group. There was a softness to his voice that seemed entirely foreign to his perpetually gruff demeanor. "It's not worth it. Trust me. It's not worth your life. I died years ago 'cause I gave it all up to chase a thing. I'm still breathing but I ain't been liv'n. It's too late for me, my days are spent, but you can still live. Don't throw it all away for a thing. Don't end up like me."

His words softened the hardened expression on Miguel's face and the anger melted away. Although he still held fast to the pick and the gun, each of them lowered slightly. In the silence that followed, Gideon watched the gun cautiously, and tried to imagine what had brought each of them to this point. He considered his own motivation, his personal desire for discovery and deep down his fantasy of fame and fortune. Until that moment, he had not allowed himself to face what was buried deep within his heart. The truth was he hoped to find Glenn, or at least what had become of him, and that is why he told himself he was there. With Jeddediah's words, Gideon had to face his own personal desire to discover the fabled treasure for selfish reasons.

Before his shame could engulf him, however, an unwelcome sound from the darkness, behind him, cut through the silence and sent a tremor of terror up his spine. A low, strong growl reverberated from up the crevasse. Gideon froze with fear and was unable to force himself to turn around and face it. Liz pressed upon his back and grasped his arm with her trembling hand. The expression on Miguel's face conveyed the horror of their new reality. Death had found them in the darkness. A pungent smell filled the narrow passage, and Gideon would have gagged if his body had not become completely petrified.

"Ya'll git," Jeddediah whispered. "I'll handle this feller."

Gideon had no intention of arguing. A single thought rose above all others and restored his ability to move. *Keep Liz safe.* He reached back, took her by the arm and pulled her beside him. As she shifted next to him a low hungry growl threatened from behind. Suddenly, a tiny bust of light sparked in the blackness near the rock floor. Gideon looked down at the match stick Cal held in his hand. The cowboy lay on his side among the lava rocks that lined the bottom of the crevasse. Cal had a wicked smile on his face as he touched the flame from the matchstick to a long wick that led back into the saddlebag beside him.

"Have some of this, you walking carpet," Cal said as the sparkling wick raced toward the saddlebag.

"You fool," Miguel shouted as he ripped the bag from the fallen cowboy. He turned and looked back toward Gideon as the wick disappeared under the leather flap. Gideon pulled Liz toward him and held her head to his chest. Miguel spun around and hurled the saddlebag down the crevasse, back toward the tunnel, and sprawled out on top of Cal as a loud boom shook the passage and knocked Gideon and Liz to the floor.

Everything went dark and there was an all out assault on Gideon's senses. His eyes were useless in the pitch black. There was tremendous pressure on his ear drums and all he heard since the moment of impact was a low humming buzz. He felt as if the air had all been sucked out of the shaft and left nothing but dust to breathe. The palms of his hands burned from the cuts and scrapes he suffered as he was thrown to the ground, but still he groped around with burning palms for the body that he hoped was still by his side. His fingers grazed against long soft hair and he was relieved when he felt her head move.

"Are you all right?" he asked.

"I think so," Liz replied.

His ears were still plugged, and it sounded as if she were answering from inside a jar. He shook the flashlight in his hand

and a faint light shone through a cloud of dust. Anxious to get up from the jagged bed of lava rocks beneath him, he rolled onto his side and struggled to his feet. As he helped Liz up, he shined the light on the rubble that covered the space where the crevasse used to be. He then shined the light overhead and said a silent prayer that by some miracle they had not been buried in the cave-in that followed the explosion.

"Gideon," Liz said as she pulled on his arm and spun him around.

They looked down on Jeddediah lying motionless on his back. Gideon quickly stooped down to assess the old miner.

"Jed," Gideon shouted as he shook him by the shoulders. "Jed, can you hear me?"

"I done told ya, it's Jeddediah," the old miner answered.

"Sorry," Gideon said. "Are you okay?"

"I've been shot at, held hostage and blowed up," he replied. "What do ya think?"

"Can you move?" Gideon asked with a chuckle.

"Give me a minute," Jeddediah said. "I ain't as young as I used to be."

It was at that moment that Gideon's light shone on the hairy body beyond the old miner. Gideon stood up slowly and pointed the flashlight at the center of the beast. The massive hair-covered monster filled the floor of the crevasse from end to end. Gideon fought hard to suppress a wave of panic that bubbled up from his gut.

"I don't think we've got a minute," Gideon replied as the mountain of hair began to move. He quickly pulled Jeddediah to his feet and surveyed their surroundings. The way back to the tunnel was blocked by the cave-in and their only path forward was blocked by a frightening creature that was stirring. Gideon leapt over the beast bracing himself on the walls of the crevasse. He turned around and motioned for Liz to follow. She deftly skirted the side wall above the monster and landed as soft as a bird by his side. Jeddediah hesitated and glanced over his shoulder at the collapsed rubble behind him.

"Come on," Gideon whispered.

Jeddediah nodded and rubbed his hands together while he sized up the jump. He prepared himself and sprang forward but only rose inches, when feet were required. His boots became tangled in the mess of hair that covered the creature's body and the old miner fell forward helplessly. Gideon reached out and stopped his fall as the monster lurched upward and moaned. He pushed Jeddediah past him, toward Liz and turned around to flee deeper into the crevasse.

They had taken precious few steps when a terrible roar exploded through the crevasse. It was so close Gideon could feel the vibrations on the back of his neck. A hand caught hold of his hoodie and jerked him off his feet. The whiplash from the sudden stop struck him right in the neck before he could even cry out. He impacted the rock floor like a meteor falling to the earth and the pressure on his ears popped. The jagged lava rocks had barely torn into his flesh when the monster was on top of him snarling in his face. Gideon gripped the flashlight close to his chest and illuminated the horror in front of him. Its eyes were set close together and dozens of red blood vessels looked as if they were attacking its black pupils. One eye opened wider than the other and it was clear from the scarring around the smaller eye that it had suffered an injury. Gideon tried to hold his breath to keep at bay the foul stench that dripped from its mouth. Its long hair circled its face like a mange lion's mane. The wrinkles on its bare forehead and exposed cheeks almost gave it a human appearance.

"Gideon!" Liz cried out from behind it.

He could see precious little but the halo of Jeddediah's flashlight framing the enormous beast. Two dull thuds drummed against its back as the light danced above them on the rocky ceiling. The monster howled and spun around with a sweeping motion with its long right arm. For a moment Gideon caught sight of Liz and Jeddediah as they were flung back by the beast. All too quickly the scene was dark again, covered by the large hairy curtain as it rounded on him again. He was pinned down, unable to move or fight back.

The only choice that remained was how he would meet his end. With eyes open Gideon looked directly into the face of this ferocious predator, determined to exit this life as nobly as possible. As he stared up at the razor sharp teeth of the snarling giant he could not help but worry for Liz. He hoped against hope that her final moments would not, in any way, resemble his.

The monster took him by the throat and pulled him up from the rocky surface toward its rage filled face. Strangely, Gideon felt momentary relief as his shoulders were freed from the stabbing volcanic rocks beneath him. He braced himself for the final blow when all at once the growling ceased. The monster's forehead scrunched together as creases in its thick skin formed around the edges of its face. Its broad nose twitched as its nostrils expanded and contracted with each tiny intake of air through the two marble sized holes in his face. Gideon had scarcely breathed from the moment he was set upon and could only guess at what the creature was sniffing at. The beast dropped its head down to Gideon's stomach and stiffed more vigorously.

With its gigantic hand, it reached into the front pocket of his hoodie and ripped out a canvas hat with a floppy neck cover. The monster held the hat to its nose and inhaled deeply. It released Gideon and looked back and forth between him and the hat. Gideon sat up slightly and shined the light more fully on the hat. He was not sure what intrigued this creature about Glenn's old canvas hat but was grateful it distracted the beast from its intent to maim and kill him. The monster reached back slowly to Gideon and stroked the top of his head before it withdrew its hand quickly in disgust. Then, without warning, the monster turned quickly and stepped over Liz and Jeddediah who had not yet recovered from being bowled over. Gideon rolled up unto his knees and shined the light up the crevasse after the departed monster.

"What happened?" Liz asked.

"I don't know," Gideon replied. "It acted like it smelled something and just took Glenn's hat from my pocket and left."

"Are you okay?" she asked.

"I'm all right," he replied. "How 'bout you?"

"My tailbone is a little sore and I've scraped up my arm pretty good but I'll live," she said.

"I'm fine too," Jeddediah piped up from behind the concerned couple. "Thanks for ask'n."

Gideon stood up and he and Liz helped Jeddediah to his feet. He and Liz grinned at each other and Gideon was happy they were both alive and well, despite the calamity they had faced today.

"Well!" Jeddediah yelped at a higher octave to draw their attention to him. "What now?"

Gideon shined the light one last time at the collapsed crevasse behind him. It was a solid wall of rock and dirt with no sign of a gap or breaks anywhere. He doubted there was any chance that Miguel or Cal had survived the blast or the fall out afterwards. Although he would not have wished them dead, he was relieved neither of them could threaten them further. He turned his light back up the crevasse where the monster had strode into the darkness.

"Looks like we've got one option," Gideon said with a wave of his flashlight.

"Sure," Jeddediah said. "Why not? Let's follow the abominable dirt man up into the dark unknown. What could go wrong?"

"Hey, you brought us this way," Gideon replied. "What was your plan?"

"I hoped we could lose the cowboy back here," Jeddediah said.

"Did you account for the howling monster in your master plan?" Gideon asked.

"I figure we was goners anyway," Jeddediah answered. "Thought there was a chance it'd eat ya'll and be too stuffed to bother with a gamey old man."

"Nice, real nice," Gideon said as he shook his head.

Cautiously, he stepped around Liz and the old miner and made his way up the crevasse. Liz reached up and took hold of his free hand as she followed behind him. Gideon had no idea what was waiting for them, or if they would ever see the light of day again. Despite the unknown, Gideon was grateful he and Liz would face it together, them and a grumpy, smelly old miner.

"Ain't nobody gonna hold my hand?" Jeddediah asked with childlike sincerity.

Liz reached back and took hold of his free hand and the group pressed on like an awkward preschool class on a frightening field trip. Gideon listened carefully for any sign of the monster as they made their way further and further into the ancient volcanic shaft. The crevasse bent sharply to the left and Gideon spotted the hairy back of the beast in the distance. It turned back and looked into his light with an unhappy grunt. Gideon lowered his light and waited for its shadow to move forward down the crevasse. There were no off shoots for them to take in a different direction. They could only follow after the gigantic creature and hope their presence would not anger it. Silently, they moved deeper into the unknown at an intentionally slow pace, as to not happen upon the monster unexpectedly. Minutes passed with no sign of their giant hairy nightmare, which was somehow worse than catching sight of it in the distant shaft beyond.

"Gideon?" Liz whispered.

"Yeah," he answered softly.

"I'm scared," she said.

"Me too," Gideon replied.

"Me too," Jeddediah chimed in from the back.

"It could be worse," Gideon said. "We could be doing this in the pitch black."

"Don't even joke about that," Liz rebuked him.

"Everything's gonna be fine," Gideon assured them. "Glenn used to say 'In time, every misadventure becomes a great story'."

"That's only if you survive to tell it," Liz said.

Their conversation halted along with their march as Gideon's light found a break in the wall ahead. He shined his light on the ground as they approached the breach. A low rhythmic breathing came from the hole in the wall as they drew closer. Gideon's hand trembled as he shuffled his feet sideways toward the opening. He turned back to Liz and Jeddediah with a nod before he stepped out to face whatever awaited them. Slowly, he lifted his light to the center of the room and it shined on the hairy back of the beast. It stood over a large pile of rocks, up against a wall at the far side of the garage sized room. In its hand, it still held Glenn's floppy canvas hat. Gideon let go of Liz's hand and began to step through the threshold.

"Gideon no," Liz whispered.

"It's okay," Gideon replied.

The monster's shoulders rose gently up and down with each breath. He kept his light trained on its back as he approached to its left. The long rock pile was nearly knee high and stretched at least as long as Gideon's wingspan. On top of the rock lay a red hiking daypack with a canteen hanging off the side and a granola bar wrapper sticking out of the top. Gideon wondered what it was about this pile that caused the monster to reverence it in this way. Then in one calm motion the beast knelt down and placed the white canvas hat on top of the pile of rocks, just above the daypack. This colossal creature patted the hat gently with its enormous hand.

Gideon's heart skipped a beat and he covered his mouth as the realization dawned on him. Tears welled up in his eyes and his jaw began to quiver as a deep and profound sadness overwhelmed him.

"Glenn," Gideon whispered, with his tear-filled eyes set on the canvas hat atop the rocky grave.

WHERE IT LEADS

With an outstretched hand Gideon approached the mound of rocks, unconcerned with the monstrous figure that towered above the stone pile. He knelt down beside it and placed both hands on the large lava rocks.

"Gideon, what are you doing?" Liz whisper-yelled frantically.

"It's Glenn," Gideon replied.

"What?" she questioned.

"Gen," the beast grunted.

Gideon snapped his head around and stared up at the hairy giant. With his head unconsciously cocked to the side, Gideon knelt in stunned silence at what he thought he heard. It almost sounded as if this creature had said Glenn's name. It reached out its giant hands and placed them on the rocks next to Gideon's.

"Gen," the creature repeated in a low rough grunt.

"Did that thing just say Glenn?" Liz asked as she entered the crude tomb.

"I think so," Gideon said without taking his eyes off the beast. He was amazed at the turn of events that had led them here and could not wrap his mind around the reality of their discoveries. Liz settled in to Gideon's left and placed her hand on his forearm. The creature to his right stood up slowly and its head nearly scraped the top of the stone ceiling.

"Well I'll be," Jeddediah said from the corner of the room. "Would ya look at this?"

Gideon turned and shined his light to where Jeddediah stood. The old miner looked down on an array of trinkets and treasures, lined up in neat rows and stacked on top of one another. There were precious metals and bars of gold next to gems and intricate crosses made of silver. Embedded in the volcanic rock wall just behind the treasure row was a thick band of sparkling white quartz.

"Ho-ly crap," Gideon and Liz gawked in unison.

Jeddediah bent down and reached for one of the gold bricks in the row. He had no sooner done so when the monster exploded in a fit of rage. A terrible scream filled the room and they all had to cover their ears from the high decimal level. With two bounds the beast was over top of the old miner and swept him to the side with one terrible blow. Jeddediah flew several feet and landed with a sickening thud near Gideon and Liz. Quickly, Gideon threw himself between Jeddediah and the monster with his hands raised submissively over his head. The monster screamed at them with its back against its treasure and its arms raised to the side in a shielding stance. The scream melded into a snarling growl as the once reverent creature had transformed in an instant back to the nightmare.

"Whoah," Gideon said. "Easy. Easy. Friends. Glenn."

He hovered his raised arms in the direction of the pile of rocks.

"Glenn," he said again slowly. "You know Glenn. Glenn was my friend. Our friend."

The creature snorted and snuffed through its nose with its sharp teeth bear. Gideon's heart raced as he tried to remain calm. He knew in an instant this beast could tear them all apart and feared there was no reasoning with it.

"Jed, are you all right?" he asked, with his eyes still trained on the heavy breathing monster.

"For the last time, it's Jeddediah," the old miner replied as he lifted his head off the floor.

"He's fine," Liz replied.

"If we're all gonna stay that way, we need to get out of here," Gideon said. "Stand up and head for the opening."

"What about you?" Liz asked.

"I'll be right behind you," Gideon replied. "Just go."

With its long arms still extended to guard its treasure, the beast slid sideways to mirror the movements of Liz and Jeddediah as they exited the nook out into the passageway. Gideon stayed still and faced his hairy foe until his friends were back out in the ancient volcanic hallway. Cautiously, he inched his way toward the rocky grave to his left. The beast snarled at him and eyed him suspiciously. Gideon reached out for Glenn's floppy canvas hat. He stopped short as the snarling accelerated and became more aggressive. It was clear that this monster was very possessive of what he deemed to be his and Gideon thought it best not to challenge its claim.

"We're going," Gideon said as he slid meekly away from his friend's final resting place. "Take good care of him."

He crouched as low as he could while still being able to exit the monster's treasure store. Liz and Jeddediah waited anxiously on the other side of the opening. Gideon backed his way to them with his eyes locked with the unpredictable creature still guarding its treasure.

"All right," Gideon whispered, out of the side of his mouth. "Let's go."

"Go where?" Liz whispered back. They all had their eyes set on the growling beast in the dark room.

"The only where we can go," Gideon replied. "Forward."

He reached into his back pocket and removed the bent and damp football card and held it in the light. With a slow but deliberate motion Gideon took one step over the threshold and laid the card on the rock floor between himself and the beast.

"Glenn," Gideon said clearly as he shined his light down on the card and backed out of the treasure chamber. He was sure to keep his eyes on the beast in search of some sign of recognition. Besides a slight calming of its breathing, the hairy giant gave no clue as to how his peace offering was received.

Slowly, they all backed up the crevasse until they could no longer see inside the room and the creature was blocked from view by the jagged rock wall of the crevasse. Gideon turned and gestured for Jeddediah to lead the way. The old miner nodded and made his way up into the unknown, as if he knew where he was going. Liz followed after him with Gideon bringing up the rear. He made frequent checks behind them to ensure they were not being followed. They made their way with purpose further and further down the rocky hallway. Several minutes later the passageway came to an abrupt end. The group stared in stunned silence at the jagged rocky slope that rose up to the ceiling above them. Gideon fought back the panic that rose from his chest and formed a throbbing lump in his throat.

"That's it," Liz said. "The end of the line."

Jeddediah spun around and sat on the rocky floor with his legs crisscrossed over top one another. He began to laugh uncontrollably, with his face toward the ground, while he pulled softly at his beard.

"What is your deal?" Gideon questioned the old miner.

"She's right," Jeddediah chuckled. "We're done for. This is the end."

"Stop laughing," Gideon ordered. "We've got to keep our wits about us or this will be the end."

"Are your wits gonna dig your way outta this?" Jeddediah asked.

"There's always a way out," Gideon replied. He remembered the last words Joe had said to them before they split up. If there was one thing he had learned from Joe's crazy stories of adventure it was that even when things looked bleak there was always another play, another move or another player they had simply not considered yet. He spoke with full faith and did not doubt the truth of his words. There was a way out. They simply had to find it.

"Gideon, let's say a prayer," Liz said. She reached out her hand and took hold of his. They knelt on the rough ground, with the jagged volcanic rocks digging into their knees. "Jeddediah, come and join us."

The old miner grimaced at them for a few seconds before he eventually complied and rolled up unto his knees. Liz took hold of his hand as well and bowed her head. Jeddediah removed his hat and he and Gideon bowed their heads in turn.

"Heavenly Father," Liz began, as if she were speaking to a fourth member of their prayer circle. "We are thankful to be alive. We ask that thou wilt receive the souls of Cal and Miguel and forgive them of their offenses toward us. Please bless Joe that he will receive the care he requires and recover from his wounds. We are in need of thy care and direction, Father. We know that if it be thy will thou wilt deliver us from this place and the dangers that lie within. Father, we ask that thou will be merciful unto us and lead us safely back to our family and friends. In the name of Jesus Christ, amen."

"Amen," Gideon agreed with his head still bowed and his eyes still closed.

"Oh, uh, yeah, same for me Father," Jeddediah added.

Gideon lifted his head and was met with an unexpected look of fear on Liz's face. When Jeddediah finished adjusting his hat and looked up, a similar look of despair broke across his face. It was at that moment that Gideon smelled the now familiar stench they had only just left.

He turned around slowly and pointed his flashlight at the center of the monster's hairy stomach. With nowhere to run Gideon did the only thing he could think of. He stood up slowly and raised his arms to shield his friends. The monster stood up to its full height and clenched its massive fists. Gideon had faced certain death before and his practiced response almost came natural. With his eyes open, and his jaw tight, he breathed through his nose and summoned a calm that only came through complete acceptance of the fact that he was not in control.

"Auhh," the monster grunted. It turned its body sideways and whipped its head back down the crevasse from where they had come. Then it turned around and headed back into the darkness. After only a couple of steps it turned back to them and grunted again with a similar head gesture.

"I think it wants us to follow it," Liz said.

"That's what it looks like," Gideon agreed.

"Ya might want to pray a little louder next time darl'n, and remember to include a menac'n Bigfoot on our list of deliverances," Jeddediah said.

"Come on," said Gideon. "I think it's trying to help."

"What gives ya that idea?" Jeddediah asked. "It could be leading us to supper, like lambs to the slaughter."

"If it wanted us dead it could've kill us right here," Gideon replied.

"Yeah but then it'd have to drag us to the dinner table," Jeddediah said. "I ain't interested in sav'n it the trouble. If it wants to eat me it's gonna have to earn its meal."

"Come on, you crazy old coot," Gideon said. "Have faith."

Liz took Gideon by the hand and the two of them moved toward their impatient monstrous guide. It gave a slight nod to them as they drew nearer and then looked back at Jeddediah. The old miner stood like a stubborn statue with his hands on his hips. Gideon and Liz turned and followed the monster's gaze back toward Jeddediah. The three of them stood quietly and waited for him to make his choice.

"Oh all right," Jeddediah yelped with a spastic shake his arms. "But if it eats us I'll never forgive ya."

Jeddediah shuffled over to them like a petulant child and Gideon shook his head and smiled at the pouting old man. With another grunt and a huff, the monster led the way back down the crevasse. Gideon held fast to Liz's hand as they hurried behind the long legged beast. They had not traveled far at all when the monster stopped and stuck its arm through a crack they had not seen on the flight through the dark crevasse. Its hair smooshed in the narrow slit and was brushed backwards as it squeezed through a previously unseen offshoot.

Gideon, Liz and Jeddediah fit much more naturally through the secreted opening than their oversized guide but this crevasse remained much more confining than the volcanic crevasse they had been traveling through. This new passageway appeared to be formed from solid rock and the surfaces of the floor, walls and ceiling were smooth and cold. The curious creature in front of them filled the hall from end to end and top to bottom. All that Gideon could do was follow the wall of hair and stink, as each step was revealed in the wake of its monstrous stride.

"Gideon?" Liz whispered.

"Yeah," he replied.

"Where do you think it's taking us?" she asked.

"Out, I hope," Gideon replied.

"First, I thought it was going to kill us," Liz said. "Then I thought you were connecting with it, then I thought it was going to kill us again and now it seems to be helping us. I don't get it."

"There's noth'n to get," Jeddediah piped up from behind them. "There's no reason'n with a creature like this. It does what it pleases and that's it."

"I think there's more to it than that," Gideon argued. "Clearly, he knows Glenn and Glenn means something to him. I think we're benefitting from that. He cares."

"He?" Liz asked.

"Or she," Gideon smiled.

"I don't think that's a girl," Liz said.

"It cares only for that treasure back there," Jeddediah said. "You saw the way he guards it. If he's lead'n us out of here it's only to get us away from his gold."

"That may be true but there's got to be more to it than that," Gideon replied. "Explain the memorial he built for Glenn."

Jeddediah did not immediately answer, as they pressed forward through the narrow confines. Gideon imagined for himself a dozen ways in which Glenn had come into the company of this beastly figure. It had to have been more than a brief encounter, or a murderous end, for the creature to have buried him in such a way and remembered his scent. He hoped that however Glenn had passed away that it had been peaceful, or at least quick, and that he had not suffered. In his mind, Gideon imagined that, in his final moments, Glenn had been cared for by this hairy enigma.

"Where do you suppose he comes from?" Liz asked breaking the long silence.

"Dunno," Gideon said. "There are a ton of myths and legends fit. Could be Bigfoot or the Mogollon Monster, maybe it was a man at one point."

"A man?" she asked.

"It was a man," Jeddediah stated as a matter of fact.

"How do you know?" Liz questioned.

"Only man's greed could come to this," the old miner replied. "Obsession can twist the mind, kill the soul, and even warp your very nature. I seen it in its eyes. The look."

"The look?" asked Gideon.

"The same look old Miguel had," Jeddediah said. "The lust what drove the cowboy to his end. I've born that lust in my heart and I'm sure I've wore that look myself. No doubt Glenn saw it on my face the last he laid eyes on me. I'm 'shamed to say the difference 'tween me and the miserable creature ain't as much as I'd like to believe. This is where it leads."

Jeddediah gestured up ahead toward their hairy guide. Gideon considered the smelly bearded recluse and all he had said. Though there were undeniable parallels between the miner and the beast, Gideon would not have connected them on his own, due to the exaggerated extreme of the cave dwelling monster. But when Jeddediah laid it out before him it was hard to argue.

"So, if you were this creature where would you be taking us?" Gideon asked him.

"Like I said, as far away from my treasure as possible," Jeddediah replied.

The monster had not looked back once since they entered the narrow passage. Gideon imagined it was due to the confined space they navigated through, which was particularly confining to the plus sized creature. There were a couple of occasions where even Gideon had to turn sideways to continue onward and he wondered how the walking mountain of fur managed to make its way through.

"This must go back for miles," Liz remarked, after what seemed liked several hours of huffing and puffing up and down the rock terrain of the subterranean hallway.

Twice they had to climb to the top of a rocky shelf several feet above their heads, which the monster had ascended with ease.

The passage stayed mostly narrow and confining but had widened briefly into a small oval room with several branches in different directions. They did not have time to explore the space, as their hairy leader had taken the offshoot to the left and continued on down a passage just as narrow as the first. It led them to a rather significant drop off which they had to work together to get down without falling. From that point their path forward was decidedly upward at a steadily rising incline.

"I reckon it does," Jeddediah replied. "I first run into this furry feller some ten odd miles from where we entered the tunnel. It was in a shaft that led back underground in a canyon. It's where I found the key, among a small collection of junk that must've belonged to it."

"Are you saying there's an interconnected group of natural tunnels under the Superstitions?" Gideon asked.

"Along with some manmade ones," Jeddediah asserted. "Yeah."

"It's hard to believe nobody has found them in all this time," Gideon said.

"Who says they didn't," Jeddediah argued. "Them Spanish priests seemed to cut a tunnel right through one. Somehow Glenn found himself down here. What if the folks that disappeared just stumbled into the wrong shaft and run into Hairy McStanky Britches up there?"

Had he not found himself currently buried among legend, treasure, mystery, death, monsters, and secret passages, he would have been delighted to have learned of such a tale and doubly thrilled to know it was all true. A proper appreciation for these strange circumstances would have to wait until they were once again safe above ground. He began to worry about the ever diminishing batteries in their flashlights. They had already burned hours, off what he hoped were fully charges batteries, and he feared finding himself in total darkness, an experience he preferred not to relive.

"Gideon?" Liz asked from behind him.

"Yeah," Gideon replied.

"Why did you get that tattoo?" she asked.

His secret keeping mechanisms were nearly overridden by his desire to share the whole truth with her. After he quickly weighed the ramifications of breaking a trust, passed down through the centuries, and sharing a secret not entirely his own, integrity dictated that he keep his true reasons from the girl he loved.

"It has special meaning," Gideon began. "There's an old African proverb about a beautiful bird named Sankofa, who left her village to see the world. She was captured and carried away to be stripped of her brightly colored feathers and kept her in a cage. In time she forgot who she was and where she came from. When her captors took all they could from her, they released her among serpents who told her she was a serpent. She believed them and stayed grounded even after her feathers grew back, until one day she met a young bird from her village. He brought her home and reminded her who she was and showed her where she came from."

He paused his storytelling as they passed through a wide-open room with several offshoots. Before he could stop and look around their tall hairy guide disappeared through the tunnel straight ahead of them. His desire to explore their new surroundings were trumped by his fear of being lost, or upsetting the beast, so he quickly hurried after it. Once inside the tunnel he continued the story.

"She had seen too much of the world to stay in the village, so she left," Gideon went on. "But from then on she always kept her head facing back to where she'd come from. That's Sankofa. Look to the past as you move forward."

"You've got to remember who you are to know where you're going," Liz said.

"That's right," Gideon replied.

They continued on down the tunnel and in spite of the sweat and trudging Gideon felt a degree of joy that she understood. There was something about Sankofa that rang true to the soul. He felt this was a gateway to sharing the entirety of his secret with her.

"But if you're flying toward the future with your head stuck in the past, there's the potential you'll miss out on the present," she thoughtfully replied.

His heart sank as if her words pressed down on it. Gideon had spent much of his time looking to the past and preparing for the future. The past had even sidetracked his trip home, which was supposed to shape his future. Unable to refute her statement he simply continued forward with her words haunting his steps.

As he looked in front of him at the hairy back of their beastly guide, he wondered how it made its way around in the darkness. Before he could finish that thought, however, the passageway widened and soft light poured down on them from above. The beast stepped to one side of a rectangular room where the passage came to a dead end. Three stone walls rose straight up to a crack high above them, which framed beautifully a star covered blanket from the night sky. Fresh air filled his lungs as he gratefully breathed in the cold winter night.

"We're gonna make it," Gideon whispered.

In the glow of the celestial stars above, the monster looked far less threatening. It looked down on them and then up at the opening to the outside world. Gideon's best estimation was that the ledge was at least fifteen or twenty feet above them. He stepped forward tentatively to stand next to the beast and gaze out through the opening. Either its smell had escaped through the shaft above or Gideon had grown accustom to the odor, as he hardly noticed it anymore. The walls were solid stone with no discernible gaps, breaks, or lips for handholds. If they were going to climb out they would need to work together. With the presumption of its blessing, Gideon turned his back to the wall and offered a nod to their hairy guide. It did not return the gesture but offered a soft grunt which Gideon took to mean he could precede.

"Come here," Gideon said to Liz as he switched off the flashlight and put in it his pocket. "I'll boost you up."

She stepped forward and stood face to face with Gideon. He smiled at her as they shared a moment together beneath the stars. Gideon bent down and made a cradle with his hands. Liz stepped into the makeshift stirrup and climbed upward as he hoisted her unto his shoulders. He could not see anything but her shoes and blue jeans but felt her body stretch and struggle to reach the top.

"I can't reach," Liz finally said.

Gideon repositioned his hands beneath her feet and with all his might pushed upwards as he lifted her as high as his arms would reach. His shoulders and arms trembled as he closed his eyes tight and tried to hold her high and steady.

"A little higher," Liz petitioned.

With no more to give he was about to lower her back down, so they could think of another plan, when suddenly he felt the weight of her body disappear as her shoes rose away from his hands. Gideon opened his eyes to find a wall of hair directly in front of him. He looked up just in time to see Liz swing her leg over the ledge and stepped out of the creature's giant hands. She disappeared over the ledge and Gideon continued to stare out through the opening, next to their hairy elevator. It looked down at him and all Gideon could see from its shadowed face was the white of its one large eye. There was intelligence and kindness in its eye he had not noticed previously.

"What should we call you?" Gideon posed a rhetorical question. "Steve? Dave? Smalls? How 'bout Gene, short for bad hygiene?"

The hairy beast snorted through its nose and blew a puff of rotten smelling air in Gideon's face.

"Gene it is," Gideon said and gagged at the foul aroma.

"Gideon," Liz called from above. "You won't believe where we are."

"Where?" he shouted up at the night sky.

"Get up here and see," she replied.

He turned back to the narrow passage where Jeddediah stood.

"You first," he said to the old miner.

Jeddediah stepped toward Gideon with his sights set firmly on the creature next to him. He grabbed on to Gideon's shoulders and climbed up the same way Liz had done moments earlier. When Gideon lifted him as high as he could, their new friend did the rest, raising the miner up and out of the shaft. There was a groan as Jeddediah rolled his body out of sight and Gideon turned his attention to the complicated creature beside him. He searched for words but found only questions he would never find the answers to. If this hairy giant could talk, Gideon would have wearied him with questions about the treasure, passageways, its age, its origin, and most importantly Glenn. Instead, he just raised his arms slowly and laid hold of its hairy shoulders and was lifted into the air like an infant being scooped up from the ground. He awkwardly climbed atop its back after finagling around its arms and shoulder. From there he was hoisted higher until he could reach the ledge and pull himself out of the hole.

Liz and Jeddediah were there to greet him, along with the twinkly city lights that sprawled out before him. They found themselves at the edge of a massive cliff that overlooked the valley. Gideon briefly exchanged ear to ear grins with his gleeful companions before he looked back down the dark shaft. He pulled the light from his pocket and shined it back down to where they had emerged from and saw only the rock floor. It left as abruptly as it came and Gideon felt an odd mixture of relief and sadness at its departure.

"Bye, Gene," he whispered. "Thanks."

"Can you believe this?" Liz said. "He brought us all the way back to where we started."

"Where ya started?" asked Jeddediah.

"Crooked Top Mountain," Gideon answered. "It's where Glenn left us the clue that led to you."

"Look," Liz said and pointed to her left. "Flatiron."

In the distance was a dark silhouette of the massive cliff face, which they had climbed just days earlier. They quietly shimmied along the ledge, until they were clear of the rock wall behind them and could set foot on safer ground. Gideon and Liz stood back and took in the majestic view of the millions of lights that lit up the civilized world below. Behind them was a dark and foreboding wilderness with plenty of danger and mystery on the surface. All of that paled in comparison to what lie beneath. Jeddediah wandered aimlessly away from the lights of the city, with his arms behind his back and his head turned up at the starry sky. The ground beneath them was still damp from the storm, but the clouds had parted and the air was as dry and crisp as any ordinary desert winter night.

"So what now?" asked Liz.

"Well," Gideon thought out loud. "We could try and make our way down in the dark or we could wait a couple hours until daybreak."

"My parents are probably worried sick," Liz said. "And I want to see if Joe's okay."

"Agreed," said Gideon. "Let's not wait."

He glanced over his shoulder and saw Jeddediah pensively staring at a large rock formation tucked back in the darkened landscape.

"Give me just a minute," Gideon said to Liz as he sauntered toward Jeddediah.

Gideon quietly walked over and stood next to the old miner. He looked up at the three towering boulders that were shadowed by the moonlight.

"Glenn called those the three sisters," he spoke softly, as they both looked straight ahead.

"Mm," Jeddediah mindlessly acknowledged him.

"It was the Pima's that named this Crooked Top Mountain," Gideon continued. "They called it Kakatak Tamai. There's a legend that says the Earth Maker called all the righteous to the top of Crooked Top Mountain and those who would not answer the call were turned to the rock formations all around here."

"Mm," Jeddediah grunted, still staring at the boulders.

"We made it to the top, and we haven't been turned to stone, so I guess that means we're the righteous," Gideon added.

The old miner turned to face him with a solemn peaceful expression that Gideon had not previously seen on his wrinkly bearded face.

"It must be hard to have been so close and come away empty handed," Gideon tried to empathize.

"Actually, I ain't felt this good in years," Jeddediah replied.

"Really?" Gideon questioned.

"I spent more than a decade look'n for someth'n," Jeddediah said. "I risked my life more than a few times, but the truth is I lost my life and I didn't even know it. Only difference 'tween me and that poor creature back there is that he does his obsess'n in the dark. See'n them young fellers get all twisted up the way they did, made me take a hard look at myself an' what I seen wasn't pretty. Nah, I ain't one of the righteous, I was one of the lost."

Gideon remembered what Liz had said about looking to the past at the expense of the future. He considered how Jeddediah spent his days, and the days that were taken from Glenn, and he silently vowed that he would not do the same.

"Even the best of us get lost from time to time," Gideon said. "Glenn was the kindest, most selfless soul I ever knew and he got swept up in all this."

"But ya see, he was right," Jeddediah said. "He told me once he felt there was someth'n out here. Someth'n unseen, someth'n hidden, someth'n he had to find. I felt it too, and we was right. That's a kind of peace no amount of money can buy."

"So, you're not tempted to go back down there after it?" Gideon asked.

"Nah, I'll let that poor soul be," Jeddediah said. "He done claimed his heart's reward and my heart's been cured."

"I'm glad for that," Gideon said. "If that's all you came away with that's enough, right?"

"I wouldn't say that's all I come away with," Jeddediah said as he stuck his hand down the front of his pants. After some maneuvering he pulled a fist-sized chunk of gold out of his jeans.

"What the...?" Gideon muttered.

"While you was hav'n a staring contest with that hairy beast, I looked down at my feet an' found this beauty just lay'n there in the passage," Jeddediah explained.

"Have you had that in your underpants this whole time?" Gideon asked.

"Nah, I don't wear underpants," Jeddediah replied with a wink.

"Gross," Gideon said.

Liz walked up beside them, and Jeddediah tucked the hunk of gold into the side pocket of his coat.

"Ready?" she asked.

"Yeah," Gideon said. "Let's get out of here."

Together they all turned and looked out at the horizon. They stood in the place between the blanket of stars overhead and a sea of street lights below. Gideon took one last moment to enjoy their brief stay in this magical mystical world between heaven and earth before they headed home.

DUTY AND THE BEAST

He stooped behind a large rock face and tried to calm his rapid breaths. If he could only breathe silently he would not have to hold back the torrent of oxygen his body wanted to consume. Despite the heat of the day, the rock he leaned against was cool as it had not yet been touched by the sun. His accelerated heartbeat was not only from this adult game of hide and seek but from the two hundred foot drop off directly behind him. Cautiously, he stole a peek around the corner in search of the stranger he fled from. It was the first time he was grateful not to be in possession of his gleaming white canvas hat, but feared his flaming red hair would be as much of a liability in his goal of concealment. Inch by inch, he peered around the corner until all at once the stranger jogged into view. Quickly, Glenn retreated to a safe distance, where he could neither see nor be seen.

"Please," the stranger's shout echoed through the crevasse that cut down the mountain's face. "I am not going to hurt you. I want to help. You won't find it without me."

Glenn had already been shot once and threatened multiple times in the space of a few days. He had barely escaped a conniving cowboy, whom he trusted and thought they shared the same goal. Now he was confronted with a man he had never met, who apparently had been following him. His one mission was to keep the promise he made and return to the old miner in the desert, but once again opposition found him. His breathing had calmed slightly but his heart still raced like the baseline beat at a dancehall.

"You need what I have," the stranger called again. "And I need the key. We can make a deal."

His nature was to trust in people but that trusting nature had been shaken by the business end of Cal's gun. He had nearly fallen into that trap again. When the stranger appeared, seemingly out of nowhere, with the old journal that bore the cross with interlocking loops, Glenn shared his mission, his plans and his travails. It was only when the man declared his supposed right to the treasure that Glenn began to fear he had divulged too much. A hasty and drastic move, to throw the old journal into a bush, allowed for his temporary escape. Only now he found himself trapped on the edge of a precipice with his options dwindling by the minute.

"Think," Glenn whispered aloud as he turned his back to the rock wall.

The view from the top of Flatiron was awe inspiring and yet his current circumstances did not allow for him to fully appreciate the expansive valley below. He slid sideways, away from the man who hunted him. His overstuffed daypack caused him to lean forward, a degree or two more than he was comfortable with, but he was confident in his footing despite the narrow sloped ledge he skirted.

"Hey," the man called as he stepped back into Glenn's view. "Stop. I'm not going to hurt you."

"People who aren't going to hurt you don't need to say it, Miguel," Glenn replied as he quickened his shuffle further down the ledge. "If that is your real name."

"Please, I just want to talk," Miguel said, as he too turned sideways and slid down the ledge after him.

The rock face bent slightly and allowed Glenn to shuffle out of sight. His relief was short-lived, however, as his right foot found nothing but air and sent him hurtling down an unseen fission in the rock ledge. He reached out to brace himself but was only able to bang his elbow on the lip of the taunting pit as he fell. An explosion of pain burst throughout his body as he landed on his knees at the bottom of the shaft. His head simultaneously struck the stone wall before he could give voice to his agony and all went dark.

"Ow," Glenn cried out as he awoke.

His eyes were open but he could hardly see his surroundings. For a fleeting moment, he feared he had gone blind but he could faintly perceive the wall beside him and the rock floor beneath him as he lifted his head. He rolled over unto his daypack and looked out through the opening high above him. The sky was a beautiful purple with brilliant orange edges that just crept into view.

"Ah geez," he muttered.

An aching pain pulsed violently from temple to temple and was only made worst when he attempted to rub his head. He flinched and pulled his hand back as he touched the wound on his forehead. Sitting up made Glenn acutely aware of each and every injury he had sustained in the fall. Both his knees throbbed like they had been hit with a sledge hammer. His dry lips stung as they rubbed together and the cracks revealed the tender flesh beneath them. Those symptoms quickly rose to the top of his list of concerns as dehydration would do him in faster than a bump to the head or a pair of busted up knees. He wriggled his backpack from his shoulders and dug into the side pocket where his warm bottle was. Without hesitation, he unscrewed the lid and drank the precious remains at the bottom. The life-giving liquid ran down his throat and he could feel it flow through his insides like a fresh spring through a dry desert riverbed.

"Aw," he sighed in relief.

He dug again into the side pocket of his pack and produced a small tube of Chapstick, which he promptly slathered over his cracked lips. After he returned the tube to its proper pouch, he flipped his pack over and removed a second water bottle from the opposite side. It was filled to the top and he gave it a hard shake to be sure. Then he leaned back against the rock wall and looked around as his eyes had properly adjusted to the mute light. He guessed the ledge over head was at least fifteen feet above him and a cursory check revealed no hand holds for him to climb. The opening at the top looked just big enough for a body to slip through and Glenn cursed his luck that he had found it at all. One good stride and he would have easily cleared the breach. Still, it was nice and cool in the stone pit which was a blessing considering it was the peak of the summer season.

His head still throbbed and his knees felt as if they were on fire but he attempted to stand nonetheless. That ambition promptly left him from the stabbing pains that shot through his legs and their inability to comply with his command.

"Oh man," Glenn cried.

With regret, he let his head fall back against the cold rock behind him, which sent a wave of hurt from the back of his brain to the front. For several minutes, he lay still and allowed the sharp pains throughout his body to settle into a somewhat dull agony. There was a tug at the back of his throat as the dry desert air had already gobbled up the last of his saliva.

"Help!" Glenn called out to the opening above. "Hello? Help!"

There was an echo that rolled out of the darkness. He turned to the side and rooted around in his pack and pulled out a blue plastic flashlight. With a flick of the switch a cone of light illuminated his surroundings. To his left was a previously unseen tunnel that led out of the shaft and down beyond the glow of his light. A nearly overwhelming desire to explore this new discovery was immediately frustrated by his lack of mobility. He kept the light trained down the fission and inspected it as thoroughly as he could from his seated position. It was very narrow and misshapen in a beautifully random way, but he had no doubt it was big enough for him to navigate through the natural passageway. His mind began reeling with the possibilities of where it went and what wonders it might lead to. Still, he knew he was in no condition to find out so he reluctantly turned his attention back to the opening high above him.

"Hello!" he shouted. "Can anybody hear me? Miguel? Hello? I need help!"

When no answer came, he set the timer on his Casio wristwatch for one minute. Each time the alarm beeped he called out again and listened for a response. His greatest worry was that he could hear nothing beyond his own faint echo, not even the breeze from outside. He wondered if his cries even reached the world above.

Regardless of his fears he continued the process for fifty three beeps of his watch, followed by fifty three shouts and fifty three desperate prayers for a reply. By then the remaining daylight had given way to night and his hopes that anyone might still be up on the mountain top had vanished with the setting sun. A night at the bottom of a hidden crevasse was not the worst thing he could think of. He had provisions and supplies to get him through and would simply have to ration his water until daybreak, when he hoped a brave summer hiker would hear his call for help. With a good night's rest, perhaps his knees would heal sufficiently for him to be able to move around once more.

All at once his mission and plan returned to his mind like the flip of a switch.

"Jeddediah," he uttered to himself.

He promised the old miner that he would return by nightfall. Now that night had fallen he tried to imagine what Jeddediah must be thinking. Glenn wondered and worried whether or not Cal had returned. If he had, did the cowboy come as a friend or foe? Even with only half of the clue there was a slight chance of the wily old man finding the key and seeking the treasure on his own. Glenn agonized at the thought of being left behind and wished he had some way of signaling Jeddediah to let him know he had not voluntarily broken his promise.

"Hello?" his voice cracked as he hopelessly cried out one more time.

His lips began to crack and peel again as he briefly deliberated between the water bottle and the Chapstick. The dry scratchy feeling at the back of throat tipped the scales toward the water bottle. He removed the lid and took a judicious sip as he was determined to make it last. A gurgling in his stomach led him back into his pack in search of food.

As he unwrapped a granola bar and took a bite, he heard a growling that did not come from his stomach. Frozen with fear he stopped chewing and listened carefully, hoping against hope that he had not heard what he thought he heard. A foul smell invaded his nose accompanied by another low growl from off in the blackness. With trembling hands, he set the granola bar on top of his pack and picked up his flashlight in the same motion. He shined the light down the tunnel and found himself looking into the furry face of terror.

The large hairy creature filled the tunnel from top to bottom and side to side. It snarled at him through its one good eye, the other was pinched shut and covered in dried blood. All at once the beast lunged toward him and Glenn jolted backwards as his preservative instinct kicked in. He fought against his own retreat as he reached back into his daypack and unzipped the top pouch. Sharp pains stabbed at his knees as the beast closed in on him. Just as it was within arm's reach, Glenn pulled his hands out of his pack and thrust them upward toward the monstrous attacker.

With both eyes closed tightly, Glenn waited for the death blow. All that could be heard in the dark shaft was the deep panting of the creature, who could not have been more than a few feet away from him. Glenn peeked through his slightly opened eyelids with his hands still held out in front of him. His flashlight lay against his daypack and shone against the gray rock wall, illuminating the tiny confines of the unfortunate pit he had fallen into. The creature had stopped and stared intently through its one good eye at the item in Glenn's hands.   His arms still shook uncontrollably but Glenn forced open his hands to better display their contents. He held his grandfather's gold pocket watch with a long gold chain. His Grandpa Bill left it to him when he died and Glenn considered it his most valuable possession, both monetarily and sentimentally. Unsure how long this shiny addition would hold the attention of the towering monster, Glenn cleared his dry throat and summoned all the courage in his racing heart.

"I'm sorry," Glenn said. "Here, take it."

He gestured to the hairy creature and leaned in its direction. The beast stood as still as a statue with only its eye moving back and forth between Glenn's face and the gold watch.

"It's okay," Glenn gestured again for the beast to take the watch. "I brought it for you, as a gift. I'm really sorry we busted into your place and stole the pick. I want you to have this."

The beast's chest rose and fell slightly beneath a thick layer of hair, as it inhaled and exhaled methodically. Glenn took the fact that he was still alive as a sign that the terrifying creature was considering his offer. He took hold of the chain and let the watch fall out of his hands. The gold circle swung back and forth in the air, suspended from Glenn's fingers.

"Please," he beckoned. "It's okay, you can have it. I want you to have it."

Its arm twitched slightly before it finally reached out and took hold of the swinging watch. Glenn flinched at its movement but steadied himself to allow for the exchange. The beast studied the shiny watch carefully while Glenn tried to remain as still and quiet as his pounding heart would allow him. After several minutes of admiring the gold watch, the hairy giant looked back to Glenn who met its eye with a big gap-toothed smile.

"I'm really sorry," Glenn said.

After a brief nonverbal exchange, the creature turned its attention to Glenn's flashlight that was still perched against his daypack. Slowly, Glenn reached out and took hold of his light and shined it at the beast's stomach.

"It's a flashlight," Glenn said. "And this is my backpack. You can have these too if you like."

Glenn lifted the pack in the air and shined the light on it. The beastly figure tilted its head to the side and looked around the pack at Glenn. He smiled at it again, but was met with the same emotionless expression as before. His stomach gurgled and he remembered the granola bar he had started. The wrapper lay on the floor next to his water bottle, with the bar a few inches away. Glenn placed his pack on the floor and, with a slow deliberate motion, reached out and picked up his granola bar. The tall hairy voyeur watched as he took a bite of the chocolate chip and granola snack. While he chewed, Glenn reached into the large middle pocket of his bright red daypack and produced another granola bar. He unwrapped it and offered it to the silent giant, who held his grandfather's old pocket watch.

"Granola bar?" he offered. "It's good."

Glenn held it out as he took another bite of his own and chewed demonstrably, as if the monster had never seen anything chewed before. The beast snatched it from his hand and shoved it in its mouth without breaking eye contact. It chewed on the bar as if to prove it knew how to do it. Glenn smiled up at it as they both finished chewing and swallowed their collective bites.

Without warning, the beast turned around and strode back down the tunnel from where it came.

"Wait," Glenn called.

It did not stop, or even hesitate, but continued on its path until it disappeared around a sharp corner.

"I need help," Glenn shouted after it. The only reply was the faint echo of his own voice. "Come back."

He waited for several minutes in complete silence. His heart rate had dropped back down to normal levels while his mind was spinning with the possibilities of where the creature had gone and what might lie just around the bend. For a brief moment, he thought about trying to walk but that ambition left as quickly as the stingy pain hit his knees. When he could think of nothing else to do, he collected the two empty granola bar wrappers and placed them in the pocket of his pack. Then he took a small sip from his water bottle and returned it to its proper pouch. He looked out through the opening overhead at the brilliant blanket of stars in the dark blue sky and tried to see if he could pick out any constellations from his limited vantage point. His wristwatch beeped and he looked down at the time. The digital display read '9:00' and he shook his head. He could not believe it had been an entire day already and that he had little to show for it, besides a bump on his head and a pair of busted knees.

Unable to think of any reasonably productive use of his time, Glenn slid his daypack up against the wall and laid his head down on it. There was a dull ache on the side of his forehead that caused him to wonder if he had cracked his skull. He closed his eyes and tried to go to sleep. Images ran through his head of Jeddediah in the old shack waiting for his return, and of Cal's threatening revolver and the stranger's journal. He thought of his fall, and the hidden tunnel, and the monster that disappeared down it.

After a lengthy struggle to rest his mind Glenn sat back up, as there was no conceivable way he would find rest. Miraculously, the pain in his knees had completely vanished. He stood up and immediately headed down the tunnel after the monster. Though the tunnel was dark and narrow, he had no trouble navigating the twists and turns and in no time he came to a large cavern filled with trinkets and treasures of all kinds. The walls rose high overhead and were lined with thick veins of white quartz, laced with glittering gold that seemed to light the entire room. His mouth fell open in awe and wonder as he gazed out on this fantastic trove.

"Ho-ly cow," he exclaimed.

At the far corner, he spotted the hairy creature standing over a pile of gold bullion. Glenn sailed to it as if he were hovering on a cloud. When he arrived by its side, they looked at one another and the beast smiled at him. He smiled back and patted it on its long and muscular arm. Just then, Jeddediah came stumbling into the cavern from an inlet to their left. The old miner removed his hat and stared at the bounty before him.

"You made it!" Glenn shouted.

"'course I did," Jeddediah replied.

Glenn was by the old miner's side in an instant as the two locked arms and danced around piles of gold and ancient treasure chests that overflowed with jewelry and precious gems. They laughed and hummed merrily to each other while they skipped through the room scooping up handfuls of gold and letting it drop back to the ground. The creature stood back in the corner and seemed to enjoy watching their celebration.

Just as Glenn thought he could not be any happier, Gideon emerged from the same tunnel he had followed to the cave of wonders. Gideon wore black dress slacks with a white shirt and red tie and a name tag in his pocket that read 'Elder Goodwin'. He held a machete in one hand and a white envelope with a blue and red border in the other.

"Gideon!" Glenn greeted him.

"I came as soon as I could," Gideon replied.

The old friends embraced and Glenn stepped back to let him have a proper look at his glorious discovery.

"You were right," Gideon said. "You were right, Glenn. Well done."

Liz and Todd appeared by his side smiling broadly at him. Todd wore the glow in the dark Yoda t-shirt that Glenn had given him for Christmas when they were ten. Liz was in the black and white evening gown she wore to prom. She leaned in and kissed Glenn on the cheek.

"You did it, Glenn," she swooned. "I knew you would."

He felt a pressure on his shoulder and a foul stench offended his nostrils. The cavern and his friends instantly disappeared into blackness as the pains in his knees and head returned. The pressure on his shoulder mounted as if something had seized upon it. He opened his eyes to find a dark hairy mass standing over him.

"Geez!" he yelped as he gagged on the smell.

The beast stepped back and stood upright only a foot or two away from him. Glenn struggled to sit up and winced from the stinging sensation that shot through his knees. He could see very little from the muted light that bled in from the starry sky overhead. Blindly, he felt around on the ground for his flashlight. When his hand grazed the plastic cylinder he took hold of it and flipped on the switch. An explosion of light caused the hairy beast to step back and raise its long arm to shield its eye.

"Sorry," Glenn said as he lowered his light.

It held something black in its hand that caught Glenn's eye. The creature looked down at whatever it was that it held in its hand and extended the gift toward Glenn. He could not be sure but felt as if it were mimicking him from when he offered the creature a granola bar. Tentatively, Glenn reached out and accepted the offering from its oversized hand. He held the light down on the black clump in his hand. It was a gushy, squishy ball of fur that leaked dark red liquid onto his fingers.

"Auh," Glenn gagged. "Thank you."

He covered his mouth and fought back the stomach acids that were erupting and burning in his throat. The creature raised its hands to its mouth and pantomimed biting and chewing. When Glenn realized it wanted him to eat its black kill, nausea washed over him.

"Oh, uh," he looked desperately for a way out. "I'm full. Thanks though."

Glenn rubbed his belly and puffed his cheeks out. The creature stared at him with its one good eye and did not move or give any indication as to its level of understanding.

"Is this a bat?" Glenn asked as he held the bloody body up by a crumpled wing. "Looks delicious."

With a forced smile, he dangled the mangled critter from his thumb and forefinger. He could not tell if the creature was displeased or if it simply always looked like that. After what seemed like a lengthy standoff, the creature turned its attention to Glenn's daypack. Eager to move on from the bloody vermin snack he held in his hand, Glenn reached into his pack and produced another granola bar.

"You want another?" he asked and subtly disposed of the bat carcass.

Before the last syllable had escaped his lips, the beast laid hold on the package with frightening speed and precision. It popped the whole thing in its mouth, wrapper and all, and chewed vigorously. Glenn pulled another bar from his pack and shielded it from the beast with his elbow, until he could open it properly. Then he turned and presented it with a fresh unwrapped granola bar.

"Here," he said as the beast ripped the bar from his hand. "It's better when you remove the wrapper."

The creature chewed just the same and did not seem to enjoy it any more or less. Glenn worried at how quickly he was running through his provisions. He looked down at his water bottle and discovered to his horror that it had been knocked over and all the water spilled on the dusty rock floor.

"No!" Glenn exclaimed. He picked up the bottle, held it over his head and tipped the last drops of liquid into his mouth. "I'm screwed."

As he looked back at the beast, a Hail Mary of an idea came to him. He sat up as straight as he could and held the empty water bottle in front of him.

"Water," he said and tilted the bottle back and forth. "I need water. Do you know where water is?"

A graveling snort burst from its marble sized nostrils. With a huff, the creature turned around and headed back down the tunnel. Glenn tried again to stand up but cutting pains in his knees brought him back down. He mustered all the strength and determination he possessed and struggled to his feet, in spite of the intense throbbing around his knees. His head was spinning and his mind felt as if it filled with a misty haze. Leaning against the wall for support he stretched his hand down the tunnel toward the departing giant.

"Wait," he pleaded.

The monster stopped just before it disappeared around the bend. It looked back at Glenn and beckoned with a toss of its head and a grunt.

"I can't," he replied. "I need help."

Like a bothered parent, the beast hastily returned to Glenn and scooped him up without warning. It tossed him over his shoulder like a sack of potatoes and reached down for his daypack. Glenn hung helplessly from its bony shoulder, with his face bouncing off its hairy torso. The smell was much more poignant at point blank range and the discomfort from his wounded legs was as tormenting as when he tried to stand, except he did not have the additional challenge of attempting to move on his own power. He held tight to the flashlight in his hand but turned it off as his transporter did not seem to need it. He could see little from his current position other than the ground beneath its feet. In his other hand was the empty water bottle which, at the moment, represented both his doom and his hope for survival. All the blood rushed to his head and caused his brain to pound and pulse to the limits of his tolerance. He felt as if he were going to throw up and almost wished he had stayed back in the shaft, though it would mean almost certain death. Without water, his chances of seeing tomorrow dwindled with each passing moment. The beast leapt down a steep drop off and a jolt of hurt struck Glenn like a lightning bolt as they landed.

"Aw!" he yelped.

The beast continued on without hesitating or checking on its cargo. Tears wells up in Glenn's eyes and streamed uncontrollably across his forehead as he was tossed to and fro. Just when he thought he could not bear another minute, the creature leapt again and they both fell weightlessly for a moment before crashing back to the rock floor.

"Oh!" Glenn shouted. "Please, stop."

His words were either unheard or unheeded as the beast rolled on down the passage with a monstrous stride. Glenn tapped its back with his elbows.

"Hey," he cried. "Hey, please let me down. I can't."

All at once their forward momentum stopped and in one motion he was lifted off his bony perch and plopped unceremoniously on the cold unforgiving floor. The beast stepped back as Glenn flipped on the flashlight.

"Wo," Glenn said as he found himself sitting at the edge of large dome-like room. There were several offshoots that extended in different directions with a set of blood red handprints over the branch just in front of him. The beast tossed Glenn's daypack down at his side and crouched down like a gargoyle directly across from him.

"Are those yours?" Glenn asked pointing to the handprints.

When he received no answer, Glenn turned his attention and his flashlight to the other dark passages. His imagination ran wild with possibilities as to where they each led. Not surprisingly, considering his circumstances, his preferred fantasy was a clean underground spring. The creature did not move from its squatted position and appeared to be studying Glenn carefully.

"Hey," Glenn said with a casual wave. "Thanks for the break. My head is killing me."

He pointed to the side of his head and squinted as his brain throbbed from the pressure between his temples. The beast imitated Glenn's squinting eyes with its one good eye.

"My name is Glenn," he said and touched his chest. "Glenn."

With its huge hand the creature reached up and touched its chest with a small grunt.

"I'm Glenn," he repeated. "Do you have a name?"

It grunted softly again and touched its hairy chest. Believing he was making some progress, Glenn tried again.

"Gle-nn," he enunciated slowly. "What are you called?"

The creature looked confused and annoyed, with a furrowed brow that drew Glenn's attention to its open wound over its closed eye. Glenn reached into his pack and removed the first aid kit. He pulled out a bandage and some ointment.

"I can fix that," he said and closed one eye while he pointed at its head. He held up the bandage and gestured for the beast to come closer. "Medi-cine."

He again enunciated slowly as if it would make his communications easier to understand. The beast tilted its head and examined the white bandage.

"Come here," Glenn said as he beckoned his hairy friend once more. "It's okay."

Cautiously, it moved toward him with its eye on the white bandage. Glenn fixed the beam of his flashlight on the medical supplies in his hand until the creature was close enough to touch. The beast reached out and ran its long finger across the soft gauze as it sat down on the ground next to Glenn. He propped the flashlight in the crook of his leg and methodically removed the cap from the tube of ointment and pressed a dollop into the palm of his hand. With his finger, he rubbed the ointment in a circle and carefully raised his hand to the beast's wounded forehead. As the soothing balm made contact with the wound, its face relaxed, and at last so did Glenn. He repeated the process several more times until the wounded glistened with the medicinal lotion.

"My mom used to do this when I fell and scraped my knee," Glenn said. When the beast did not acknowledge or protest his sharing, Glenn continued. "I used to fall a lot when I was younger. I guess you could say I never stopped falling."

Glenn chuckled to himself until he met with the unamused eye of his monstrous patient.

"There was this kid, Ivan Decker, who used to trip me whenever he saw me. I never told my mom that's why I fell so much," Glenn continued as he gently unrolled the bandage and laid it over the deep cut. "One day Ivan took my chocolate milk and knocked my lunch unto the floor. That's the day I met Gideon. He helped me pick up my tater tots and gave me his sandwich. At recess he hit Ivan in the head with a basketball. Ivan never bothered me again."

He wrapped the side of its hairy head until the gauze was exhausted and then flashed a bright smile at the beast.

"There," he said. "Doesn't that feel better?"

The beast reached up and touched the clean white cloth that covered its dirty matted hair. Glenn searched for some sign of appreciation but found the same emotionless face staring back at him.

"You're welcome," he said as the beast slid back to its crouched position on the other end of the room. Glenn returned the tube of ointment to his pack and picked up his flashlight.

"I never wanted to be a bully," Glenn continued as tears welled up in his eyes. "I'm sorry we took the pick. I can get it back for you. I will get it back for you. If I make it out of here."

Glenn's head throbbed. His cracked lips and dry throat reminded him of his dire need for water. He picked up his water bottle and bounced it lightly up and down. The thought of his painful journey to this point made him question whether he could bear another stretch. If he could only know how long his afflictions would last, he could make a more educated decision on whether or not to carry on.

"Water," he said shaking the empty bottle at the creature. "How much farther to water?"

The beast stood up and walked back over in front of him. As it reached down to take hold of him he pushed at its hands.

"No, no," Glenn protested. "I can't. Hurt. Ow. Too painful."

He held up his water bottle and gestured for the creature to take it.

"You go," he pleaded. "Take this. Please."

At its full height, the creature's head nearly scraped against the rising rock wall, which Glenn rested against. He could not be sure if it understood him at all. He was about to give in and let the beast carry him onward, if it meant relief from the pounding sensation in his head. The extreme dryness started on his lips and drove right down through his body like a withered root of a dying tree. Before he could do or say anything more, the beast reached out and took the water bottle from his hand. It turned and headed for the tunnel to the left under the giant handprints.

"Thank you," Glenn called out, just before it disappeared out of sight.

He sat there alone in the domed cave and listened for signs of the creature's return. His mind drifted from his current predicament to the circumstances which had brought him there. The mysterious man with the journal, the old miner and his mule, the cowboy and his dog, all floated in and out of his thoughts. He felt as if he could no longer swallow and strained against the tug at the back of his throat. It felt as if his brain had swelled to occupy every inch of his cranium. Unable to focus on any one thing, Glenn flipped off his flashlight and lay his redhead down on the cold rock floor. He remembered his dream and thought of his friends and how much he was going to enjoy telling them this story one day. A smile broke across his face as he imagined each of them listening intently, Gideon appreciating his tale while Liz politely humored him and Todd skeptically challenged every detail.

In time, every misadventure becomes a great story, he thought with a grin.

Then Glenn closed his eyes and, in an instant, all his pain evaporated as if it had been a bad dream.

THE RETURN

"Bull," Todd said as he swiveled around on a padded rolling stool.

"It's true," Gideon replied.

"You're telling me that you found a secret passage to the Spanish treasure vault," Todd questioned.

"An empty vault," Gideon interrupted.

"And then Cal and the man in the cloak blew each other up," Todd continued.

"I think Miguel sacrificed himself, but yes," Gideon added.

"Then the Mogollon Monster led you to the treasure and Glenn's grave?" Todd concluded.

"I don't know if it was the Mogollon Monster, but yes to the rest," Gideon replied. "I called him Gene."

"But it wouldn't let you near the treasure?" Todd questioned.

"That's right," Gideon said. "Gene chased us out."

"Before it came and found you, and led you through an underground subway system that spans the Superstitions?" Todd stated skeptically.

"Yep," Gideon replied.

"This is like the time you tried to convince me that aliens made Papago Park to hide their spaceport," Todd said.

"First off, that Papago thing is plausible," Gideon said. "And two, this is not like that."

"Todd, he's telling the truth," Liz spoke up from the armchair beneath the large oval window. "I wouldn't lie to you."

She giggled and Gideon's heart skipped a beat. Even beneath the muted light from the cloudy sky beyond the window she seemed to glow. Her smile lit up the tiny oblong room with the sterile white walls.

"That's crazy," Todd said with a shake of the head.

"We've seen crazier," Gideon replied. He raised his eyebrows at Todd and his blonde friend smirked and nodded knowingly.

"Fine," Todd conceded. "I'll believe it when you take me back to the entrance with the loopy cross key thing."

"Deal," Gideon agreed. "Just as soon as Joe's ready we'll all go."

"Good deal," Joe smiled from his hospital bed. "The doctors said I should be out of here in a day or two."

Joe wore a pale blue gown and was nestled snuggly within a pile of pillows with layers of blankets over him. Gideon could not ever remember a time he had seen Joe so clean and well groomed. His dark beard was trimmed and his unruly hair combed. He looked well rested from his stay at Good Samaritan Regional Medical Center, where he had been helicoptered directly from Weaver's Needle.

"You sure you're gonna be up for it that quick?" Gideon asked.

"Of course," Joe replied. "This ain't the first time I've been shot by a greedy bushwhacker in the middle of nowhere."

He winked at Todd and they all laughed. After a hard chuckle, Joe winced in pain and grabbed at his stomach. Although the smile never left his face, they all stopped laughing in deference to his healing. A steady beep from the monitor beside his bed was the lone sound in the tiny room once the laughter ceased. Gideon looked out through the oval window to the east. In the distance, he could just make out the face of Crooked Top Mountain on the cloud covered skyline.

"Hey Joe?" Gideon asked breaking the strangely comfortable silence.

"Yeah?" Joe replied.

"What do you think we should do?" he asked.

"About what?" Joe replied.

"About what we know," Gideon answered. "The key, the treasure, the tunnels, the monster, Glenn. All of it."

"Are you asking if I think we should take another go at it?" Joe grinned at Gideon.

"Yes," Gideon said. "And no. Do we have a responsibility to do something? To tell someone?"

"Well to the first thing," Joe began thoughtfully. "I think the old man was right. We ought to leave it be, the creature and its treasure. As for the second thing, you already told the police what happened to Cal and that dude in the cloak."

"But I left out the part about the Spanish gold and the monster," Gideon added.

"And you were right to do that," Joe said. "If word got out that you found gold in the mountains there'd be even more fools out there look'n for it and more lives lost."

"And what about Glenn?" Gideon asked as a lump formed in his throat.

"Well that's a tough one," Joe said as he pulled at his beard. "If that were my son, I'd want to know what happened to him for sure. But if we tell Ms. Bicklesby she's likely to ask questions that you don't want to answer."

"Like where his body is," Liz added.

"Right," Joe said. "I guess you gotta consider, what good will come from sharing."

Gideon considered Ms. Bicklesby and all the pain and heartache she had been through. He knew the personal loss he felt paled in comparison with that of a mother. However, he imagined that the unrelenting torment of the unknown must visit her daily, as it had with him for so long. Although there was still much he did not know about Glenn's final days, it did help to know where he was laid. As he weighed that peace of mind against the opening of old wounds there was a knock at the door.

"Come in," Joe called.

The heavy wooden door pushed open and in walked a short round-faced woman. She wore a green and red sweater and was followed by a slender older gentleman with a navy blue dress shirt and a black tie. At the bottom of his tie was the Looney Tunes Tasmanian Devil wearing a Santa costume with a word bubble over the cartoon that said 'I don't do chimneys'. The woman had a soft white complexion with pink rouge on her face while the man had deep grooves on his leathery clean-shaven face. Gideon looked back and forth between the mismatched pair as they tentatively shuffled into the room. The gray-haired man fidgeted slightly and looked at the floor while the woman raised her hands across her plump frame as she slid her purse into the fold of her arm. She looked expectantly at the gray-haired man and pressed her lips together into a pleasant grin.

"Hello," Joe finally said.

The woman tugged uncomfortably at her green and red sweater as she waited for the old man to respond. He did not look up but pulled anxiously at his collar like a toddler on his first day of Sunday School. She cleared her throat and turned back to Joe.

"How do you do?" she said. "My name is Nancy."

"Pleased to meet you, Nancy," Joe replied.

"He wanted to come and see you," she said with a furtive look at the gray-haired man. When he did not immediately respond she continued. "To see that you were all right."

"Oh," Joe said as they all looked curiously at the scrawny old man.

At last the man looked up from the linoleum floor and grinned awkwardly with his slightly crooked teeth. His smile quickly faded as he was met with four blank stares.

"Well don't look at me like we ain't never met," the old man barked.

"Jeddediah?" Gideon gawked at the old man.

"Call me Jed," he replied and took hold of the woman's hand as he beamed lovingly at her.

"You shaved," Todd remarked.

"I clean up real nice, don't I?" Jed replied as he straightened his tie.

"You sure do," Liz said as she stood up from the armchair. She walked over to the curly haired woman and gave her a hug. "Pleased to meet you, Nancy."

She gave Jeddediah a squeeze and a kiss on the cheek. Gideon and Todd stood as Jeddediah led his lady friend to Joe's bedside. The two old treasure hunters shook hands, and Joe gave him a wink and a nod toward Nancy.

"So, what happened to you?" Gideon asked. "And what's with the 'call me Jed' stuff?"

"Well, Nancy here prefers Jed," he replied. "We met at the bank."

"The bank?" Todd asked with his mouth hanging open. "Were you there to rob it? Ma'am, are you his hostage?"

She covered her mouth as a snorted laugh exploded from her lips.

"No," she replied with a squeaky giggle. "I work at the bank. Jed came in for a loan."

"A loan?" asked Todd. "You work at a bank that caters to crazy old hermits? No offense."

"None taken," Jed replied. "I got collateral."

The old miner winked at Gideon as Nancy stifled another giggle.

"I'm still not convinced she's not his hostage," Todd said.

"What's the loan for?" Gideon asked Jed.

"The RB Ranch is for sale," he said. "With a little work it could be something nice."

"You're gonna live there?" asked Joe.

"Yep," Jed answered. "Plan to run a full service operation outfitt'n tourist and guid'n folks all back through in the Superstitions."

"*All* of the Superstitions?" Gideon asked.

"Well, no," Jed said with a wry smile. "We'll keep to the upper half."

"Did you take care of that thing you were going to look after?" Gideon asked.

"It's all closed up," Jed assured him. "The cross is back at Nancy's place. You can speak freely, she knows all about it."

"Jed swore me to secrecy," Nancy added as she moved her fingers over her lips in a zipping motion.

"Let's see if he tells the same story," Todd said as leaned on the foot of Joe's hospital bed and folded his arms defiantly. "What do you know?"

"Well," Nancy began with a hesitant glance over at Jed. He nodded his gray head back at her and she turned to face Todd. "There's gold hidden in old lava tubes under the mountains and guarded by a hairy monster. Jed found the gold following a series of clues but had to leave it to save all your lives."

"Wait," Todd interrupted.

"That's more or less how it went," Jed put his arm around Nancy and shot a wide-eyed look at Todd.

"A lot more and a lot less," Todd responded with a shake of his head.

"Sounds about right to me," Gideon said. He stepped forward and shook the old miner's hand. "I never did thank you. For everything."

They exchanged a long heartfelt look. Jed nodded his gratitude to Gideon and released his hand. He thought for a moment he saw a tear form in the corner of Jed's eye, but the old miner quickly brushed it away.

"Well, we'd better git," Jed said. "The auction's this afternoon and we don't want to be late. Glad to see you're all well. When ya git outta here Joe, come and look me up."

"I sure will, Jed," Joe replied. "You take care."

Jed pulled the heavy door open wider and Nancy smiled at each of them and turned to leave. With a slight bow Jed spun on his heels and followed her out of the room. Gideon smiled at Joe who chuckled to himself as soon as the old miner was out of sight.

"Can you believe that?" Todd said.

"Who knew he was such a smooth operator," Gideon said.

"I'll say this for him," Joe added. "He's one of the most interesting characters I've ever met and I've know some real pieces of work."

"Speaking of which, how is old Stewart," Gideon asked not particularly caring for the answer.

"Same," Joe replied.

"We'd better be going too," Gideon said. "I promised Brother Hunter I'd have Liz back before dinner, and I don't want to get deeper into the dog house with him."

Gideon reached out and shook Joe's hand as Liz moved around the bed next to him. She leaned in and gave Joe a kiss on his scruffy cheek.

"We'll check in on you tomorrow," she said.

"Are you going to bring that boy there with ya?" Joe asked with a nod toward Gideon.

"I don't think I have a choice," Liz winked. "We're kind of a package deal."

"Well if you must," Joe smiled.

"You need anything, Pops?" Todd asked. "I'm going to walk them out and come right back up."

"Nah," Joe said. "I'm fine."

"You sure?" Todd asked again.

"Well, if you like, you could sweet talk the nurse into bringing me an extra pudding with my supper," Joe replied.

"Chocolate?" Todd asked.

"Of course," Joe said.

"Done," Todd said.

As Gideon made his way to the door the phone in the room began to ring and a red light on the receiver started blinking. Gideon stepped to one side and gestured for Liz to go first. She turned back and waved to Joe as he picked up the blinking phone.

"Joe's room," he answered and paused to listen. His smile sunk into a look of concern. "Well hey there, darl'n. What's the matter?"

Gideon stopped, with his hand on the door, and waited. Todd stood beside him as they both listened with great interest to Joe's conversation. There was a tug at Gideon's stomach, just behind his navel, and a tingling sensation on top of his ears. He could tell from Joe's tone and the look on his face that something was wrong.

"I'm so sorry to hear that," Joe said as he raised a finger toward Todd and Gideon, silently petitioning them to wait. "Yeah, he's right here. Just a second. Gideon, it's Tara."

He walked slowly back to Joe's bedside. His curiosity was tempered by the feeling in his gut that no good news awaited him on the other end of the receiver. Joe gestured again for him to take the phone and Gideon reluctantly accepted it and lifted the phone to his ear.

"What's wrong?" Gideon said, wasting no time.

"Gideon, 'im gone," Tara said with a crack in her voice.

"Who's gone?" Gideon asked. "Corey?"

"No man," she replied. "Corey's right 'ere. Mi fadda, 'im gone."

"Bammy?" Gideon asked. "What do you mean *gone*?"

"Marcus called to tell mi Bammy died yesterday," she said.

"What? How?" questioned Gideon.

"Mi na know, 'im wouldn't say," Tara replied. "'im just say wi must come 'ome."

He stood in stunned silence and looked around the small hospital room. Todd leaned against the foot of Joe's bed and Liz ambled back into the room and stood beside him. They all looked on with concern as Gideon struggled for words.

"Tara, I'm so sorry," he finally said. "We'll get you home. I'll make arrangements and call you back."

"A'right," replied a crackling voice on the other end of the phone. "T'anks."

"Of course," Gideon replied. "Stay by the phone, mi soon call, ya 'ere."

He handed the phone back to Joe and stared blankly, for a moment, at the interwoven pattern on his blanket.

"Bammy's dead?" Todd asked.

Gideon answered with a slowly solemn nod. He looked up into Liz's compassionate brown eyes and fought back the tears that welled in his own eyes.

"I've got to go back," Gideon told her.

"I'm so sorry, Gideon," she said. "Bammy was a friend of yours?"

"He's Tara's father," Gideon nodded and choked back a lump forming in his throat.

"How did he die?" she asked.

"She didn't say," he said. "I need to book us on a flight back to Jamaica."

"Count me in," Todd said.

"Me too," Liz added.

Gideon snapped his head toward her. From her expression, he realized the surprised look on his face, as her eyebrows lowered slightly along with the corners of her mouth. He quickly composed himself and studied her for a moment.

"I mean, if you don't mind," she continued. "I've never been to Jamaica and I…"

Her words trailed off as she grimaced and looked down at the linoleum floor. She folded her arms across her chest and fidgeted with her sweater.

"No, that would be great," Gideon blurted out, as soon as he recovered from the shock. "Are you sure?"

"Yeah," she replied. "I think I'd like to come along. Maybe you could show me the estate you manage. And I could be there for Tara. I think I'd like that."

Todd raised his eyebrows at Gideon and shook his head softly. With her full attention on him, Gideon did not acknowledge Todd's reaction but he imagined similar thoughts were running through their minds. There were a handful of people in the world who knew the truth of Gideon's purpose in Jamaica. One less now that Bammy had passed away. As much as he wanted to, he knew that it would not be wise to bring Liz into that particular circle, at least not yet. He simply smiled at the girl who owned his heart, and chose to cross that particular bridge when it arrived.

"Okay then, grab your passports boys and girls," Gideon declared. "We're headed back to The Land of Look Behind."

Aaron Blaylock

Acknowledgements

Hello there, reader. I'd like you to know a couple of things. First, my wife is incredible. I could not do this without her patience and support. Second, my children's interest and enthusiasm for my stories gives me the fuel I need when things get difficult and I want to stop or take a break.

I am also blessed with tremendous friends, many of them are reflected in the characters in my books. I'd like to single out a couple of friends in reference to this story. My friend Mitch for his love of mystery and these mountains, he was an inspiration for the direction of this story. And to my friend Mike for his generosity and willingness to haul me back in the mountains for research and good times.

Lastly, thank you to Brock, Janette, and Randy for allowing me to juvenilize the Ready, Set, Write Podcast and for their encouragement and support. Also to the ever-growing list of authors who have taken me into their ranks and treated me like one of their own. And don't worry Alyson, Kevin, and Heather, I won't mention that thing that happened in Layton. That will stay in my non-sensual head.

About the Author

Born and raised in Arizona, Aaron is proud to call the desert home. He came of age in the suburbs of Sacramento, California, and as a missionary for The Church of Jesus Christ of Latter-day Saints in Jamaica, where he fell in love with the people and their culture, but he was always drawn back to the valley of the sun.

He married his childhood crush, and the girl of his dreams, in 2001. Together they are raising four beautiful and rambunctious children. He worked as a freelance sports reporter for *The Arizona Republic* for nearly ten years, combining his love of writing and sports. When not working, writing, or serving at church, Aaron volunteers as a soccer and baseball coach for his children and enjoys chasing a small white ball around a golf course.

His storytelling draws heavily from his love of history, adventure, his faith, and his own life experiences. *Crooked Top Mountain* is his third full length novel and a follow up to his debut novel *The Land of Look Behind*.

Aaron Blaylock

Visit www.aaronblaylock.com
Or follow Aaron on social media channels @AaronBlaylock